ONE OF THE FOUNDERS

ONE OF
THE
FOUNDERS

A Novel by P. H. Newby

∽

Philadelphia

J. B. LIPPINCOTT COMPANY

New York

Grateful acknowledgment is made to Sam Fox Publishing Co., Inc., for permission to quote one line from the song "Bless 'Em All" by Jimmy Hughes, Frank Lake, and Al Stillman.

Contents

ONE OF THE FOUNDERS

CHAPTER ONE

The Usual Scandal

For some moments after the girl came his mind stuck. She arrived so unexpectedly. There he was, doing—he could not remember what he was doing. Nobody indoors. The old man was down the garden burning crisp pea haulm. She must have found the front door open and walked right through the house. According to the calendar, it was high summer and she was dressed for it: white shoes and a cotton dress. Against her tow-coloured hair and the lemony dress her arms and face showed up like a Red Indian's. But she had blue eyes.

"Mr. Hedges," she said, "I thought I might find you in."

She was one of the teachers. That was what had stunned him. Teachers just didn't drop in casually. He tried to remember her name.

"Can I give you a drink?"

He himself was drinking bottled beer. The glass and the bottle stood on the ironwork table and, looking at them, he remembered what he had been doing before this girl arrived. He had been thinking how cold it was for the time

of year. The full foliage of the garden limes stirred patches
of chill light over recesses of dank gloom, and he ought to
be indoors with a coal fire instead of (it was coming back to
him now) sitting there in knee-high rubber boots and a
seaman's blue jersey enjoying the feeling he was on the
point of making an important discovery. He had this feeling
perhaps half a dozen times a year. He was just tottering on
the edge of discovering something crucial about—well,
about life; something that was so self-evident and marvellous that no one had been able to get it quite in focus. It
had to do with the way people are born. Usually, this sense
of near discovery sprang up with no warning. Sometimes
gin on an empty stomach did the trick. Tonight it must
have been the cold summer garden and the lime-flower
sweetness mingling with the bitterness of the flaming pea
haulm.

"I've been busy with the hose. You're Miss Styles from
St. John's Road."

"I want to say something." She hesitated.

"Shall we go indoors? It's cold out here."

"No, I'm all right. I'm not cold. I just——"

She was standing so close he could feel her breath on
his face, and her eyes were wide open, unblinking, bold, and
blue.

"I like the town," she said. "I'd be more than happy to
stay here. But is there any way of changing schools? I mean
without making too much fuss?"

He persuaded her to sit in the beer-barrel seat by
explaining how he had made it himself: a saw, wood-chisel,
hammer, nails, purple paint, white paint, patience, taste, a
sense of humour. He had painted the slats alternately purple
and white because he had seen a picture of a desert beetle
with this particular colour scheme—it was in the *American*

Scientist—and he'd thought, I'll have a seat coloured like a desert beetle.

"I'm not too happy about the rust-coloured cushion," he said, before going for her Toi Pepe, "though it's correct anatomically. This beetle had rust-coloured mandibles."

She sipped the drink politely and put the glass on the table. Plainly, she did not want it. She was too uneasy. "I'd rather be in a school where the Head is a woman."

"Saundersfoot is all right."

"He pesters me."

"Saundersfoot?"

"It's really rather horrible, a man of that age."

Sitting in his canvas chair, Hedges sighed and scratched himself. Saundersfoot had a couple of years to go before retiring. Assistant and then Head, he had been teaching at the St. John's Road School for thirty-five or -six years. He had started there, fresh from college, ten years before this girl had been born.

"He used to teach me," said Hedges.

"I'd really rather be somewhere else in the Michaelmas term."

Hedges just went on staring at her. "You're a bit Edwardian, aren't you? I mean—no, don't get angry. Saundersfoot's wife beats him. I thought you could have knocked him down, a strong young woman like you, and kept the whole thing personal."

She stood up and appeared to be gathering herself for a spring back into the house again and so away. "Thanks for the understanding advice."

"I mean," said Hedges, "I can't just switch teachers about as easily as all that. Saundersfoot's harmless. Anyway, why did women get the vote and all that if they can't fight off a few earthy passes? It's the price of emancipation."

11

"It was in the stationery store," she said, "where voting wouldn't have done much good."

"As an old soldier I'd say one thing. Keep out of the stationery store, that's my tip. And any other place where there's no room to manoeuvre."

She seemed to have changed her mind about going, but she was still on her feet and Hedges had to look up at her. Those eyes caused a lot of trouble, no doubt. They were causing trouble now. Hedges would have liked to take one of her hands in his. He knew how the delicate contact would strike to the stomach. Wasn't it what she wanted? He'd been pretty damn rude, but she hadn't taken offence the way he might have expected. Why hadn't she called at the office? He reckoned she had called at his home and not the office because it was not so much official action she wanted as private talk and comfort. He was ready to give it. He did not believe that Saundersfoot had been chasing her. Knowing Saundersfoot's wife, who would? She was a restless, energetic, endlessly curious old woman who still kept Saundersfoot at the holiday rock-climbing he would rather have given up a dozen years ago. His energy must have been drained away. He'd been kept on the trot. Hedges couldn't imagine him pawing young women.

"Do you mind if I ask what your first name is?"

"Yes, I do, on the whole."

"And you've been here——"

"A year last Easter. This is my second job."

At this point Hedges did what he had been fancying for some time. He stood up and took one of her hands. She immediately withdrew it, but he was just fascinated to note that she didn't actually go. She had her chin up and her cheeks pink.

"Either I'm irresistible," she said, "or just by chance I've struck another of 'em. Perhaps I'd better go."

Hedges noticed how the wind shook the wet leaves, and the slender, unopened green cones on top of some very late blue, yellow, red, white lupins turned one way in the chill stream; and he heard the old man's fire, hidden behind the runner-beans, crackling like a basket.

"No, don't do that. When men get old—I'm thirty-nine—they want to keep proving they're still young again. Assuming what you say about Saundersfoot is all true, haven't you thought he's lonely and his children have grown up and Mrs. Saundersfoot probably doesn't keep on saying she loves him?"

"No, frankly, and I don't love him either. All I want is a change of school. I'll just have to put the request in writing. I've had quite enough of that sort of behaviour."

"What does he do?"

"If I have to see him about something he holds my hand."

"Like this?"

"Yes."

"And you don't like it?"

"No." But this time she didn't withdraw her hand.

"What else?"

"He squeezes and pinches. It's the look on his face."

"Why bring me into it?"

"If I knew before coming into this house what I know now, I wouldn't."

"You thought to find an official and you found a man. Have you a lover?"

"I've got a friend. He's in the Air Force, in Aden."

"My wife left me too. She married a man called Brush.

A literary critic." He thought for a while, absent-mindedly squeezing her hand more tightly. "He reviews books in the papers."

"I'm very sorry—about your wife, I mean."

"I think Brush gives her a hell of a time."

He could see that she thought she had achieved nothing by her visit, and her slight bewilderment why this should be made her, in Hedge's eyes, more enchanting than ever. If instead of this damn silly desert-beetle seat he had made a rustic bench, she might have been sitting on it now and he could have moved over to sit at her side and slipped an arm around her waist. If they were not to go on talking about Saundersfoot for the rest of her visit (and the subject had become a bore), some such coup would have to be brought off.

"I can see you're probably more sensitive than most people," he remarked. "You don't like to cause pain, and that is why you are, so to speak, tolerating Saundersfoot's brutish advances. You tolerate them to his face and then stab him in the back."

For the second time she twisted her hand away. "You think I'm making a fuss about nothing. Perhaps I am. I came here with the idea of getting out of St. John's Road School. Because you're the Education Officer, you've given me the idea of getting out of the town altogether. I've got other things to use my energy on than fighting off old men."

"Such as?"

"I'm writing a novel."

"Then don't turn your back on experience, my dear. Accept the fact of man in all his sinfulness. We are as we are and can be no other. You exist and I exist in the only form we possibly could. If we were in other guises we'd be other people. Everything exists under this necessity. You

and I are standing here talking, I am attracted to you, and
you are a little attracted to me in spite of the disgusting way
I have received you, because there are really no alternatives."

She said, "Thank you for listening to me so patiently.
I'll go now."

"Stay to supper. We've veal-and-ham pie. I'd like you
to meet my father."

"No, thank you."

He had not the slightest intention of letting her get
away so easily and, gripping her firmly by the right elbow,
steered her towards the house.

"My name is Ian and I wish you'd call me by it. What's
your name?"

He was delighted to see she was breathless with surprise.

"Prudence." She tossed the name at him as meat might
be tossed at a tiger, to facilitate an escape.

"Indeed," he said, looking at her with renewed interest.
"A beautiful name and, if I may say so, an appropriate
one."

Fifty years ago there had been less than thirty thousand
people living in the borough of Perstowe, but now the
figure was ninety-seven thousand odd. In the twenties there
had been migration from the Welsh coal-fields and from as
far away as Tyneside, men looking for work on the trading
estate established on the site of the old Ordnance Depot.
During the war the almost forgotten medieval port on the
estuary was brought to life again, and now Canadian grain
ships tied up against the new mill. The Shell refinery, built
on a one-time marsh between Church Hill and the sea,
would be in production by the end of the year. The West

Indians had arrived. Bungalows and red-brick semi-detached houses flared over the hills. The local broad vowels were thinning and bus-conductors sounded their aitches. The four-teenth-century church lost half its graveyard to the road-wideners. The corn-chandlers, the ironmongers, the little shops shelling sherbert suckers and stationery, all these came down in fountains of dust, out of which emerged the multiple stores. One effect of all this change was to make Hedges, naturally rather a secretive chap, feel he had a duty to be more open about his private life and ambitions.

He looked at it this way. When his grandfather was a boy, everybody in Perstowe had known everybody else. Even his own father, in the years just before 1914, could stand at the door of his shop in his butcher's straw hat and apron and nod familiarly at nearly everybody who passed by. But now the town was full of strangers—strangers to the old families and strangers to each other. Hedges went about saying this was a transitional phase. The town plan provided for a population of one hundred and five thousand. After that God knew where the people would go to! A new town on the other side of the moor, that was one idea. Perhaps procreation would slow down. Anyway, so far as Hedges could see, Perstowe was in the process of digesting its finite increase of population. It was important that the process be speeded up by as many people as possible getting to know each other *personally*. In his more extreme moments, quite bizarre ways of bringing this about would come into his head: meetings, for example, in which people would get up and talk about themselves. He had spoken about this to Minchin, the borough librarian, who said it was what people were doing on television all the time. So long as the confessing took place in a studio miles away, probably no great harm would be done. But as soon as people met under a roof to do it, religious fervour would descend upon them and exhibitionism of all sorts—the seeing of visions, possession by devils, fits, conversions, and the like—would take place.

Minchin was, in fact, a medieval historian by training. He had despaired of the twentieth century the moment he became conscious of living in it and believed that the optimum size for any town was some fifteen thousand inhabitants, for preference enclosed in a stone wall. Hedges looked upon him as an obscurantist because Minchin apparently believed that these fifteen thousand people should be self-supporting, spinning their own cloth, tanning their own leather, and so on. Hedges could not bring himself to insist on anything of the sort, but he did insist that a happy society depended on its members knowing each other, preferably by their Christian names, and that the public servants of that society were under a special obligation to wear the faces of human beings. He also believed that a proper show of frailty helped. Nothing vicious of course— no actual dishonesty, no corruption—just the recognition, and the frank confessing, that a Borough Education Officer was a man like any other man: the son of the town butcher, backward at his elementary school because of asthma; a conscientious objector for the first six months of the war (then he had changed his mind); a good teacher during the three years he had in the schools (he saw no reason to conceal his good points); a useful fly-half until four years ago, when he had broken his leg; fond of dancing and traditional jazz; an irrational supporter of Newcastle United (irrational because he had never been to Newcastle, never seen the team play, was not interested in soccer as a game, but stayed at home on Saturday evening until he knew whether they had lost or won); an occasional, but pusillani-

17

mous, gambler on the Stock Exchange; the possessor of a Scottish Christian name because his mother (cook in the household of local gentry) had come from Dumfries. And he had been a cuckold. He was ready to talk about all this not only because the subject interested him but because it helped him to communicate. If he was explaining to a parent whose boy had failed to get into the Grammar School that the Eleven-Plus exam was a splendidly accurate way of assessing a child's potential, Hedges thought he could put it across just that much better if the parent was thinking, This is only Ian Hedges, poor chap, whose wife ran off. He could think of himself, by talkativeness and candour, turning strangers into friends.

"The smell of the lime-trees at this time of year," he said to Prudence Styles, "frightens me, really. You see the little lime nuts hanging there at examination time. My recurrent dream is to be sitting for some examination, and then at the last minute I discover I haven't prepared for one of the papers at all. Do you ever smell anything when you're dreaming? Then, of course, another reason why this lime-tree smell is so menacing. You won't remember those crisis summers before the war. . . .

"Oh," he said, as they heard heavy footsteps approaching from the garden. "Have you met my father? Dad, this is Miss Prudence Styles from St. John's Road Junior."

"Ah!" Mr. Hedges did not step into the room. He lowered his eighteen stone on to a bench and sighed as he bent to unlace his gardening boots. The sweat washed red channels through the bonfire grime on his face. He exuded a steamy, rustic glow. They could see him, looking up now and peering into the darkness of the room, screwing up his eyes under the hay-coloured froth of a continuous eyebrow. Once his hair had been thick. Now it hung round his head like mist. The enormous raspberry of his tongue protruded as he worked his grey-socked feet out of the boots.

Then—blessed release and the feet, steaming, rested on the concrete.

"What's that you say?"

Hedges pushed the girl forward. The old man, taken by surprise, tried to hide his stockinged feet. He also tried to stand up.

"Miss Styles. St. John's School."

"I thought I could hear somebody talking," said Mr. Hedges. "St. John's School—that school, I tell you, was built on the finest bit of agricultural land in these parts. I've seen wheat up to my shoulder. A man called Weeks used to farm that. Course that was fifty years ago. He's dead now. Where's your home, eh?"

"Brewchester, actually," said Miss Styles.

Mr. Hedges stretched out his legs. He had recovered from his embarrassment. He wiggled his toes. "Brewchester? I know it well. That's where our mob was before we got posted to France, and I went round with the officer buying horses. Swear? You never 'eard such language! A lot of old nags, you 'ad to 'old 'em up while the officer looked at 'em. Thirty, forty, fifty quid. This officer says to me, 'Hedges, we've arrived late on the scene,' and too bloody true we had, I'm telling you; it was the Service Corps, they'd been before us. We was Gunners. But that's a nice place, Brewchester. You got any family there?"

"My father. I've got a brother in Canada."

"He did right," said Mr. Hedges. "If I 'ad my time over again that's what I'd do, I'd emigrate. Your dad working?"

"He's retired but he's very busy with this committee—you know, this University for Brewchester committee."

"What's that?" asked Hedges, professionally interested.

"Dad left school at thirteen. He was a saddler. He's always been obsessed with the idea of education. That's why I'm a teacher. He's a tremendous autodidact. His shop—it was his workroom too—was lined with books on two sides, and when he retired he dreamed up this idea of Brewchester having its own university. It was entirely his own idea. But there's a committee now and he's chairman of it. He's an absolutely marvellous man."

"Brewchester? A university in Brewchester?" Hedges was incredulous. The place was just over the county border about fifty miles away. It had a splendid airy position on a hilltop with pine-trees, but it had never really got over having its big monastery dissolved. There was the Abbey church, interesting ruins, a lot of pubs, and a cattle market still held every Thursday in the enormously wide High Street. "You couldn't start a university at Brewchester," Hedges said. "It hasn't even got a railway-station, has it?"

The moment Dad came into the conversation Prudence relaxed happily, apparently forgetting old Saundersfoot and even the brusque way Hedges had received her slander. The main point she tried to make was that Dad had no equal for intelligence, energy, or a sense of humour; once he made up his mind to plant a university on Brewchester Hill, the job was as good as out to tender. Hedges could accept all this testimony to the old chap's ability, but what made him stare was the girl's sudden bubbling over with enthusiasm and—yes, obvious adoration. It wasn't natural. She must have some terrible father-fixation. Hedges naturally thought back to Saundersfoot. Perhaps it wasn't just Dad. Perhaps she was capable of fastening on to anybody who was the same age as Dad, and the truth of the affair in the stationery store was not that Saundersfoot had been making advances to her but that she had been making passes at him.

"Do you know what book he used to teach me to read?" Miss Styles's blue eyes drew his own hypnotically. "Darwin's *Voyage of the Beagle.*" She was Dad's girl, all right.

"And he was a saddler?"

"He had prizes for his saddles."

"Plastic saddles, that'll be the next thing," said Mr. Hedges.

"But you can get them already! It was one of the reasons Daddy retired, that and so as he could have more time for the university."

" 'Strewth!" Mr. Hedges picked up his boots and, groaning under his own weight, made his way into the house. asked Miss Styles to excuse him. Hedges noticed she was following his father's progress with an affectionate attention that more than ever convinced him she had a passion for the older man. But perhaps she lacked the self-knowledge to be truly aware of her condition. She had matured only to the point of imagining a situation that would crystallize it and possibly bring about her rescue. Was she making an unconscious appeal for release from the spell that had been cast over her and making it to the one man who combined enough personal charm and official power to be an effective white wizard? Was she saying, "Wake me with your kiss"? If she didn't *know* she was saying it, Hedges thought he'd better treat her like a real Sleeping Beauty and wake her very gently indeed.

Mr. Hedges could be heard walking about upstairs. The grey, damp wind pressed into the room. Hedges shut the French window and with the toe of his rubber boot flicked the switch for the electric fire. The reading lamp over Buddha came on, too, and the light dripped like butter on to the bronze cheeks and thighs. The fecundity of full summer was blighted. Through the window he watched the sea of foliage heaving in the wind. That misty powdering on the glass might well be the drying brine. Upstairs the old man paced from bedroom to bath-room. Hedges poured more sherry and thought it must be the Norse blood in his veins that persuaded him there was any beauty in summer weather like this.

For the third time Prudence said she must go.

"Not yet. You must let me think. What you tell me has been a great shock. Look at it from my point of view."

"What more is there to say?"

"Everything. We scarcely know each other."

"The fact is you don't believe me, do you?"

Oh, for God's sake be careful! he very nearly shouted.

"Whether or not," he said, "people believe one another at moments of crisis—and this is a moment of crisis—depends on the degree of confidence they've been able to establish in one another before the crisis developed." Hedges thought that the safest course would be to establish a few general principles. "I've a great dislike of commercial advertising for this very reason. Please don't be cross. *Please* be reasonable. After all, you've made an accusation that could get a lot of people into a lot of trouble."

Prudence sat down again and appeared to be breathing once more. "Why don't you like commercial advertising?"

"You've met my father. You wouldn't go far wrong, would you, in taking my old man as typical of quite a lot of people?"

"Typical in what way?"

"Just typical. The other evening we were watching the

commercial telly. You know that floor-polish ad? You see a dirty floor, a mop is passed over it, and the floor is clean, shining, bogus. This long-handled mop is——"

"I know the one you mean."

"My father looked at it and said, rather sadly, really, 'I suppose the bloody dirt's sucked up the handle.'" Hedges continued. "My point is this. I'm not down on the advertisers because they tell lies. What bothers me is the way they're caught out. They're making us into a nation of sceptics. You start by not believing the adman. You end up by not believing—oh, I dunno, that Hitler started the war, for example."

"Or that what I say about Mr. Saundersfoot is the truth."

"Exactly."

Prudence put down her glass—it was still full—picked up her bag, and made for the door. Hedges walked after her, explaining that scepticism was certainly very necessary if we were not going to be led by the nose by politicians, trade-union leaders, businessmen, journalists, and the like, but that he could not believe that a society like ours, in which scepticism is fostered by advertisers, could possibly hold together.

"You've got to remember," he said, "that the language of the adman is becoming the pricipal method of communication between the leaders of society and the masses. It can only lead to an estrangement at the heart of the community. This is the estrangement we ought to be worrying about, not Snow's two cultures or highbrow writers failing to sell a lot of books. I prefer the word estrangement to alienation. Communication is corrupted. We don't know what to believe, who to believe——"

"Will you please let me open this door?"

"No," he said. "When I say *what* to believe, I'm not speaking metaphysically. I mean quite simply the ordinary facts. How much radio-active fall-out is there in the bones of Welsh mountain sheep? Is So-and-so who is said to be a security risk really a security risk? The simple things of life."

"If you don't let me go, Mr. Hedges——"

"Call me Ian, Prudence."

"—I shall write to the County Director of Education."

"Beresford? He's as innocent as a monk. He wouldn't know what you were driving at."

They were standing at the front door. As Hedges had his arm round her waist, the more easily to restrain her while he voiced his social criticism, Prudence was trapped. Her left arm was caught between her body and his, and he had a firm grip of her right wrist. Her one resource would be to stamp on his foot, and this she now did.

"It's outrageous that I should come here to complain about Mr. Saundersfoot's behaviour and find you regard this as an invitation to be beastly too. What's the matter with education in this town?"

Her stiletto heel had punctured a hole in his rubber boot. The pain dazed and then he felt sick. He looked down at the hole, expecting to see an upwelling of blood. Prudence, now released, could have made her escape if she had wished, but she too stood looking down at the hole in his boot. He supposed she had felt the stiletto piercing flesh, tendon, and bone. Perhaps she felt sorry now. Her complaint about Saundersfoot seemed to be called into even graver question. If this weapon had not been brought into play (and he hadn't heard of Saundersfoot being off sick), the fellow couldn't possibly have gone very far.

"Are you all right?" He was glad to hear a less hostile

note in her voice as he stood there on one foot, feeling his face go long and grey.

"The next best thing to an embrace," he said, "is a blow."

To prevent him falling, Prudence tried to support him, and in the tangle he managed to kiss her on the back of the neck.

Prudence visited him twice during the three days he spent in Perstowe General Hospital. On the first occasion he spoke on the subject of nurses and sensuality, saying that the erotic feelings they aroused in the average Englishman were disguised nostalgia for the happy days before the emancipation of women. The second visit he said that gangrene had been arrested, and now there was every hope of leaving him with at least one of his toes. Prudence was terrified.

But Hedges's real thoughts were elsewhere. On the third day he was discharged with his bandaged foot in an ordinary carpet-slipper and, under his right arm, a crutch that made him feel young again, that his rugger days had returned. He took a cab to the office. It was later in the afternoon than he had thought, past five-thirty, and the building had emptied. Instead, then, of climbing to the second floor, he sat on the steps at the entrance, still gloriously hot in the sun, and gazed at the Market Square through half-shut eyes. Sooner or later some smartie would drop a penny into his cap, and Hedges decided he would just put the coin in his pocket.

He had very nearly to close his eyes against the glitter of the cobbles, but he knew everything from memory: the clock tower dated 1887, the cast-iron lion on its plinth, the car-park attendant's wooden hut, the plane-trees, the magpie half-timbering of the Royal George, the multiple tailor's, the multiple chemist's, and that one untenanted spot at the north of the square, to the right of the war memorial, where he had in his boyhood imagined the equestrian statue of Field Marshal Hedges. Later it became Colonel Hedges, dressed as an Arab, imperiously dragging a stone revolver out of his holster. Still later, the bronze bust of Ian Hedges, Secretary-General of the United Nations, looked out of a marble niche. And what did he see there now? Surely he was not too old for visions? What about a piece of wire sculpture to the memory of Ian Hedges, M.A., Hon. D. Litt., "but for whose advocacy the University of Perstowe might never have existed"?

He could see Fred Amos come out of the *Advertiser* office and look about him. He lifted his crutch and shouted. When Amos came over and stood between him and the sun, Hedges suggested they should go over to the Royal George for a drink.

"You sure alcohol is all right for that foot?" asked Amos. "My father had phlebitis in his foot and had to keep off the drink."

"This isn't phlebitis."

"There's no need to make such a mystery of it."

Across Amos's waistcoat ran a fine gold and platinum watch-chain. He wore a detachable white collar over a striped shirt. He was going bald. The scalp sparkled under the thin hair. His long jaw was blue. The reading-glasses, too, with their little half-moon lenses that had slipped down his thin beak, argued the older man. But he was not. In fact, he and Hedges had sat under old Saundersfoot together.

"It isn't very often I speak to you seriously," said Hedges, as soon as they were sitting in the window-seat of the public bar in the Royal George, "so I want you to pay

26

particular attention. Yes, a pint of draught bitter, if you please."

Amos came back with the glasses and said his wife was giving a dinner-party that evening, so Hedges need feel under no complulsion to buy him a pint in return.

"As editor of the local paper," said Hedges, coming to the point at once, "you ought, I think, to start a campaign to have one of these new universities established here in Perstowe."

"I don't own the bloody rag. I don't start campaigning just when and how I like, you know—though of course," said Amos, "I have a completely free hand. I wouldn't tolerate any interference. Arrowsmith knows this with the kind of certainty that needs no reinforcing." He put down his glass. "What I like about beer is the way it brings you out in a sweat. Anyway, why should there *be* a campaign for a new university?"

Hedges was sitting sideways with his right leg stretched out on the window-seat. There were three other men in the bar, but they were all at the counter. Hedges and Amos had their end of the room to themselves.

"Don't you believe in higher education?" Hedges demanded.

"*Turpe nescire*. Bachelor of Arts, Perstowe in brackets. Architect, Sir Basil Spence." Amos had drunk enough of his beer to be able to wave the glass about without spilling any. And to speak impressionistically. "Royal Chancellor, foreign students, rag days, scandal involving chemistry student and professor's young wife, town faction, gown faction, great tension, students' magazine suppressed by Vice-Chancellor, another scandal involving the members of the Music Society, students strike over bad food, inaugural lectures, lectures—oh, what visiting celebrities would they have?

Intellectual industrialists and Philistine academics. Or foreign politicians. M. Mendes-France, now, he'd be a good choice. And apart from these high-powered lectures there'd just be the ordinary lectures. Arguments about how *to* lecture. Tutorial experiment at Perstowe! I can just see the headline. Of course, if instead of a Chancellor you had an elected Rector like they have in Scotland, then you'd see some fun. Yes!" Amos finished his pint and set his glass down carefully. "I can just see it all. As an individual, I'm in favour. As the editor of the local organ of intelligence, I ask the simple question, 'What's in it for me?' "

Hedges was accustomed to the way Amos allowed his mind to romp through imaginary landscapes and dramas, describing volubly what he thought he was seeing and hearing, and paid little attention to this outpouring. He sucked at his beer and wondered what Amos had meant by referring to his injured foot as "a mystery." Had someone been talking?

Amos's face was bacon red, above the blue bristle, and steaming. The half-moon lenses were opaque.

"What's in it for the *Perstowe Advertiser?*" Amos repeated. "Anyway, I haven't the slightest idea how to start a university, so I should look damn silly, shouldn't I, campaigning for something I didn't know how to start. What if someone came up to me and said, 'All right! You've convinced us! Go ahead!' How? Eh? You're the Education Officer. Why don't you campaign?"

"That's just what I'm doing."

"In trying to win me over?"

"If a Borough Education Officer got up on a soap-box and preached the need for a university in his administrative area, the county authorities would have kittens."

"You mean a new university would mean something on the rates?"

"Too true it would, and that's politics."

"Myself," said Amos, "I didn't go to a university. You did. Now look at us! Here we are, drinking beer on a summer evening. What difference did it make? Well, I'll tell you. You had three years' more play. Play is the great thing in life. Not games! Play! Let the mind play! Let it accept this possibility and that possibility and play with them as if they were true. My mind," said Amos, "is such a chameleon I would, I think, be puzzled to know the right answer if you were to ask me what its real colour was. I ought to have been an actor. Do you know what my gift is? Empathy! But I've no will of my own. All right! You've talked me over. I'm with you. We'll campaign for the university together. But now I've taken the decision you must tell me why we're campaigning, eh? Well, somebody might ask me."

"Not for a bloody play-centre, I tell you that straight, Fred, my boy."

"In higher education," said Amos, "everything that is not vocational training is play. Religion is play. Literature is play. Everything that is not of immediate practical value is play, according to my definition. Any intellectual activity is play if it starts from an unanswerable question and then proceeds as if the question has been answered. 'Does God exist?' for example. For the sake of the magnificent game that then becomes possible you say, 'Yes, He exists.' Myself, I'm a sceptic. I'm prepared to play all these games. I am ready endlessly to suspend my disbelief. When a university isn't teaching its students to be doctors, scientists, teachers, lawyers, and parsons, that is precisely the function

29

I expect of it, to induce a suspension of disbelief over as wide an area as possible."

"Palmistry and astrology not excluded."

"Palmistry and astrology do not start from unanswerable questions; they start from lunatic affirmations that are demonstrably wrong, and the very fact, I might say, that you bring them in shows you haven't understood a word I've been saying! Ian, you must ask yourself the serious question whether a chap with your intellectual limitations is the one to start campaigning for a new university."

"I'm not starting out with a theory of knowledge. I have a certain view of society, that's all."

"Isn't it your turn to buy a round?" Amos had been talking so quickly and vehemently his pinched nose could not supply him with enough air, and he was having to breathe through his mouth. His dark face glistened. "What d'you mean, I said I didn't want any more? What if we are giving a dinner-party? A man can have a drink before a party, can't he? Look, gimme the money. I'll hop over and get 'em. Forgot about your foot. Remind me to ask about your foot, there's a good chap."

Amos plonked the two pints down on the table, spilling some, and said, "So, you've got a certain view of society, have you? That's an O.K. thing to have. We may not know about God and all the other value-judgements, but *people* are there all right. It is very respectable to be a sociologist. I regard sociology as the great anti-play activity of our time."

The bar was filling up, and both Amos and Hedges were having to lift their voices in order to make themselves heard.

"It's obvious," said Hedges, "from the way you've been talking, you've an untrained mind."

"Buttocks!"

"A university here in Perstowe twenty years ago, you'd have been drawn in and we'd have been spared all this half-educated talk. Admit you're an ignorant phoney, Fred. Don't fight against yourself in this way."

"Mr. Amos!" It was the bartender shouting. "Your wife's on the telephone, and she says you're to come home right away."

Amos stood up. Hedges, more laboriously, followed suit, and the two men clinked glasses before emptying them.

"My view," said Hedges, as they emerged into the evening and glided gently over the hot pavement, "is something like this. Once upon a time a town owed its character to its local industries, its football team, and its dialect. Well, the tanning and brewing have finished in Perstowe. We've got the kind of light industries you'll find anywhere else. The local speech, too, has been sicklied over. Nobody watches football much any more. The one thing that'll make a town stick up above the murk of what was England and is now an endless suburbia is a university."

"You hurt your foot or something?" Amos stopped and peered. "You're using a crutch. I can see it clearly."

"—all the more important it should be a university with a distinctive character. Myself, I'd like to see a slant towards the social sciences."

"Nuts on the social sciences! You're wearing a slipper. You got gout?"

Hedges wanted to keep the conversation strictly to the point. "There's nothing the matter with my foot, at least——"

"Liar! Let me give you a lift."

"You're drunk."

"I am not *very* drunk. If I'm drunk you should stop me from driving. It's your duty, as a citizen."

31

"I'd drive you myself if it wasn't for my foot."

"You said there was nothing the matter with your foot."

Amos was trying to unlock the door of his Zephyr. Hedges took the key from his hand. A thought had suddenly struck him.

"Look here, Fred. You won't need your car this evening if your wife's giving a dinner-party. If I drove you home can I borrow it for an hour?"

"Now you mention it," said Amos, wiping his face with his handkerchief, "I do feel a bit boozed."

Hedges found that driving with his injured foot was greater torture than he had feared. Once he had dropped Amos and had the car to himself, he allowed himself to scream quietly. But he drove on up the hill.

While in hospital Hedges had got his secretary to find out Prudence's private address. He had made a note of it in his diary, and he now discovered it was one of the little Georgian terraces of colour-washed houses, each with portico and pillars, that stood on the very crest of Mythe Hill, commanding a fine westward view. Waiting for Prudence to come down, he was able to sit at one of the great windows in the drawing-room, with his foot on a stool to mitigate the throbbing, and look down at the square church tower, red-brick façades, blue slates, steel and glass office blocks, the railway-station, and, away to the estuary with its pink warehouses, the silver tanks at the Shell refinery and, behind them, the hills. He wondered if she would mind if he didn't stand up. The driving had left him with a pain up to the hip.

She wore tartan trousers and sandals and seemed scared.

"What's happened? How's your foot?"

"Discharged as incurable."

She looked at him with none of the relief in her face that he had expected. The same iron-complexioned woman in tweeds who had admitted him to the house and shown him into this room now put her head round the door and asked whether he would like a cup of tea.

"Not for me, Mrs. Kidwelly," said Prudence.

"It was your guest I was thinking of, Miss Styles, dear."

"Mr. Hedges is not staying."

The head was withdrawn, and they listened to the landlady making her way to the back of the house, coughing like a man. If he had asked Prudence's permission to sit she would have refused it, he suspected, so he said nothing and settled himself with his slippered foot up in the air, just as he had been before she came in. She stood over him.

"You mean they're not going to cut any toes off?"

"I must apologize for having made light of my injuries."

"I haven't slept for two nights."

She looked, he thought, more attractive than ever. He ought to have been cowed and apologetic, but he was only admiring. He would have liked to draw her down to his knee and compare Mrs. Kidwelly with the melancholy marabou stork, a bird into whose eye came the dull gleam of merriment only when cracking a crocodile's egg. "Surely you'd rather have me gay than gloomy?"

"It isn't being gay to make jokes about having your toes amputated."

"All right, I apologize. Now you don't trust me any more, do you?"

This sudden thought was terrible. He always wanted people to trust him, as he trusted them. No secrets. He

33

wanted to be in everybody's confidence. He just hated not knowing. If he was dying of cancer he would want the doctor to tell him. No beating about the bush. That winter night he had come in from the office, stood in the hall, knocking snow from his shoulders, and Nell had given him a glass of sherry and blurted out (after looking at him for some moments) that she wanted a divorce, he just said, "But what's going on? Why doesn't anyone tell me anything?"

Maybe all this talk about living in a society where there were no lying advertisements and everybody knew the truth about everybody else was just part of his cure. He had never considered it in that way before. This concern to have people look each other squarely in the face was just a technique for getting over the shock of learning that Nell had been going to bed with Brush. He didn't want to be deceived any more. He didn't want to discover that someone he loved was shockingly different from the person he thought she was.

Prudence was right. He shouldn't have joked about his toes. The extraordinary thing was that she appeared to be getting angrier and angrier.

"You joked in that lying way about your foot just to show me you thought I was a neurotic liar too."

"Oh, come——"

"You thought I was lying about Saundersfoot."

"Hell, Prudence, if you told me you could do the Indian rope-trick I'd believe you. I don't think you invented the bloody story, but then I've known old Saundersfoot all my life and I've got to believe him too. That's the sort of state of mind I'm in. You're not helping one tiny little bit."

"If I didn't invent it and you've got this complete confidence in Saundersfoot, where does the truth lie?"

"Truth? Are you asking me what truth is?"

"Don't blow my question up into something big and unanswerable. You give me no alternative but to resign."

She turned and marched off towards the door, but Hedges shouted, "Oh no, you don't! Come here at once!"

With one hand on the door-knob she stopped and looked back in astonishment. "What's that?"

"Come here!" His jaw had gone so stiff it was difficult to get the words out. "If you don't come I'll crawl after you and bite your ankle."

Mrs. Kidwelly opened the door at this moment, carrying a tray with one cup of tea and a plate of plain biscuits. She appeared to be moving her legs only from the knees down, but Hedges decided this must be an optical illusion brought on by the feeling that she was really rough-hewed and inanimate, proceeding on wheels, and the tray when it came near enough would show itself to be carrying not tea and biscuits but strange votive objects: iron nails tied with ribbon, dentures, messages in code for the divinity. In spite of his sudden gloom, Hedges could allow his fancy to play around. When, however, she stood squarely in front of him, with one trembling lower eyelid the only sign of life, he accepted the tea and biscuits hastily and stood there drinking and crunching the biscuits fiercely so that the crumbs spluttered out over his jacket.

Prudence had returned some distance into the room. He had never seen such enormous eyes. He sensed that some change had taken place. He *thought* she was laughing.

"You know perfectly well you're under a contract and you've got to give three months' notice. You don't want to be sued for breach of contract, do you?"

Yes, he could see she was laughing.

"What did you say you'd do?"

"Bite your ankle."

"No," said Mrs. Kidwelly, moving her shoulders like a wrestler under her masculine-looking jacket, "if I saw that going on in my house, Mr. Hedges, I should feel called upon to interfere."

"These last few days my mind has been rather taken up with an important new venture." Hedges addressed Prudence. "You think I've been brooding over my foot. Not at all. I say this only to explain why I should have misled you over the gangrene and the amputations and all that sort of thing. My thoughts weren't really on the subject. They were elsewhere."

"You spoke without thinking."

"I was preoccupied."

"With no matter that concerned me, of course?"

Hedges hesitated. "Well, no." He might have been even more uncertain about this than he looked, because he changed the subject and went on to say that although he did not expect any more surgery his foot would probably never be the same again.

CHAPTER TWO

The Idea of a University

From time to time Christopher Brush would turn up, usually a bit tipsy, to borrow money, and Hedges would give it to him, ten pounds at the most, sometimes as little as ten shillings, thinking that if Nell didn't receive any part of it herself (and the usual story was that Nell wanted a new dress, or a holiday, or she couldn't pay the gas bill) at least it would relieve the strain on her of Brush's continual sponging. Hedges remained fond of his ex-wife and could not bear the thought of her being unhappy. She worked as secretary to Gideon Toplis of Toplis Mouldings, because Brush couldn't earn enough to keep them. He did book-reviewing and wrote chatty biographies—of anyone he thought might catch the public fancy: Cagliostro, Laurence Oliphant, and Lord Rutherford were the most recent. He was a small, podgy man with prominent, wistful, dark eyes and a lot of black hair not only on his head but on the backs of his hands.

That Nell should have preferred this ursine, promiscuous, drunken scribbler to himself still puzzled Hedges. At

the very beginning, when Nell first told him she'd been
sleeping with Brush, he had been so incredulous that the
more natural anguish of betrayal had been muted. Incredulity modulated to bewilderment, finally to perplexity. But
for this aberration Nell had been a nice, sensible girl. If he
could only catch up with the implications of all this, they
would surely be very damaging to his self-esteem. As soon
as he had the time he certainly meant to work them out. He
might even, quite bluntly, ask Nell herself.

This time when Brush walked in Hedges was lying on
the settee with his foot supported by a cushion. He was
watching the Old Trafford Test on television and was not
at all pleased by the interruption. Dexter was thrashing the
Australian bowling.

"Here comes Christopher Brush," he said, "hanger-on,
drunkard, and adulterer."

"No idea you were following my career so closely."
Brush cared nothing for cricket, and he stood with his back
to the television set. He had the throaty bleat of a hunting
duchess. "I can tell by your tone that you think I'm after
your money. Well, maybe I am. But first of all I want to
tape a bit of conversation with you on this machine of
mine."

Hedges now noticed that Brush had a sizable black box
supported by a leather strap that went over his right
shoulder. Brush dropped the box on to a table. He opened
the lid and produced a microphone like a tin toffee-apple
which he gave Hedges to hold.

"Get out of the way, there's a good chap. Benaud's just
come on to bowl."

Brush leaned backwards and switched the television off.
"Be reasonable. I can't record with that row going on." He
tinkered with the controls of the recorder. "Natty job, this.

A battery job. Real portable. Take it anywhere. Borrowed it from the B.B.C."

Hedges knew from experience that if he suddenly put his foot to the ground the pain would run up his leg and daze him. It was through force of argument alone that he was going to get a sight of the cricket again.

"You mannerless bastard!"

"Har! Har!" Brush belched a laugh. "Wanted to see how you were, old chap. Nell saw the piece in the paper about you sticking the garden-fork in your foot——"

"What?"

"We saw in the paper about your accident, and Nell jumped to the conclusion you were dying, so——"

"What accident?"

"Your blasted foot!" Now Brush was annoyed. "That thing wrapped up on the end of your leg. You stuck a garden-fork in it, you oaf."

Hedges was so interested that he forgot about the tape recorder and he even forgot about the cricket. "Have you noticed that if ever you see in a newspaper some account of a happening you yourself know about at first hand, the newspaper will *always* get it wrong? There's always some detail, as often as not an important detail, that is simply untrue. Take my foot. I didn't stick a garden-fork in it."

Brush had found a cigar-box. He had unwrapped a cigar and lit it with extraordinary rapidity. "What happened then?"

"That's immaterial. Now if the newspapers are wrong about small things like my foot, what about the big things? What about the Berlin crisis? How do we know the stuff we get served up about the great issues of our time isn't wrong too?"

Brush slipped the cigar to the side of his mouth. "Do you mean to say you have large doubts—LARGE DOUBTS—about the honesty, the objectivity, and mechanical efficiency of the British press? You appal me!"

"I merely said——"

"You actually think it would be a good thing to have papers you can believe?"

"My point was——"

"Because I don't! That's what I meant when I said you appal me. You appal me because you have these expectations. And where do they lead you? Censorship! The official hand-out!"

It occurred to Hedges that he could hammer Brush with the microphone if he wanted to. He was sorry he had started this subject. Brush went on talking excitedly. Cigar ash fell on his brown pull-over, and there was a smell of singed wool.

"Broadly speaking, there are two types of intellectual: those who believe in the possibility of some kind of absolute truth about mankind and his destiny. And there are those who don't. You, Hedges, believe in truth with a capital T. You believe that this truth has been revealed. You believe that the press and the mass media are the channels through which unsullied truth should pour, even about such insignificant matters as your right foot. You remember the two categories William James divided people into?"

"No."

"He said people were either tender-minded or tough-minded. The tender-minded are theoretical and idealistic. They believe life can be understood as a whole if only you get the right angle on it." Hot ash fell from his cigar and scorched his pull-over. The stink seemed to work on his passions. His nostrils broadened and quivered. "You're so tender-minded it's scarcely credible. You'd allow yourself to be destroyed for a principle."

"And what are you?"

"I'm tough-minded. I'm materialistic, pessimistic, and irreligious. I don't believe what people tell me; I don't believe anybody came down from the mountain with any particular revelation. I distrust all people who think they've got some vision of the truth. More hell has been let loose on this planet by men with tender minds than by tough-minded people like me who believe in selfishness and getting what you can while the going's good. And remaining scoffers. I don't want to reform the press. Let corruption flourish. You can be free only in a corrupt society you know to be corrupt. That's why Satan led his hosts out of heaven."

"Then Christ was tender-minded."

"And look what happened to him! What's the matter with your foot anyway?"

"A girl trod on it with her stiletto heel."

Brush nodded, waved his right hand dismissively, and did not press his inquiries. The implication was that he was often trodden on by girls with stiletto heels. "I've come to see you about this university idea. I thought I'd tape the whole campaign and sell it to the B.B.C. It'd do for 'In Our Time.' "

Hedges was irritated that Brush had not taken him up about this girl stabbing him with her stiletto heel. Did the fellow think that because he had pinched Nell with so little trouble the forsaken husband was sexually of no account at all? He wanted to get through to Brush with *this* particular truth anyway, and he hoped Brush would pass it on to Nell.

"Actually," he said, "I was kissing this girl at the time."

41

"You rake, you!"

"She was not so unwilling as you might imagine. The kick was a reflex action, really. In point of fact she was after *me*."

"A handsome man like you must have lots of trouble with the women."

"I certainly don't bore them with the kind of obscurantist rubbish you've just been churning out."

Brush blew cigar ash off the tape recorder and prepared to start it up. "I match my conversation to my audience. I don't talk to the women like that."

"*And* she came to the hospital to visit me."

"You devil, you! When you grow up you'll be a proper sex maniac. Now, sober up, man, and talk to me about this bloody university. Some chaps've got to earn their livings."

Hedges remembered now that he had from time to time heard Brush on the radio, apparently talking to a lot of people with off-beat jobs or personal histories. He hadn't realized Brush collected them on his tape recorder and, in any case, didn't like the idea that Brush privately classed him as so much entertainment value, on a par with flea trainers and junkies. On the other hand the fellow had to live.

"This university project isn't a joke, you know. Anyway, where did you hear about it? It's very confidential."

"In your own words, Mr. Hedges," said Brush, putting on his professional-quizzmaster-type smile, "perhaps you would tell us how the idea first came to you of establishing a university in Perstowe."

Startled by his change of manner, Hedges looked up and saw the reels going round on the tape machine. He held the microphone up in front of his face as though it were a mirror, cleared his throat, and began enunciating with great clearness what now seemed to him to be the truth of the matter:

"As a native of Perstowe who happens to be more concerned with the future than the past, I consider that the establishing of a university here will give the town a splendid stimulus and make the people who live here understand that the exciting things of the twentieth century are not away on the other side of the horizon but can be right here in their own town. You ask me where the idea first came from. Where do ideas come from? I sometimes think the really good ones come by themselves. This one is so obvious I marvel nobody had thought of it before. We need money, of course. This is not a one-man job. We'll need a University Promotion Committee. Industry will have to come in. Leaders of opinion will have to rally round. It'll be a long hard pull, all right." Hedges lowered the microphone. "I say, this does sound balls."

Brush pressed a button and the reels stopped going round. "I hope I got that final remark."

"You're not going to put *that* out?"

"These programmes need personality. You ought to hear Amos. Nell's going to get old Toplis for me. I've got an appointment with Supple this afternoon, and then I suppose Jimmy Pigge and old Primrose are good for some high-minded cock—well, Primrose is, anyway. Actually, I rather like Jimmy Pigge. He'll be against the university."

"But these people don't know anything about it yet."

"They will. I don't think I've quite made it clear to you, Hedges, that in this programme I'm after something new. Not a snapshot. It'll be a portrait in depth. How long d'you reckon it'll take before this promotion takes off? Months. I'm going to chronicle it. I'm going to record

43

people like you and Toplis and Supple over the weeks. When your case goes before the University Grants Committee, I shall put my programme on the air. And d'you know what it'll show? It'll be a social document. It'll show how a few far-seeing people in a community can create an appetite, a sense of purpose, an ambition, where there was nothing before. It'll show how society actually works in our so-called democracy. I'm going to probe Perstowe. After the radio programme I'll write a book called *The Articulation of a Late-Twentieth Century Social Anatomy*, and a copy of it will be buried under the foundation-stone of the university Senate-house. Good day to you, old sport. I'll be back."

Before Hedges could ask him the sharp question or two that would have revealed whether Brush was trying to pull his leg or not, Brush had hurried out of the room. Hedges hesitated over chasing him. He sat up, put his foot to the ground slowly, and waited for it to stop throbbing. By this time the front door had slammed, so Hedges went hopping in search of the *Perstowe Advertiser*. He found it stuffed into the fuel hod in the kitchen. Surely Brush had, as usual, been lying? But when at last he found the report of his accident in the crumpled pages, it stated with a curtness that carried an authority even Hedges himself found himself respecting—*can* there be something in it?—that "Mr. Ian Hedges, M.A., the Borough Education Officer, was admitted to Perstowe General Hospital on Tuesday with a puncture wound in his foot sustained by lifting new potatoes, part of the first crop of the year."

Why had Amos done this to him? It wasn't just drunken carelessness. It wasn't just a matter of putting down the first thing that came into his head. Hedges thrust the paper back where he had found it. He had caught

44

himself in the very act of deciding that a deliberate motive must exist for this printing of a false report. That way lay paranoia.

Brush's remarks about an anarchic society in which a certain amount of corruption was readily accepted as the price of freedom had made a deeper impression than he would have liked to admit. Had he leanings towards authoritarianism? Or was he just neurotic about the free flow of truth? Was it the old wound? Was he just struggling to recover from cuckoldry? Would he become ever more watchful and suspicious? Surely he was half way to the belief in some conspiracy to suppress or pervert the truth? From there you went on to believe in secret sources of information. He saw himself subscribing to private and expensive news agencies that professed to give it to him. He'd go in for the occult. He'd find himself believing that the history of the world was hidden in the dimensions of the Great Pyramid.

For the second time he pulled the *Perstowe Advertiser* out of the fuel hod. This time he put it into the empty boiler and set fire to it with the gas poker. He was determined to cultivate a sunny disposition.

His father, that very day, came home with the news that he had given Prudence Styles a lift. Mr. Hedges's interests these days were divided fairly equally between his garden and his new scarlet Miniminor. He went off for daily joy-rides. Returning from one of these he had spotted the girl carrying a haversack of books, so he picked her up and told her about the Australian stock-whip he used to have. It just came into his head, that's all. He could take a cigarette out of a man's mouth at twenty-five paces.

"You remember that whip, don't you, Ian? It was in

the loft for years. Them brass carriage-lamps, too, what became of them? The stuff that got turned out. There was a four-poster bed in that loft when I was a boy. And the horse brasses! You know what you could've made with those bedposts, don't you? Standard lamps."

Mr. Hedges frequently forgot that his son was a Borough Education Officer, and he now asked him whether he realized Miss Styles was a teacher at St. John's Road School under old Saundersfoot, whom he then went on to describe as a man he had never liked nor trusted. "Face like a kite and always bobbing about like one, too. Real false-looking chap. Looks as though he takes to bits at night. Screw off arms, legs; remove teeth, moustache, wig, eyeballs. You know 'im? But, o' course, what am I thinking of, he was the master when you were at school there. That'll make him near retiring age. But he don't take to pieces. He's flesh and blood. *Do you know*, my father bought a horse from the man as owned the field Saundersfoot's house stands in? Big grey. Went like a stag."

Hedges was worried to think Prudence and his father had discussed Saundersfoot, and he asked whether she had said anything special. Why this dislike of Saundersfoot? What had he done wrong?

"She's a real nice clean young woman, I'd say, Ian. Before I die that's the sort of young woman I'd like to see you married to. I told her. I said you were free. ' 'is wife divorced him,' I said, 'but 'e was really the innocent party, and they did it that way round because 'e's a gentleman.' "

"Do you remember anything special she said about Saundersfoot?"

"Saundersfoot? What's the matter with him then?"

"Did Miss Styles say anything about him?"

"He's the master at the school where she works. That's what I'm telling *you*."

"She didn't say anything else?"

Mr. Hedges looked puzzled. "Well, I was telling her about this whip, you see?"

The more he thought about Saundersfoot, the more his foot hurt. There was something very odd about the way his foot gave him hell and then, half an hour later perhaps, the pain subsided and he was able to walk about quite normally. Before his father came in, his foot had been so mysteriously free from pain that he had taken his slipper off and prodded his instep. Now the rat was gnawing again. He thought of it as a real rat—no, not real, a sort of phantom rat trapped in his slipper that bit into his foot like so much cheese. He would address it obscenely, though not if his father happened to be present. When the rat was not biting, life seemed pretty good, and then, thinking about Prudence, he saw her as someone who fancied him and lied (or exaggerated anyway) about old Saundersfoot as a way of provoking him. When the rat gnawed he knew better.

Mr. Hedges closed one eye and looked at his son steadily with the other. "I told 'er judging by the injury she'd done you she must've taken a running jump. There ain't room, not in this house. So I told her, 'D'you know what I reckon? There you were, 'opping about on top of some article of furniture—a sideboard, we'll say—'opping on one foot, and then you 'op over the edge, with your leg stiff as a poker and at just the right angle.' She didn't 'alf look!"

"It wasn't like that at all."

"She must've 'it you like a train."

The sensible thing would be to ask Saundersfoot into

47

the office under some pretext and just try the name of Miss Prudence Styles on him and see how he reacted. A guilty start? Well, what then? What if he broke down and confessed? Why shouldn't he hold her hand and give her toffees? Even a pinch? Well? Hedges brooded over the problem, the rat gnawed, but he did not even feel jealous. But what if Saundersfoot became dissatisfied with merely caressing Prudence? What if he tried something really serious, and the scandal was too big to hold down? Prudence might reveal she'd reported Saundersfoot while he had still been on the nursery slope, and it would not look well in court if Hedges had to get up and admit she was quite right. Under examination he could hear himself confessing that even he had tried to embrace the witness and been severely wounded in the attempt. A reputation tarnished like this, and he would stand as much chance of successfully promoting the University of Perstowe as he would of realizing one of his really secret fantasies, like winning a Cup Finalist's medal with Newcastle United or discovering the manuscript of *Hamlet* and refusing to sell it to the Americans for a million pounds. A divorced man who has confessed to an assault on a young woman teacher trying to start a university! Hedges thought of the pleased horror that would run through the town.

In spite of the rat, he walked out of the house without the help of his crutch and found that the afternoon was still hot. He opened all the windows of his Triumph Herald and drove north, making for the by-pass when he knew perfectly well he ought to have been going back to the office to do something official about Prudence. Just what he did not know. But something.

The road ran in the shadow of a thirty-foot-high railway embankment. He drove south and west along this road.

The sun was still high enough to look over this embankment and turn the road metal blue. He could smell the hot tar above the petrol fumes of the traffic, homeward bound now that the factories had shut down for the day.

He was coming up to the turn at no more than forty, his leg throbbing right up to the hip, when suddenly he was scared. He even yelled.

He went round to the front of the car, expecting to see the fellow and his bike caught up in the wheels. He wore a black jerkin, white helmet, and goggles. But there was no sign of him. He had come out of the north-bound lane of traffic, cut across Hedges's bows, shot under the railway bridge, and by now was a couple of miles away. Two other motor cyclists, also in white helmets and black jerkins, followed under the bridge, and Hedges looked after them with the taste of vomit in his mouth.

"You wanna give some signals, mate." This was from the driver of a small delivery-van which had been behind Hedges. Once he had gone, there was nobody left who cared one way or the other. For some moments Hedges watched the traffic stream by. He was quite cold. The sun had heated the car bonnet like an oven door, and he would have liked to lie across it and warm his belly. He might have killed that fellow. The corpse might have been lying there in the dazzle.

He would give up driving. The kind of near miss he'd just experienced was happening a dozen times a day, but he'd had enough. He wouldn't expose himself any more. At this very moment he could be riding in the ambulance with the dead kid. Then there'd be the inquest. No, he'd walk everywhere. He'd crawl everywhere on hands and knees so long as he didn't have that kind of scare again.

Then he was thinking, Hell, I can't crawl everywhere.

He supposed about thirty seconds had passed, and already he was thinking of Prudence and Saundersfoot again. This could only mean he'd a pretty thin skin. Or, to put it differently, the nasty side of life took a bit of getting through to him. His reality-threshold was high. Prince Gautama saw a sick man, an old man, and a corpse and was converted to a life of piety. That was what you might call a low reality-threshold. But Hedges had only to miss homicide by a whisker, and just as though nothing had happened at all he was considering some local scandal. He had a trivial mind. Reprieved in front of the firing squad, like Dostoevski, he was the sort of man who would immediately start wondering whether his job had been kept open; or he'd be preoccupied with some small inconveience—a blister inside the nose, say, or an aching foot. His foot was aching, wasn't it? But a job and a blister in the nose and an aching foot shouldn't add up to some bloody great barricade you had to clamber over before you could really see what was going on in the world, all this birth and this copulation and this death. A man can put up with only a little reality at a time. O.K. O-o-o.K.! But sixty seconds after a near killing he ought to be sweating it out a bit more.

He was no Prince Gautama or Dostoevski, but you'd think he'd want to go into some church and thank God he hadn't destroyed anybody that afternoon. But it wasn't a killing of his contriving, was it? He'd witnessed a near suicide, and the law would have held him guiltless. Sure, but you still think he'd wanted to go into some church. The incident showed up his preoccupations to be of gnat-like importance. You'd think they'd be driven out of his mind.

Not a bit of it. He drove back to the office, and all the time his foot throbbed so that he felt like screaming. He wondered whether his brooding on this Saundersfoot affair was just a defence mechanism or whether he really was the sort of tough who heard the plane he'd missed had just crashed with no survivors and simply went on picking his teeth quietly and reading the comic strips. Yes, that's precisely the sort of stupid, unimaginative bum he was.

Once in the office he sat back in his chair, extended his right leg on the desk in front of him, and closed his eyes. The rat went on biting inside the tartan slipper, and he gave up the pretence that he was relaxing. He wiggled his toes. Curiously, the pain seemed not quite so fierce. He opened his eyes, drew his foot towards him, and removed the slipper. He wondered whether his nervous system had been affected. The exposed toes looked pink, and when he touched each one of them in turn with a pencil he could feel the contact normally.

Abruptly he began to concentrate on Prudence. After a while he could see her with some clarity beckoning him into the thickets like some irresistible wood-nymph.

"As a friend," said Amos, settling himself into the armchair on the other side of the desk, "I must tell you extraordinary rumours are flying round the town about you."

"What rumours?" said Hedges.

Amos cut judiciously this way and that in the air with the edge of his hand. "You've got to understand that there's bound to be a certain amount of prejudice against you. In the first place, you're the butcher's son who got himself a posh job on the Council, and you understand, Ian, we're conservative about such things as social station in Perstowe. We think you're a bit jumped up, you see, though if anybody asks us straight out we're always ready to say how proud we are that a local boy from the Grammar School, et cetera, et cetera. And the other thing, of course, is this business of your divorce. Nobody minds you being divorced, lad, but what shocks us all is that you're still friendly with the woman. You meet her! Worse than that, you meet her husband! You're friendly with 'em. Well, we don't like it. It's countenancing immorality. So the general opinion now is that Nell was probably right to leave you, you having these immoral, pagan views."

"What rumours?" said Hedges.

"To start with, there's the one about you having some sort of disgraceful affair with one of the teachers and her father giving you a warning by slashing the tires of your car and saying next time it would be your throat."

"I can confirm every word of that."

"And this story of stabbing your foot while lifting potatoes is a lot of hooey. It was *him*, getting that bit nearer to your throat."

"What else?"

"The university promotion is seen as sheer self-aggrandizement."

"All that," said Hedges, after he had thought about Amos's revelations, "only goes to show it isn't too late. Where there is gossip there is a real community. It shows Perstowe is still a real town. There's no gossip in suburbia. It persuades me I'm cut out to play a real role in the parish. I hope *you* didn't make these lies up."

"Unless it's the truth, somebody's got to."

"No, it isn't the truth. The truth about me, Fred, is after all not terribly interesting." He fished the key of the hospitality cabinet out of a drawer and tossed it over. Amos caught it and crossed the room to the cabinet with an air of having put other questions out of his mind. "When we were kids, can you remember us doing anything really nasty?"

52

"You used to pinch sausages out of your father's shop, and we used to go up on the moor to fry them."

"Is that all?"

"There was that smoking in Fenner's barn when the place got burned to the ground." Amos handed over Hedges's scotch and water and stood looking out into the square, sipping his own. "You know, years after, Cuthbert Simms told me it wasn't an accident. He deliberately put a match to the hay."

"What, the Reverend Cuthbert Simms?"

"Yes, the Reverend Cuthbert Simms."

Hedges sat up straight, he was so interested. "I never knew that. Well, after all these years! You mean Cuthbert set fire to that barn out of sheer bloody nastiness?"

"Yeah! He said it was what made him a Christian. Original sin."

"Marvellous blaze, though."

Hedges lowered his feet from the desk, stood up, and began to walk about. His injured foot did not so much as give him a twinge. "I couldn't have done that, Fred. I'd have been afraid. Pinching sausages is just about as wicked as I can get. Do you ever get the feeling you understand yourself?"

"I understand myself continually."

"Some people are just afraid to face truths about themselves. You know what, Fred? I'm ready to admit there's a certain amount of self-aggrandizement in this university-promotion idea of mine. What's the harm in that? Let's be honest about ourselves. Bedrock. I've got to get married."

"Pregnant again, uh?"

"I need a woman, that's all. I'd make a damn good husband. Don't listen to Nell. I'm just so aware of myself I think Freud would have been incredulous—I mean, that I

53

hadn't been analysed. Basically, that's why I thought up the university project. I'm the type who's never fully himself until he's got a cause. I've even stopped dreaming. That's a good sign."

"What did you dream about?"

"Well——"

Hedges was not quick enough off the mark; Amos was able to cut in.

"Sorry, what I really meant was I've been talking to Toplis about the university, and he's worked it out that for every student four extra workers would be needed in the town. So that economically——"

"The problem, really, Fred, is just one of keeping my spirits up. There are times when I hear nothing but the still, sad music of humanity. I've the tragic sense of life. And then I go about saying, 'What's the use? Who cares? What does it all matter?' In some ways I wish I could have been more like old Cuthbert. Wonder where he is now."

"Whatever vineyard old Cuthbert labours in will have to be a prosperous one. Always did have expensive tastes. Remember the silk shirts? So I reckon he's a regular megalomaniac these days. Betcher he's a high priest of some splinter group in South London, or Worthing, or Bournemouth, with a real heresy all of their own."

"I liked the man. A real prig if ever there was one. I was drawn to him."

He supposed that if Cuthbert, cheerful and intelligent extrovert that he was, could burn down a barn and then lie about it, Man had indeed fallen. If Cuthbert was a sinner then everyone must indeed be a sinner. He remembered hearing Cuthbert argue, after the Old Boys' Match one year, that as a result of his own experience he was convinced nobody could be saved but by the unmerited favour of God. Now that he knew Cuthbert was a fire-raiser, Hedges saw the force of this remark for the first time. He knew that he could never be religious and follow in Cuthbert's footsteps. His religious instinct, such as it was, stirred only when he felt gloomy. He loved to play his Kathleen Ferrier gramophone record and hear that splendid voice sing out, "He was despised, He was rejected." Hedges knew jolly well she wasn't actually referring to him, of course, but it was plain she knew how he felt.

The one chance he had of religious faith lay in his refusal to put up with this feeling of being an outcast. When Nell had cleared out, the feeling had, he supposed, got him down. What rejection was there so complete as that of a woman of her husband? She rejected house, money, personality, body, relatives, everything. He ceased to exist for her. In a weird kind of way, he had, for a while, ceased to exist for himself. He scarcely knew what he was wearing, doing, or eating. He even forgot how he liked his eggs boiled.

The anybody-can-kick-my-behind feeling was the great emotional hazard he would have to master. He saw life like a track through a great forest. At intervals were pits of self-disparagement which someone or something must keep him out of. And he thought, once more, of Cuthbert— and wondered whether it was conceivable that what a burning barn had done for Cuthbert, losing a wife might do for him. Not only losing a wife. Life was making a series of derisive and contemptuous gestures—producing a girl like Prudence, for example. He was *terribly* fond of her, but she, poor girl, understood herself so little that she simply didn't know how fond she was of him in return. Yes, it was contemptuous, because just at the moment he wanted to throw himself into this university campaign, Life had tugged him by the sleeve, saying, "You're human after all."

"Three's one thing, Fred," he said, as they finished up their whisky and prepared to leave. "It will never be said of me that I lived the unexamined life."

The telephone had been ringing in the outer office for some time. Hedges paid no attention until he realized it was nearly half past six and that Beryl had gone a long time ago. Hard to imagine who could be phoning at this hour unless it was the old man, asking him to do some shopping on the way home, or Amos's wife, perhaps, having failed to locate him at the Royal George. Anyway, Amos went out and answered it.

"It's a Miss Styles!" he shouted. "Shall I switch her through?"

Prudence? At the thought of speaking to her he lit up with joy. Sweet girl! He was so excited that she had been talking to him for some moments before he realized she wasn't gently cooing remorse, asking after his foot, and withdrawing her threat of resignation. She was in a blazing temper, for some reason that he couldn't understand calling him an opportunist rat.

"What's that, Pru? What's that? What?"

He heard Amos replace the receiver in the other room, and the slight rattle—Amos contrived to make it sound apologetic—conveyed desertion. Hedges would have liked to shout to Amos and get him to pick up the phone once more. This was no time for betrayal. But Prudence would not stop talking, and as long as she talked Hedges had no time to say anything but yes and no. She was forcing him to admit that he had put forward the idea for a university in the town.

"Your father?" he said incredulously. "What's he got to do with it?"

"Do with it?" There was a note in her voice that forced him right on to the defensive. Incredible that a girl who spoke like that could have allowed him to kiss her on the back of the neck. Unimaginable that she should have been put upon by old Saundersfoot! "You know jolly well you'd never have had the wit to think of starting a university in Perstowe if I hadn't told you about Daddy starting one in Brewchester."

"But, Prudence——"

"You're absolutely beastly. It was Daddy's idea first."

"There's no reason why——"

"So I want you to stop it, because the Government would never start two universities in towns that are only fifty miles apart. What sickens me in all this is your fearful duplicity. Daddy's coming over to see you."

"But there's no copyright in——"

"You only make it worse by being legalistic."

"—and in any case"—Hedges had been thrown into confusion—"to tell you the truth, I can't remember anything about a university in Brewchester. When did you tell me? I'm *not* calling you a liar. I'm just saying I put this scheme forward as my own in perfectly good faith. I did it innocently. But there's not even a railway-station at Brewchester. It just hasn't got the facilities for a university. Whereas, here, in Perstowe. . . ."

Surely, he was thinking uneasily, he had said this all before about Brewchester? He was pretty sure he had mentioned the lack of a railway-station somewhere to someone.

"But it's one of those ideas that might come to anyone at any time."

"I despise you," she said and put down her receiver.

The effect on Hedges was to make him for the first time talk candidly to Amos about the history of his own

relations with Prudence, her account of Saundersfoot's behaviour, the manner in which she had injured his foot, and
about his sudden uneasiness that in saying he had pinched
her father's idea she might have some puzzling shreds of
evidence to back her up. He still believed it was his own
notion and that he had been cherishing it for months. His
memory was not what it was. He had lapses. Something to
do with wanting to forget the divorce and all that unplea-
santness—going off to that hotel with that sordid woman
and being horrified to discover they'd been given a double
bed. Experiences like this were bound to damage a chap's
memory. There was so much he just wanted to wipe off the
slate. He explained all this to Amos and went on to say that
one thing was pretty evident, whether he had pinched Mr.
Styles's idea or whether he hadn't, and that was the deep
feeling Prudence had for her father and possibly all other
old men too. This must be faced. It was a real sign of
immaturity.

"Tell me," he said as an afterthought, "how did you
come to print that story about me sticking a garden-fork in
my foot?"

"Your father told us," Amos replied.

Hedges very clearly had the feeling now that some
kind of catastrophe was gaining momentum and that there
was one simple step he ought to take before matters got
worse. He really ought to have a quiet chat with Saundersfoot. The difficulty was how to give him the tip-off that
Prudence Styles *might* be dangerous without embarrassing
the old chap—or himself, for that matter. He did not want
to do anything ostentatious, like going to the school and
taking Saundersfoot on one side. For one thing, Prudence
might spot them and guess what was going on. Fortunately,

Hedges was able to meet the Headmaster in the heightened atmosphere of the Peacock affair. This permitted him to slip in the news about Prudence almost as a postscript. Certainly with great delicacy.

The following morning a certain Mrs. Peacock and her son Walter were shown into his office. Hedges was sitting parallel to his desk with his right, slippered foot (hurting again!) resting on the seat of a chair and the *Financial Times* draped across his knees. (He loved studying prices. He was not on the make. He had about a thousand pounds invested in five different kinds of shares and watched the prices fluctuate, week in, week out, feeling all the time he was tending some queerly fascinating plant. He didn't understand the feeling. That was something else he meant to get to the bottom of.)

"Sorry to hear about your accident," said Mrs. Peacock, a small, intelligent-looking woman with her head tied up in a yellow scarf like a fortune-teller; and after Hedges had excused himself from rising she sat down in the leatherette-covered, stained visitor's chair. Walter looked as though he could not possibly have anything to do with her. He had broad pink cheeks and small eyes set rather close together.

"What's this I hear, Walter, about your not wanting to go to the Grammar School?" said Hedges.

Walter was now watching the flower-seller shake a watering-can over her bunches of carnations and sweet peas on the clock steps. "My mates are going to the Secondary Modern," he remarked in a bored but sturdy voice, "and I wants to stick with 'em, sir."

"But *every* boy wants to go to the Grammar School. You want to get on in the world, don't you? What are you going to do when you leave school?"

"He's just silly," said Mrs. Peacock.

"I'll go to the Grammar School," said Walter, "if Fred Thorne and Arthur Wisdom and Reg Hill go too, but I'm not going by myself. We wouldn't want the gang to be split up."

"Look at Mr. Hedges when you're talking." Mrs. Peacock caught Walter by the elbow and gave him a shake. The boy turned his head slowly and stared mournfully at Hedges.

"These other boys *can't* go." Hedges pitched the *Financial Times* into the waste-paper-basket and tried to sit a little more upright. "They failed their Eleven-Plus exam. I mean," he corrected himself quickly, "the examination showed that the right kind of education for you was provided by the Grammar School. Book-learning, Latin, algebra, that sort of thing. But your mates will be happier with other kinds of work."

"So would I," said Walter. "We don't want to get split up, see, sir."

"What other family have you, Mrs. Peacock?"

"Walter's the youngest; there's Nigel, he's sixteen, and Lorna, she's fourteen; and Walter's the only one to pass into the Grammar School."

"His brother and sister went to the Secondary Modern?"

"That's right. It's enough to make you feel you want to knock 'is head off. I'd set my heart on one of 'em going to the Grammar School." She pitched her voice a little higher to talk to her son. "If it was the other way round, and Fred Thorne or one of the others got a Grammar School place and you didn't, you don't think he'd chuck up the chance of getting on in the world just for your benefit, do you?"

"Yes, 'e would," said Walter. "We swore an oath, see?"

Mrs. Peacock brought her glossy black handbag up to chest level and gave it a good shake. "You swore an oath not to go to the Grammar? You silly little idiot! You didn't tell me! That's the first I 'eard of it."

"We swore an oath all to go to go to the same school," said Walter.

"Their Headmaster should never have allowed it." Mrs. Peacock's self-control was beginning to give way. There were pale patches as big as half-crowns under her eyes, and she shook her handbag as though it were Walter himself.

"Let me see, who is Walter's Headmaster?"

"Mr. Saundersfoot."

"Indeed." Hedges lifted his telephone and said, "See if you can get Mr. Saundersfoot for me, will you? and if he's engaged leave a message for him to ring back." He replaced the receiver. "St. John's Road is the school I went to myself, Walter, and Mr. Saundersfoot was Headmaster there then. But I wasn't a clever boy like you."

"I'm no more intelligent than Reg Hill." Walter spoke with unexpected savagery. "It's only that he don't put down the working. He does the sums in 'is 'ead, only nobody believes him."

Hedges consulted the papers again and saw that Walter had an I.Q. of 148.

The phone rang. Saundersfoot's voice whinnied down the line, excited as always. "Are you calling me or am I calling you?"

Hedges asked the boy to step out of the room for a moment. When the door had closed, he said, "Hallo! I've Mrs. Peacock with me, mother of Walter Peacock, remember? I suppose we've just got to insist on his taking the Grammar School place."

"It's the boy's father."

"Eh?"

"It's the boy's father behind it all. Look, I've a free period, Ian. I'll hop in the car. I'll be with you within five minutes."

While they waited, Mrs. Peacock and Hedges drank coffee and talked about Mr. Peacock. Hedges thought it prudent to keep Walter in the outer office, where he ate a doughnut and read the cartoons in Beryl's *Daily Mirror*.

"My 'usband is very, very conservative," said Mrs. Peacock. "He's an electrician, and what was good enough for him's good enough for Walter. *He* thinks! Mind you, he's a collar-and-tie electrician. He dresses you wouldn't know he wasn't going to a real white-collar job. And *his* father, who was *not* a collar-and-tie electrician (he wore a blue boiler suit), said, one day, 'Tom, you're the first member of our family as earned 'is living with a collar and tie on,' and I could see it was really quite a nasty shock to Tom, to be told that. His father didn't mean anything. If anything, he was *proud*, but Tom thought his father was accusing him of class treachery, I reckon. The Peacocks 'ave been electricians right 'ere in Perstowe for 'undreds of years."

"Oh, but electricity hasn't been invented all that long."

"Excuse *me*," said Mrs. Peacock firmly.

"And he wants Walter to be an electrician too?"

"I must say they earns good money. But I've set my heart on young Walter being a research biologist."

"What?"

"The rate the population of the world is going, we're going to need a lot more food. Blessed is he who makes two blades of grass grow where one grew before."

Hedges was sorry, when Saundersfoot arrived, to hear him suggest that Mrs. Peacock withdraw for a moment while the two men had a quick word together. He didn't like discussing the affairs of such a serious-minded woman behind her back.

"Ian," Saundersfoot cried, the moment the door was closed behind her, "I'd forgotten it was today you were seeing the boy." He leaned forward and rested the tips of the fingers of his left hand on the plaster of Hedges's left foot, signifying: I have taken note of this object. I heard of your accident. At the appropriate moment we shall discuss it. But more important things first.

Saundersfoot was a tall, nervous man in his late fifties with a peculiarly cracked and worn pink face under his rough, sandy hair and untidy moustache. This is how he had always looked. When Hedges first knew him, thirty or so years ago, his face had had this same parched and floury pink surface. It was like old clay, dabbed on none too neatly. And where the hair of his head and of his moustache broke through the clay surface, there were tiny crinklings where the skin had been forced aside. The round blue eyes stood out on the surface of the face. It was horrible to imagine such a face coming closer and closer in the stationery store, or wherever it was poor Prudence alleged his rutting ground to be.

"I wanted to be quite sure," said Saundersfoot, "that you made no idle promises, Ian. I know you. I know how easily swayed you are. That boy *must* go to the Grammar School. Are you aware that old man Peacock is the local branch secretary of the Electrical Trade Union?"

"Mrs. Peacock said he was a Conservative."

"He's a Commie, my boy, and that's why he doesn't want young Walter to go to the Grammar School. I know Peacock. He's in the Bowls Club. He's one of those hard-bitten, unforgiving, paranoic Communists. He doesn't want

Walter to go to the Grammar School because he knows that's how he'll lose the boy. The boy will get some bloody scholarship, go to the University, move up the social scale, and be one of *them* bastards. That's how Peacock talks. He's got a theory the trade-union movement needs all the intelligence it can get. I'm out to defeat this. I'll bleed 'em, I will. I'll bleed the intelligence out of the class that makes trade unionists, so long as I'm in the teaching profession, I will!"

Saundersfoot's flamboyant Toryism was well-known in Perstowe, though this was the first time Hedges had heard him bring politics into the actual business of teaching.

"Well, perhaps Mrs. Peacock and the boy can come back in now," Hedges said and pressed his buzzer. "Mrs. Peacock," he said, when the pair were standing on the other side of his desk and he had apologized once more for not rising, "I think Walter had better go back to school now. And I'd like to see Mr. Peacock himself, if that's possible, because after all, if Walter does go to the Grammar School, he's the one who has to sign the form guaranteeing to keep him there until he is sixteen."

"There won't be any difficulty about *that*, Mr. Hedges, I can assure you."

"Dad won't sign," said Walter, and his mother turned and slapped him open-handed across the side of the head. He neither moved nor changed expression, but Mrs. Peacock shook her hand as though she had burned it.

"It is illustrative of Peacock's cunning," said Saundersfoot, after Mrs. Peacock and the boy had gone, "that he should allow this Grammar School issue to go forward simply as Walter's disinclination to leave the gang. All the time, there he is, behind the scenes, pumping a lot of seditious nonsense into the boy. I mean, this talk of solidarity with one's pals. What's more, Ian, I don't believe this is an isolated case. Up and down the country I've not the slightest doubt there are Commie trade unionists standing in the way of their children's Grammar School education. They don't work alone. Peacock would not strike out by himself. There is a conspiracy."

"I don't believe that, Ted."

"I've taught for very nearly forty years, and I have never known a boy refuse a Grammar School place because he wants to stick with his pals. I'm not sure that Peacock, Wisdom, and Hill *are* pals anyway. They're always fighting each other like bloody hell."

"They fight, do they?"

"Especially young Peacock. Unless we get that lad into the Grammar School and off to the University and on to the social escalator he will—mark my words, I won't be here to see it—be one of those big noises in the T.U.C. who get their dental treatment in a Moscow clinic, take their holidays at a Black Sea resort, and then have the effrontery to try and dictate British Government policy! Try? If it's a Labour Government in power he *will* be dictating policy. And it's all based on rigged ballots. I won't be here to see it, Ian, but I've got children and I love this country. It's a good place to live. I've travelled about—France, Belgium, Scotland. I know! Young Peacock goes to the Grammar School if it's the last thing I do. His mother is, of course, a natural ally. I don't mind telling you I've thought of taking her aside and telling her I was up to her husband's game. But then, I don't like mixing teaching with politics."

"I wouldn't do that, Ted," said Hedges.

"Then what are you going to do? And another thing! It's the being defied I don't like. Peacock is trying to defy us."

"Well, after all, it's *his* son."

"Peacock doesn't think of him like that. He thinks of the boy as a pawn in the political game."

"But, Ted, if you *do* believe education puts people on what you call the social escalator and makes working-class boys into middle-class white-collar workers, then you're really agreeing with Peacock."

Beryl brought some more coffee in and Saundersfoot put his buffalo-head pipe on Hedges's desk, where it remained upright, supported by one of the curling horns.

"Of course I agree with his analysis. Peacock is an intelligent man. I'm just determined to frustrate his purpose, that's all." He sucked in a quarter of a pint of coffee. "No, on second thoughts, I don't really agree with his analysis. Peacock's is an entirely nineteenth-century conception. The so-called working classes of tomorrow will *be* the white-collar workers. Peacock is in the intellectual position of a Cobbett who was against, you'll remember, poor boys having a lot of schooling because it made them discontented with the hewing of wood and the drawing of water. He simply lacked the intelligence and the imagination to see what the nineteenth century was to bring. Peacock has no conception of what the *next* industrial revolution will bring. I don't suppose he's even heard of cybernetics."

"Funny you should mention that word," said Hedges. "People are always telling me what it means but I keep forgetting."

"I take it you've powers to direct young Peacock to the Grammar School?"

Hedges was letting his coffee get cold. As Saundersfoot had been talking, so his sympathy for the Peacock school of thought had been growing—Peacock, junior, that is to say.

He kept thinking of young Walter's sturdy remark, "I want to stick with my mates"; a wise remark, surely—one that sprang from a sure social instinct. Hedges was beginning to see he ought to be on Walter's side rather than against him.

"There's not much wrong with the world," said Mr. Saundersfoot. "I've no sympathy for the self-pitying gloom that people go in for nowadays. It's naïve and ignorant. Your belly-aching intellectuals who go stalking across Hampstead Heath talking about the splendid days before the dissociation of sensibility set in and people were happily ignorant of the difference between thinking and feeling, they just get on my wick! I don't believe in the Golden Age before the Industrial Revolution. I think, to be specific, that Minchin is a fool. There are far too many people about suffering from a sense of guilt over the mere fact of being alive. Instead of dancing on Dante's grave, which is the healthy and sensible thing to do, they say, 'Poor chap, you may be dead and we may be alive but you have no cause to envy us. Just the reverse. We are living at a time when the consciousness of man, once upon a time a great crystal dome refracting in splendid colours the radiance of eternity, is shattered around us.' At least," Mr. Saundersfoot continued, "they would say something like that if they'd read Shelley, which nobody has these days, and had some shreds of native eloquence to support them in the modification of a metaphor."

Hedges had been familiar with Saundersfoot's oratorical style since the time when he would have found it inconceivable that there was any other, but he still had a lot of anxiety when Saundersfoot launched into what was obviously going to be an elaborate sentence and had to look away, or shut his eyes, so that he could pretend not to have noticed if Saundersfoot failed to bring it off. But usually Saundersfoot did.

"And as for the Ancient World," said Saundersfoot, "when an intelligent man scarcely knew where his body ended and the rest of nature began, that is not an epoch when I would have wished to live. I believe in a high standard of living; I believe in a plentitude of consumer goods; I believe in sanitation, hygiene, anaesthetics, and an absence of irrational religious belief. Man's life need not be nasty, brutish, and short. The fear of the H-bomb is less, to most of us, than the fear of the plague was to the inhabitants of Perstowe in the fourteenth century. Ian, have I spoken to you on this subject before?"

"Yes," said Hedges.

"Then you'll know my belief that society has evolved to a fine flower when the poorest boy can grow up to be Prime Minister. Today, in England, we are in that happy position. And then people like Peacock arise who don't like this free and open society. They don't like *individuals* going up the social scale. It has to be the whole bloody working class going up. And that is why I am against them. I am against everybody who thinks in terms of classes and categories. You know me, Ian, I've always thought of the individual. How did we get on to this subject?"

"We were talking about young Walter Peacock as an example of the kind of intelligence you were determined to drain out of the working class. You were going to put him on the social escalator."

"As I put *you* on," said Saundersfoot, "and I don't suppose you've regretted it, eh?"

Hedges supposed that Saundersfoot's eloquence was all the fiercer because of the way it was dammed up at home.

There, Mrs. Saundersfoot scarcely allowed him to raise his voice.

Throughout this interview, Hedges had been waiting for an opportunity to mention Prudence. He was on the point of doing so when, to his surprise, Saundersfoot beat him to it.

"Now I'm here, I may as well mention another little matter that's been on my mind. You know Miss Styles on my staff? You remember the girl? I'm worried about her."

"Prudence Styles? Yes, I know her."

"Prudence? Is that her name? That's as may be." Saundersfoot's pipe bubbled like a cauldron. "No disciplinarian. I've had to sit at the back of her class and clout a few heads, I can tell you. Slack at her marking. The other day I found a stack of exercise books she hadn't marked for a month. D'you know what her explanation was? Said she was writing a novel."

"What about?"

"She said her pen-name was Richard Derby—I don't like it, Ian. I said I wouldn't have it."

"As a matter of fact she called on me in hospital."

"She did, did she? What for?"

"She put me there. She trod on me with her stiletto heel. I was trying to kiss her at the time."

"Good God!" Saundersfoot looked at his pipe as though it had spoken.

"What's more, she says you've been making passes at her yourself."

"Me?" Saundersfoot was still watching his pipe, but his pink, crumbling face flushed even brighter. "The little bitch!"

"I suppose the real question is, How do we shut her up before there's a scandal?"

Saundersfoot, who was probably thinking of his wife, did not look like the man who had referred to Shelley's crystal dome.

"How *do* you propose dealing with her?"

"Once my foot's better," said Hedges, "I thought of asking her to marry me. Though I doubt whether I'm old enough. She's got this fixation on old men. It's her father's fault. Do you know, Ted, she seems to think he's the only man in the country capable of a new idea."

Hedges woke in the middle of the night. He lay in the dark, listening to the wind in the poplars and thinking of all the people around him in the sleeping town. All but he were observing the truce. Come the morning and each man, woman, and child would pick up the old, familiar personality and start rushing about again. You had to be an insomniac to marvel at the continuity. The man he was the day before seemed already a stranger. Tomorrow?

70

CHAPTER THREE

The Promotion Committee

Hedges doubted whether he could now stop the university idea going ahead, though there came a time when he would have liked to. For one thing, it was somebody else's turn to be convinced that the whole thing was his own brain-child—Gideon Toplis, of all people. That very evening Toplis was giving a dinner, to which Hedges was invited, where the Promotion Committee would be launched officially. For another, it was understood that Christopher Brush would be present at the dinner to preserve the speeches with his tape recorder for posterity.

Doubts too arose about his own role in the affair. Had he simply pinched the idea from Brewchester? The more he thought about it, the less he could be sure. It was distressing to have his lack of self-knowledge underlined in this way, he who had boasted that Freud himself would have examined him with incredulity. Not being able to think of anything better to do, he decided to go and look at Brewchester for himself, hoping, frankly, to reassure himself about the place being absurdly inadequate as the site of a university. His experiences at Brewchester and while returning from there gave him doubts about Perstowe University that were even more fundamental than those raised by the way Gideon Toplis had horned in, by the thought of Brush as the Recording Devil, or even by the simple wish to put himself in the clear with Prudence again.

A gazetteer told him that Brewchester was a picturesque old town on a hilltop with a broad High Street, a fine Abbey, a population of 7,480, and early closing on Thursday. The nearer he approached the more shrewdly did the rat bite into his foot. By the time he was driving down the High Street and looking out for a saddler's, he had already decided he would go back to Perstowe by train. That was something else he had discovered from the gazetteer. Brewchester had a railway-station. He parked the car in the station-yard and went loping round the town, thinking that old man Styles must be really crazy to imagine that such a one-eyed place could sustain a university. There were sweet-smelling lime-trees in the market-place, enormous yews in the Abbey yard, pollarded beeches in the bus-station. There was a Woolworth's but no Marks, Boots with a library, and an extraordinary number of pubs. The local industries were cheese-making and light engineering. In the White Lion, the bartender said he had never heard of any idea to go in for college building in Brewchester, but, at the Marquis of Granby, Hedges got into conversation with the licensee himself, who said, Yes, Mr. Styles had a letter every week in the local paper about a new university, and the Bishop was now talking about making church land on the other side of the Abbey available as a site. If Hedges took the first turning on the right he'd come to Mr. Styles's house, a red-brick building set back from the lane, with a banner over the front gates.

Hedges was looking up at this banner—it was supported by what looked like a couple of bean sticks and said *Floreat Brewchester*—when he became aware of a foxy-faced man in a white panama watching him from between two rows of sweet peas in cordon. It was noon, cloudless, hot. Water gurgled in the shadow of a crumbling wall, and the man, with a band of blue shadow across the eyes, went on staring with such intentness that Hedges turned away and walked back to the High Street. Just the sort of chap who might use *The Voyage of the Beagle* to teach his daughter to read. And the next time he saw Hedges he would know him! Hedges even wondered whether he ought to go back and introduce himself. What as?

Over lunch in the Marquis he reflected he might do more harm than good by telling Prudence he had been over to Brewchester and that, as he had suspected, it did not compare with Perstowe as the site for a university. Too late he realized he should have made himself known to Mr. Styles. Man to man they would have been able to decide pretty quickly that there was so much talk of new universities in the air nowadays it didn't make sense to accuse anyone of pinching the idea from anyone else. On the other hand, Mr. Styles looked the sort of man who might already have had a word with the police about a stranger who'd been inspecting his house and garden.

He could not understand why he should have this sense of big trouble ahead. Perhaps it was just one of the effects of the anti-tetanus jabs they had given him for his foot. Certainly his foot was playing him up again. All this pain on a full stomach made him feel sick. He opened his *Express* and looked to see what guidance Lord Luck had for him. Pisces subjects, he learned, would impress people in authority. Who were people? What was authority? He thought of the night when he had awakened and listened to the deep breathing of every unconscious puppet in Perstowe. There was a moment in the middle of every night when their roles were easily interchangeable. Hedges could imagine himself switching the little psyches and then watching Amos, say, set off to play Saundersfoot's part with as much fire as Saundersfoot would play his. Hedges looked up to see whether anyone had spotted he was reading Lord Luck. He once thought a belief in luck was the philosophy of the spiritually destitute. Well, call it realism.

For the journey back to Perstowe, Hedges found himself alone in a first-class non-smoker with a young, red-faced clergyman who was reading the *New Scientist* and smoking a brier pipe with a bowl as large as a good-sized coffee-cup.

"I hope you don't object to my smoking," the parson said, lowering his paper, "but this is the only corner seat I could find."

Hedges wondered if he knew Cuthbert.

"I smoke myself," Hedges said, "but I got in here not to."

"Good! Good!" The parson returned to his paper.

The train rattled past a disused brickworks, then a timber-yard where tens of thousands of rough-sawn elm strips were stacked to dry. The bitter, forest smell could be detected even through the two-inch gap of the open window.

"Coffin wood," said Hedges.

"Eh?" The parson lifted his eyes in surprise.

"All that wood. For coffins." Hedges had some scarcely formulated idea that this was a subject of reasonable professional interest to a clerk in holy orders, but he must have been wrong because the fellow just went on puffing his

74

pipe, and looked at him out of bright, attentive, darting eyes.

"You going far?"

"Injured my foot. So I left my car and took the train."

"I'm going right through to London. You may be interested to know I'm staying the night in Lambeth Palace."

Hedges was trying to measure him up. "Afraid I don't go to church much."

"Neither do I," said the parson unexpectedly. "I go to Communion, of course, but I assume you are referring to the ordinary religious services. They are a great embarrassment, I fear."

"Embarrassment?"

"Terms of reference all wrong." The parson emptied his dottle on to the floor and filled up again straight from the tin. "Trouble with non-smoking compartments is they've got no ash-trays."

Hedges, who really was out for balm for his bruised spirit, muttered something about the emphasis Christianity placed on believing a lot of impossible things.

"Well, of course"—and the parson, looking cautious, gripped his pipe-stem the more tightly between his teeth—"I could recommend a few books to you, if you like."

"I haven't got time to read a lot of books."

The parson would clearly have liked to pick up his *New Scientist* once more. "Why don't you see your parish priest?"

By now Hedges had observed the name-tab on the suitcase, the Reverend W. D. Warp, M.A., and he said with great urgency, "Mr. Warp, I beg you to tell me something here and now."

"You have the advantage of me."

"Hedges."

"Mr. Hedges, I don't see your difficulty. You're obviously an educated man. It's all very, very simple."

Hedges kept one eye on the corridor. He would have been very upset if a stranger had butted in at just this moment. "The Creed, you know, dead and buried, the third day. Then there are all those miracles. It's all impossible, isn't it?"

Mr. Warp was now beginning to frown heavily. "From one point of view, yes. From another point of view, no. If the supernatural side is difficult for you, why don't you demythologize it?"

"What's that?"

"Read the Gospels not as historical records but as doctrinal and liturgical documents for the Early Church. And it is for us to discover what they mean to the twentieth century."

"Mr. Warp." Hedges put out his hands with the absurd idea at the back of his mind that perhaps Warp would grasp them in brotherly love. "Do you believe that Jesus rose from the dead?"

"I don't see how any rational man could be certain about problems like this. The evidence simply isn't there. No, I don't believe that in the ordinary sense of the words there was a physical Resurrection. In point of fact," said Mr. Warp confidentially, "the modern theologian believes awfully little, really. You can take it from me the division nowadays isn't between the believers and the unbelievers. You know, Christians and atheists, that lark! The division is between those who are dogmatic, one way or the other, and those who aren't. Me, I'm not dogmatic. Indeed, I think the modern Protestant theologian believes so little nowadays there's very little *doctrinal* reason why everybody shouldn't be Christian. Compared with you, Mr. Hedges, there are some eminent Christian theologians—and I could name them—who are almost atheists."

The Reverend Warp had been talking so much he had been unable to get his pipe going. He abandoned the struggle, thrust the tobacco down with his thumb, put the pipe in his pocket, and stood up. "I'd like to say how much I've enjoyed our little chat." He loosened his clerical collar. "No, I insist. I'm quite capable of getting my own case down." He lowered it to the floor and picked up his black Homburg.

"I've just realized I've been smoking my pipe in a non-smoking compartment, and as I've quite a journey in front of me. . . ." He stepped into the corridor. "Pipe a great comfort. Intellectual stimulus. Glad to have met you, sir."

With a wave he disappeared.

In his haste he left his *New Scientist* behind him, and for the rest of the journey Hedges wrestled with an article on the conservation of parity in fundamental particles. He didn't understand it, and he reflected he was not preparing himself very well for the dinner that night. He would certainly be called on to speak. Perhaps Toplis was looking to him to whip up enthusiasm. But instead of preparing his speech he had tired himself out with a pointless trip to Brewchester, set his foot throbbing like mad, and engaged in a conversation with an agnostic parson that made him feel it didn't much matter what happened. This was when his more serious doubts began to take shape. Perhaps he had better say, "Gentlemen, it's all a mistake. My interest in the founding of a university was purely social. I thought it would help to make Perstowe into a real community once more, but I see now that it is more likely to destroy it. A

77

rush of strangers into the town would be a real social shock."

He even began turning over a few reasons why Brewchester's claim might be supported; what's more, he now thought Prudence had been right all the time and he ought to go and apologize to her for the calm way he had tried to elbow Brewchester to one side.

What Toplis's dinner-party ought to address itself to was something more fundamental than the whys and wherefores of a new university. Let them consider the nature of the good life. Had they the social set-up that made it possible? All right, talk communism if you wanted to, but who was it said communism was a Christian heresy, and hadn't it been well argued that Christian society itself had a fatal flaw? The unit was the family and it was too small. If the family didn't happen to work, you had Mods and Rockers. But if the social unit was the tribe or the clan, there was a much bigger pod for the individual to shake about in. Outside Christendom, juvenile delinquents didn't exist. So, down with the family! Tribalize Britain!

But Toplis would expect him to be practical. Hedges tried to think of some way of persuading Toplis's guests to drop university promotion and go in for some basic thinking about the good life, but the more he thought the more his foot hurt.

He arrived home to find Prudence waiting for him. She was talking to his father in the garden. As soon as they were alone, she said, "I want you to forget what I told you about Mr. Saundersfoot. He's been pestering me again, but I want you to forget all about it."

The sun was trapped in the bleached yard, and Hedges, who sat in the beetle seat with his right leg on a kitchen chair in the hope that blood and pain would drain away, thought the sun was attacking his very substance. It bored through him. He doubted whether he was casting a shadow. The unripe plums gleamed like green bullets in the shining trees.

"Is Mr. Saundersfoot going to the dinner tonight?" Prudence was asking. "Well, I hope the food chokes the lot of you."

"Pestering you? Again?"

In his surprise and pain he had forgotten to ask her to sit down. He peered at her through his nearly closed lashes and formed the impression she would not have sat down anyway; she was standing, rather boyishly he thought, with a brief-case in one hand and what looked like a leather binocular-case in the other, though it might have been a camera. Her radiant, bronzed, beautiful face seemed to wobble, but this was an effect created by his quivering eyelashes. The hot sun, that was reducing him to dust and air, only slipped on the surface of her wide, staring eyes and came back at him like two blue daisies. He slackened his tie and licked his lips. His carpet-slipper fell off.

"Saundersfoot's not coming to the dinner."

He was quite right, she wouldn't sit down. She stood there with the sun in her face, saying, yes, Saundersfoot had put his arm round her in the stationery store, mumbling incoherently but not so incoherently that she had been unable to gather he, Hedges, had spoken to Saundersfoot about her previous complaint. She wished to God he'd done nothing of the sort. Obviously the old man had been wounded. If Hedges had more understanding of human nature, he would know Saundersfoot was more to be pitied than blamed. He was lonely. Prudence said that she took no particular pride he'd picked on her. She just happened to be around, that's all. On her, as a result, fell the burden of response to this aging male animal. Mr. Saundersfoot was helplessly caught in a sexual current. If Hedges hadn't enough understanding of human nature to know what was going on, could he not have a little sympathy for a man who, by all reports, had been singularly kind to him over the years? Look at it this way: in twenty years' time Hedges himself might be going through exactly the same trouble.

Good God, Hedges would have liked to say if only she would stop talking, there had been no reproaches from him. It was her complaint, not his.

The sun burned his unprotected foot, and his imagination had been surprised into such nervous sensitivity that he thought he could smell roasting flesh. He sat up and covered his foot with his father's straw boater which lay conveniently to hand—the same old butcher's boater with the red and white ribbon that in years gone by had been worn in the High Street shop.

Prudence went on to say in effect that she hoped she understood the rules of sex warfare as well as anyone. She hadn't asked for protection. She took the greatest pleasure in looking after herself. Her life, she seemed to imply, was a succession of vigorous encounters with the opposite sex, thank God, and just because Hedges had been physically injured in one of them that didn't mean he'd carved out any special status in her eyes and he wasn't to deceive himself, not for one second, on the score of having a painful foot.

She pressed the attack. "Talking about me," she said, "about something I consulted you in confidence about, talking behind my back! Do you think that if I wanted that sort of thing said I'm not capable of saying it myself?"

"What sort of thing?"

"I was complaining about his attentions."

"That's not the language I'd use."

"And that you'd kissed me and we were going to be married." She brushed the moist hair back from her forehead with her wrist and actually wagged a finger. "Your common sense ought to have told you that Mr. Saundersfoot was infatuated. The very thought of an *affaire* between you and me would upset him terribly. It upsets me a bit. And there's Edward."

"Edward?"

"He's in Aden."

Hedges was stupefied by all this.

"I am not, I'd like you to understand"—she was speaking quietly, and it made her anger all the more impressive—"a little girl in need of care and protection. By what right do you try and interfere with my private affairs?"

She didn't even ask him how his foot was. The fact that Hedges was reclining and she was standing no longer seemed odd. He really felt he had been laid low. She looked as though she had laid him low. The tremendous sun went on grilling them until—time passed, even at a meeting like this—the shadow of the plum-tree rose like water to touch his dangling hand, and he felt the coolness creep up his fingers.

Shut up! he wanted to say to her. Come and sit by my side and let me pass my water-cooled hand over your beautiful naked knee. You're wearing no stockings. I can see that much between my lashes. Let me caress your sun-dried thighs with my reassuring hand, only for God's sake stop this hysterical, meaningless talk! Let me kiss your (if it has to be admitted) rather thin, boyish neck, so thin that to my way of thinking your golden head rocks like a rose on its stem.

But in her present mood there was not the ghost of a chance.

"Say good-bye to your father for me."

These were the last words of some rigmarole, to which he did not properly listen, about how easy it was to bring really sensitive people (she meant Saundersfoot again) to the point of suicide. Thank heaven Mr. Saundersfoot was too well-balanced even to think of such a step, but Hedges ought to understand that he had been playing with some highly explosive material. His official position was no licence for lunacy. Let him look out.

And she went.

Normally Hedges loved a dinner-party. He loved putting on a black tie, standing about with other guests while they waited for late-comers. He liked lifting full glasses off a passing tray and putting them back again empty. He liked the faint smell of roast from the kitchen. He liked green olives and the aroma of somebody else's whisky when he himself was taking gin. The dress, the drink, the buzz of conversation—all this normally gave him a feeling of buoyancy on a sea of well-being. The calm expanse of a shirt-front and the glitter of cuffs could usually make him bubble with optimism. But fatigue after the trip to Brewchester, the fact that this was a stag-party (the sight of figged-out women would have helped), the shock of Prudence's outburst only a couple of hours before, the sight of a blue-chinned Christopher Brush in tails, like a waiter, setting up a battery of microphones down the centre of the dining-table, and his embarrassment over having one foot in a carpet-slipper—all this took the zip out of the occasion. For God's sake, what was he going to say?

The tape recorder was set up on a table in the corner of the dining-room. Presumably that was where Brush would sit during the course of the meal. To make sure, Hedges walked round the table to inspect the names on the cards. It would have been most disagreeable to find Brush actually taking a speaking part in this Perstowe University Promotion Committee dinner. For one thing, Hedges did not wish to hear Brush uttering on the subject; for another, his presence at the table could only mean that someone else would be working the tape recorder, and that someone else could only be Nell. Fortunately Brush's name did not appear on any of the cards.

"If you get hungry," Hedges said to him, "give me a shout and I'll throw you a chop or something."

"I've had mine already," said Brush, "in the kitchen, and I don't mind telling you the chicken's like boiled rubber."

Gideon Toplis, the host, was an elderly jockey of a man—a brown-faced, stringy, slightly bow-legged bachelor —who had been a regular soldier and come into the family business unexpectedly. He stood with his back to the fire, shaking words over Arrowsmith, who owned the *Advertiser*, and Fred Amos, who edited it. Others present included Sam Primrose, Conservative and Unionist M.P. for Perstowe; Jimmy Pigge, whose family had at one time owned Lack Park; and Arthur Supple, the grocer, recently elected Mayor and Chairman of the Education Committee. Toplis had already made it clear he expected this gathering would set up a committee to promote the establishment of a university in Perstowe, and Hedges had

83

already had enough conversation with him to realize that Toplis was convinced the whole thing was his own idea. Well, perhaps Amos *had* said something to show he was fumbling towards a plan for higher education in the town; but it had been he, Toplis, who had at once seen the possibilities.

He had a wiry voice that cut through most conversation. "Look here," he said over the smoked salmon, "you don't get a university simply by putting your hand up. There's some cut-throat competition about. Stamford has offered to put threepence on the rates."

" 'Strewth!" said Jimmy Pigge.

"And Canterbury is ready to put a hundred thousand quid down on the counter. They've got a site, too. Four hundred acres. You can see I've been doing my homework on this, Primrose."

Arthur Supple was using his smoked salmon and brown bread and butter to make sandwiches. "Well, if it means money on the rates the folk won't stand for it."

"Supple, we must have vision." Primrose looked up and down the table to see if he had attention. "If Canterbury can have a university, why can't we, eh? Why should Perstowe be left behind? I hope you're not suggesting"— Primrose became flushed and excited at the thought—"that Perstowe isn't on a level with Canterbury!"

"If the Government wants new universities then let the Government pay for 'em," said Supple.

Toplis put down his knife and fork. "Are you aware, Supple, that a student population of three thousand means ten thousand jobs going for the men and women of Perstowe?"

Supple said that he did not believe it. And, in any case, there was no unemployment in Perstowe, so even if there *were* ten thousand more jobs who was going to do them, remembering that the town plan provided for a population of one hundred and five thousand, which they'd pretty nearly got? It would mean tearing up the town plan, a new university would, if the argument about jobs held water. But it didn't. Supple said he was against the idea of a university. He had every respect for Toplis, and that was why he had come along to this nice dinner. He had every respect for the other gentlemen present, too. They must excuse his plain speaking. He had known Mr. Pigge's family all his life, and so had his father and grandfather before him. He used to play football with Toplis's brother. He knew these gentlemen, and he wasn't puffing himself up and trying to claim as he knew better than they did. But he had to speak his mind and if you put the question to him squarely, he would have to say, no, he was against this Perstowe University idea. He stopped Toplis's butler from giving him any wine and asked for water instead.

Supple was a big-headed, awkward-looking man with a clean chin but patches of hair over his cheek-bones. Toplis's eyebrows shot up. He stared at Supple but said nothing. Nobody else spoke either. A couple of women in black nylon went round with the chicken and vegetables. And there was suppressed groaning. Why the hell hadn't Toplis won Supple over beforehand? You couldn't enjoy this food and argue at the same time. If Supple was against the university, why not simply leave him off the Promotion Committee? But you couldn't. He was the Mayor. Sam Primrose, who was more used than the rest of them to talking and eating at the same time, began speaking about his recent visit to the Soviet Union, where a child had a one-in-eight chance of going to a university as against a one-in-thirty chance in Great Britain. He had been *enormously* impressed by the standard of English-speaking. Where did they acquire such good accents? To his mind it was conclusive proof that they listened to the B.B.C. in spite of the jamming. He wished Supple had been with him to hear the kind of English spoken in Moscow.

"A lot of bloody, dishonest rubbish is talked about universities," said Supple. While Primrose had been talking, he had cleared his plate with extraordinary rapidity and could now lecture while the slower eaters had their mouths full. "I ask myself how many people have a disinterested belief in the value of university education. Precious few. The idea has always got to be sold for some other reason. For example, competition with Russia. And another thing. Towns have universities these days the way some folk have two cars and holidays in Greece. Not because they can afford these things or even really want them, but because they're big-headed and think people in their position owe it to themselves. If they don't have these expensive luxuries, how will other people know how important they are? I make no apology for bringing religious values into this. We whore after false gods. So long as I'm Mayor of this town, I won't be party to establishing a university just because it'll bring employment, or it makes us more competitive with the Russians (which I doubt), or because it's the latest in status symbols. I've got to be persuaded it's good *in itself*. And it's my earnest hope there's somebody here tonight as can do this service for me."

After a pause, Toplis said he was glad Supple had raised this point. If the Promotion Committee were to develop *drive*, they obviously had to talk all their differences out beforehand; but speaking for himself he thought it would be a poor look-out for the human race if before deciding on any course of action they went in for a lot of philosophic discussion about whether it was good or not. He was a practical man. It was his military training.

"Hear, hear!" said Primrose.

"What's wrong with competing with the Russians?" Arrowsmith spoke for the first time, his large copper-coloured cheeks shaking. "Or the Americans, for that matter? I mention the Americans because I don't think we ought to let politics get into this. I think we ought to be neutral."

Toplis said he had just landed a quarter-of-a-million-pound contract for supplying switch-gear to the Ukraine, and he'd never been one for letting politics interfere with trade. "You see that picture up there?" He pointed to a portrait over the fire-place of a man with mahogany curls and a green waistcoat. "My ancestor was one of the Governors of the Levant Company. He traded with the Grand Turk, which was almost like trading with the devil. Wool out, mummies back."

"Mummies?"

"They used to grind 'em to powder for medicinal purposes. When the natural supply ran out, they used to knock somebody on the head and store the body in antimony for a couple of years. Indistinguishable from the genuine article. What harm came of it? None." Turning to Supple, "If Perstowe University had a good medical school, you wouldn't be against that, would you? You wouldn't ask what is the good *in itself* of turning out a lot of doctors."

"If they were trained on taxpayers' money and then shot off to America as soon as they qualified, I would" said Supple. "Anyway, there's a lot more to a university than training doctors and chemists and engineers and the like. I can understand that. What I can't understand is all this history and literature and philosophy. And I won't pay lip-service. I'm open to persuasion, but I think it's just the education of people to be gentlemen and we've no time for gentlemen in the second half of the twentieth century."

Before Supple had even finished, Jimmy Pigge, having listened to little that had been said so far, had started baying a confession that he couldn't understand why universities had to be deliberately started. He thought some pundit set up house in a provincial town and pupils gathered at his feet.

"Jimmy, it's all changed since the Wars of the Roses," said Toplis, who had a deep respect for Pigge's ancestry, "and all the feudal aristocracy were killed off. I'm not a snob, Supple, but the turning-point came when the grocers and wine-merchants, like the Cecils, for example, took over in the sixteenth century. Wandering scholars are definitely out. To get a university going nowadays you've got to demonstrate to the University Grants Committee that you've got at least some of the money and you've got a site with buildings to form a nucleus. Gentlemen, let me put my cards on the table. The firm of which I am managing director is prepared to put down ten thousand pounds. We're ready to launch the Perstowe University scheme with ten thousand smackers."

"Bravo!" cried Amos, pounding the table.

"I'll go five hundred," said Arrowsmith, "but this really does come out of my own pocket, you know. I can't write it off against profits like you can, Toplis."

"Who said I could write it off against profits?"

This, from Toplis, was a shout. It created a silence in which nothing was heard but the whirr of the tape machine in the corner. Hedges decided to step into this silence. He secured a degree of attention that would have embarrassed a soberer man. But he had enjoyed his gin, his smoked salmon, his chicken, his hock, his strawberries and cream, and his brandy and was at last aloft in a gale of genial feeling. Even his foot did not hurt. He saw that his earlier plan to sabotage the university scheme by way of preparing the ground for a fundamental debate on post-Christian society was altogether too ambitious. The world—or those representatives of it now watching him—were not ready for him. Nevertheless there was a way of affirming his deepest beliefs and, at the same time, giving the university idea a good shove too.

"The answer——"

Christopher Brush jumped up. "Hold it, brother! Twenty seconds to put on a new reel. I'd just hate to miss what's coming, whatever it is." There was a pause, during which Jimmy Pigge was heard to say he didn't know they were being broadcast and Arrowsmith said this was a violation of privacy the press never went in for. Toplis explained that Brush was documenting the rise of Perstowe University just as that film had recorded the growth of Coventry Cathedral. And then Brush shouted, "O.K., everybody, you have the ear of posterity! Speak up, Hedges."

Jimmy Pigge said he'd a damn good idea to smash the tape recorder, but he was shushed down and everybody looked at Hedges.

"The answer," said Hedges, as though he had not been interrupted, "is that we shall be building the New Jerusalem."

"I like that," said Supple.

"We've got to look farther than our own noses. I agree with Mr. Supple that narrow self-interest is no reason why

we should try and start a university. We've to think not of
ourselves but of future generations."

Toplis smacked his hand down and said, "Hear!
Hear!"

"Mr. Toplis and I," Hedges went on, "have one thing
in common. The future generations will include no progeny
of ours. Mule-like we stare down the centuries."

There were guffaws, and Toplis said he didn't know
how to take that remark.

Hedges continued. "We're both bachelors, that's what
I mean. I say with special feeling, then, the New Jerusalem."

"That's talking!" said Supple. "That's real talking! I
approve of that."

The butler was removing the bowls of roses, so that if
the diners had been unable to get a sight of each other
before they could now. Hedges sat, rather stiffly, gripping
his coffee-cup with one hand, his brandy glass with the
other. He breathed deeply to control his excitement. Over
Amos's shoulder he could see through the huge casements,
down the sloping lawns, to the buff waters of the lake and
the bone-white pillars of Toplis's Folly, a ruin in the Greek
style, where it stood on its sedge-infested island. With
encouragement he would have stood up and made a formal
speech. Words that on other men's lips would have sounded
pompous humbug now seemed simple truth. He wasn't
drunk. He had taken only two glasses of wine, and his
second brandy rippled untasted in the balloon before him
as he felt the skin of his mind rippling under the afflatus. If
he'd been a Hebrew he would have prophesied. Being
English he spoke of his childhood.

"I was born and brought up in this town. When I was a

boy, I used to walk on the hills and look down at it and out to sea. It was—you know, it made me feel sort of helpless. I'm a local patriot, a very local patriot. Now, that's only one of the reasons I want a university here."

"Ignore that tape recorder," said Amos. "Be honest for once."

"The New Jerusalem!" Supple smiled to himself and rolled the words over his tongue.

Toplis leaned back in his chair, sucking a cigar, his eyes watering because of the smoke and flashing in the light from the pink table-lamps that had been just turned on.

"I'm not afraid of saying it." Hedges lifted his voice. "The New Jerusalem! When it's built, my guess is it's a town like any other town. But it's what you get out of the building! We've had the idealism scorched out of us by the wars. It sounds just vulgar: the New Jerusalem. Utopia, that's another dirty word. But if there's no ideal, how do we know where we're going? If we really got this university idea going, and we really got every Tom, Dick, and Harry in Perstowe behind it—not just the sort of people sitting in this room— if it could be a real ambition for everybody with a vote, you'd see the town transfigured."

"What I didn't like," said Supple, "was the thought of self-interest."

"This would mean sacrifice," said Hedges.

"If you're agreed, Supple," said Toplis, "then we're all agreed, so the next stage is formally to constitute the committee."

Supple nodded and permitted the tip of his nose to lift in a smile. "I hate hypocrisy, and I just wanted to get straight the real reason for a university. Prestige, employment, competition with the Russians: they mean nothing to me. But Perstowe as the New Jerusalem means that God is in it, and I'm thankful to Mr. Hedges here for drawing my attention to the fact. As long as it means sacrifice."

Sam Primrose now proposed Gideon Toplis as Chairman of the Promotion Committee, Jimmy Pigge seconded, and, nobody opposing, Toplis was duly elected. He rapped on the table with his knuckles and said, "Talking of the New Jerusalem, shouldn't we co-opt some churchmen onto this committee? We ought to have the Bishop."

"Nothing can be done without the representatives of the Free Churches," said Supple.

It being agreed that a few parsons should be brought into the committee, Hedges was elected Secretary, and Supple was argued into sponsoring a motion in due course to be placed before the Borough Council that its property, Lack Park, and twenty-four acres of ground should be made available as a site for the new university.

As the committee moved off to the drawing-room, Toplis took Hedges on one side, saying, "It did the trick! I'd never have believed it."

"What did what trick?"

"Telling Supple we were building the New Jerusalem. He's an obstinate bastard, but it swung him round. I don't know how you guessed it would swing him. But you were right! By God, you were right!" Toplis had the lapel of Hedges's jacket between thumb and forefinger. "We've disposed of the main business. Think we could get up a foursome for croquet?"

"Croquet? You mean outside, in the garden?"

"Well, I didn't say billiards."

"But it's dark."

"We'll get the cars out and switch the headlights on."

He told the butler to take the balls and mallets out to

the croquet lawn. "Hedges and I will take on any two of you," Toplis then shouted. To Hedges's annoyance, Brush immediately said he was a croquet Blue and would be glad to show anybody round the course for five quid.

"Done!" said Toplis, and ten minutes later the whole party were out in the summery darkness, moths dancing in the headlights of Toplis's Jaguar and Bentley.

Toplis banged his yellow ball into the pool of darkness where the first hoop lay, and when eventually Hedges followed him with the blue he was able to say, "I meant what I said about the New Jerusalem, Major Toplis. I wasn't just trying to win Supple over."

Their other opponent, besides Brush, was Primrose, and they had both overshot the hoop into a rose bed. Toplis could be heard shouting orders for the Mercedes to be driven on to the terrace, from where it could clear some of the heavier shadows that still remained. There was a shout, the click of mallet on ball, and a ball came skidding across the lawn to finish up at Toplis's feet. He bent down and flicked his cigarette-lighter at it.

"A red 'un. That's Primrose's." He stood square on his own yellow ball and hammered it with such ferocity against the red that the red shot off into the night again and his own yellow rolled neatly through the hoop. He raised his mallet in the air and cheered. Hedges's carpet-slipper was wet, and as he could not believe the dew was as heavy as all that he could only suppose that he had stepped in the lake. Anyway, it was pleasantly cool. A bat flickered in and out of the light. The Mercedes crunched over the gravel, and a weeping willow, thirty yards away, was transformed into an emerald waterfall.

"Myself," said Toplis, "I don't trust do-gooders. I don't like their talk. The less said about the New Jerusalem the better. Supple's a religious maniac. He goes for that kind of talk. But it puts most people off. It would put the Bishop off." Toplis's eyes flashed out of his shadow-pocked face. "I'll knock my ball in behind yours. With a bit of luck I can just hammer you through the hoop."

But he missed and swore.

Brush appeared in the wake of a green ball which struck Hedges's gently. "I'm sorry about this, in a way," said Brush. He set his ball squarely behind Hedges's blue, and the upshot was that Hedges had to go down to the edge of the lake to look for his ball while Brush screamed with laughter. Toplis followed to give advice.

"I'm sorry you take such a poor view of idealists, Major Toplis. I should have thought a bit of idealism was just what we wanted."

Toplis poked about with his mallet. "You don't think it went in the water?"

"I heard a plop. Fish jumping, I reckon."

They found the ball sitting quite pretty, and Toplis advised Hedges to hammer it straight at Brush's head, which they could see silhouetted over the top of the bank. Every time Hedges moved his slipper squelched. There was no pain at all, and he wondered if it was because his foot was numbed.

"Think I could do it?"

"Sure," said Toplis. "He'd never know what hit him."

The shot went wide, of course, and Toplis—who had known that it would—guffawed. Hedges was always to remember that he had taken deliberate aim and been disappointed that he had foozled it.

"Idealism is all right," said Toplis, "provided you're serving your own interests at the same time. In these conditions I've got nothing against it at all. Still, it takes all sorts!

You know the saying." They were climbing the bank. "I like you, Hedges. We ought to see more of each other. Nice wife you've got, too."

"If you mean Nell, she's not my wife, she's Mrs. Brush."

"Quite right," said Toplis. "Matter of fact, she was telling me you were marrying again and how she thought it was all going to turn out badly."

"Was she pleased or sorry?"

"Oh, sorry! There was this scandal. She said you were sacrificing yourself. What's it all about, eh? Well, some other time, maybe. I wasn't listening. Never had any sex life myself. Never felt the need. Discipline. That's why I took your reference to mules in such bad part. It's nothing constitutional. It's the will. Mind you," said Toplis, as they came up to Brush, "there'll come a time when the kid will have to know who his real father is."

"Did you try to hit me with that ball?" Brush said to Hedges.

"What scandal?" Hedges asked Toplis, a bit wildly. "I don't know what you've been talking about."

"Never talk scandal, gentlemen." Toplis made it sound like a rebuke. "Remember the three wise monkeys. Time to go back in the house for a drink. Croquet. I enjoyed that. A good game. Expands the chest."

"Did you try to hit me with that ball?" said Brush insistently.

Hedges was so perturbed by what Toplis had told him that he replied absently, "Yes, but I missed, you know."

The drink was in the Victorian conservatory. The glass winked like black oil. Bunches of unripe grapes could be seen through the trembling leaves. Hedges was so preoccupied that he was still carrying his croquet mallet in spite of attempts made by the butler to take it from him. He had told Toplis that whatever the scandal was it was untrue, and Toplis had replied that he was very glad to hear it. But he had become rather grim, like a magistrate acknowledging a profession of virtue from the dock.

He sat in a basket-chair to remove a shoe and sock. Disregarding the others, he sat with a white foot resting on his left knee while, completely absorbed, he turned the sock inside out. Everyone, even Hedges, watched the foot with the dulled, cow-like interest of men who had dined and drunk well and were now really thinking of getting to bed. Absently, Hedges was swinging his mallet round and round his body, changing hands fore and aft and so marking out a circle with a couple of yards' radius inside which nobody could venture.

"Buttocks to the ordinary people!" Jimmy Pigge was saying to somebody who had said they ought to be interested in the university. "Ever noticed what balls gets talked when 'ordinary people' get mentioned, particularly by chaps who've never been in a public bar in their lives?"

"I had one sock on inside out," Toplis was explaining calmly.

Hedges beat the floor with his mallet. "I was born in this town, as you know, Pigge, son of a butcher. And *his* father was hard put to it to sign his own name. That wasn't through stupidity, either. There are quite a few families in this town just a couple of generations away from near illiteracy and near hunger under the stately shadow of your family, old cock."

"Your meat was always better than your manners."

"I don't want to quarrel with you, Pigge. But I'm ready to do it if it means getting this university right—I mean, right from the town's point of view. I wasn't talking hot air about the New Jerusalem, you know. I meant it." A number of things were angering Hedges, and he thought he might as well mention them. "It'd mean an end to juvenile delinquency, for one thing." There must have been a cellar underneath the conservatory, because the stone floor boomed like a drum as Hedges hit it with his mallet. "And the kind of emptiness and boredom that makes so much gossip possible. You sometimes get a feeling of some diabolic force at work."

"And how are you going to build the New Jerusalem?" There was a lot of animosity in Primrose's voice. Pigge had his mouth open. Arrowsmith was scratching his chin and trying to read Toplis's expression; Supple had been persuaded to a couple of whiskies and was somnolent; Amos was smirking. All the attention that had been directed at Toplis's foot was now turned on Hedges—all except Brush's: he was leaning back in a chair smoking a cigar with his eyes closed. The charitable ones thought Hedges was drunk. Anyway, he was shouting.

"In the first place, you don't have students shut away from the town in halls of residence. One year out of their three it ought to be statutory for them to live in digs. And if you ask me where, I'd say from now on every new house on the Council estate should include a student's bed-sitter. People who aren't Council tenants could have building grants."

Hedges was almost as surprised by this proposal as Primrose himself. He wasn't even thinking about the university. He was thinking about Toplis's confused remarks in the garden. Somebody was having a baby. Who?

"Students billeted in council-houses!" said Toplis. "What a bloody horrible idea."

"There'd be trouble with the Housing Committee over *that* one."

"Inverted snobbery, I call it."

"They'd never have the quiet."

"Too political for me to touch."

"Speaking as a politician," said Arrowsmith, "I can see the social theory, so to speak, behind this suggestion. But surely what we want is a fine range of buildings on a hill. The young mind should be given the chance to develop in dignified and spacious surroundings. No, I don't go along with you, Hedges, on this one. Don't forget the U.G.C. and the other sponsors will want to see something for their money. A lodge at the entrance, handsome gate with a crest, that sort of thing. Eh? What do other people say?"

"Hear! Hear!" said Arrowsmith.

"They'd never put up with the cooking, Mr. Hedges, these students wouldn't." Supple looked on Hedges as an ally and tried to state his objection as gently as possible.

"Gentlemen," said Hedges, "we shall all have to think about the character of this university a bit more closely. My view is it should be much more of a social experiment than anything you've got in mind. If I don't carry you with me I'll bow out."

"Good riddance!" Jimmy Pigge muttered to himself.

Toplis heard him and said, "Oh, shut up, Jimmy. We're trying to run before we can walk. We can't argue about the character of the university before we try the idea out on public opinion and see whether there's any life in it."

"I don't agree," said Hedges. "Getting a university will be a real battle, and you can't fight without knowing what for. Frankly, I think this committee needs strengthening. We're going to need some real intellectual horsepower."

Toplis said they had talked enough business for the

night and invited everybody to inspect his goldfish pool. A large spider was observed by all walking across one of the lily leaves.

"Wake up," Hedges said to Brush. "I'm coming home with you. I want a word with Nell."

Brush opened one eye. "What about?"

"I want to ask her what she's been telling Toplis about me."

"It's one o'clock. She'll be asleep."

But as Hedges volunteered to help carry his recording gear down to the car, Brush made no serious resistance, and after Hedges had said good night to Toplis and apologized for losing his temper they drove back to town in silence.

Until Brush said, "I suppose you know you made some enemies tonight?"

"Demythologizing," said Hedges. "You ever heard of the word?" He went on until Brush had to confess—no, he hadn't, and then Hedges explained it to him.

The Brushes lived in the old part of the town near the station. A coaching inn with rooms opening on to a central yard had been rescued from collapse by a grain-merchant-*cum*-baker who had put steam-ovens into what had once been the dining-room and bar, torn down the dividing walls on the first floor to make a grain loft, and, on the other side of the yard, transformed the first-floor bedrooms into living quarters. The merchant being long since dead and his successor living in a red-brick villa near the river, Nell and Brush occupied the living quarters. As Brush and Hedges walked into the yard, they saw a rat sitting in the moonlight. It did not move until Brush shouted at it. One of the bakehouse windows was open, and they could smell yeast and wet coke.

"Light's out," said Brush. "She's gone to bed. I'll have to doss down on the trough."

There was no light anywhere except from the full moon.

"I'm going to wake her up," said Hedges.

He was making for the steps when Brush said, "No go, once she's locked up she doesn't let me in, even if she is awake. But as no doubt you well remember, once she goes off—well, I've had to give her a real punch, you know, to wake her. It's a kind of death. I mean that, Hedges. She likes death."

He went into the bakehouse and switched on the light; Hedges, puzzled by all this, followed him. Brush was already taking his clothes off. Black beetles rustled out of sight behind the sacks of flour and ten-gallon tins of raspberry jam. The sealed, blank face of the oven breathed out damp heat.

"Bloody baker comes in at five-thirty. Must get some sleep," said Brush. "I'm shacked, listening to all you lot. Must get at least two hours."

"Does Nell let you in then?"

"She won't open up before seven," said Brush. "Oh, I'm all right. I walk about a bit. Or I make tea for the baker. We get talking, you know. I give him a hand with the scaling off."

"D'you mean to say—" Hedges couldn't swallow all this.

"Switch the light off as you go out." Brush was already in his socks, vest, and underpants. He rolled up a sack for a pillow at one end of the trough and brushed away some flour with a filthy towel. He was roughly the same length as the trough, and when he had stretched himself out on top of it, arms folded over chest, Hedges thought he looked like a Pop-art version of a medieval tomb and effigy. There was another trough, and Hedges supposed he could have made himself comfortable on it until five-thirty, but he did not fancy walking the streets for an hour and a half until Nell took the milk in. Anyway, he wanted to see her without any more messing about. He could not wait. He decided he'd give Brush time to fall asleep and then go and knock at Nell's door. He could not remember her being a heavy sleeper. Being married to Brush he supposed she just had to drug herself.

"Good night, old man," he said.

"Made a fine bloody fool of yourself, all right, you did," Brush answered, with his eyes shut and smiling. Hedges put the light out and went into the yard. Thank God it was a warm night.

On the way down to the river he was stopped by a policeman in the deserted street, attracted, possibly, by the slipper and shoe pad-tap.

"This just goes down to the quay." He added "sir" when he saw Hedges's dinner-jacket.

"That's all right. I'm just walking," said Hedges. No doubt he *was* just a bit drunk or he wouldn't be cherishing this idea of waking Nell up and questioning her. But not really drunk, presumably, or the copper would have pulled him in. He walked on, pretty steadily, watched by the copper until he could see the moonlight on the estuary and the illuminated clock over Harper's: ten past one. What did he want anyway, waking Nell up at ten past one in the morning? Congratulations?

He did five minutes' pad-tap to the station and studied a poster of the Northumbrian coast in the second-class waiting-room. His foot ached but he was determined to take no notice. There seemed to be nobody about. The gate to the platforms was locked. He sat on a wooden seat, listen-

ing to the gas popping in its glass bowl, just as though
Queen Victoria was still at Osborne, and thought: right, I
wake her up, Nell, and ask her about this gossip. What will
she think of me, waking her up in the middle of the night?
She'll think I'm drunk. What did Brush mean, anyway, by
saying she liked death?

By now it was nearly three, time for Brush to be sound
asleep, so Hedges walked, not hurrying, back to the yard
and without hesitation climbed the wooden steps to the
balcony where the baskets of geraniums hung and rapped
with his knuckles at Nell's door. The creaking of the
boards under his feet made more noise. So he rapped louder.

The graining of the wood in the door, the basket of
geraniums, the leaded windows, a foot-scraper, a black knot-
hole next to his right foot—all this had the sharpness of
hallucination. The red geraniums were purple in the moon.
A window flap was open. By sticking his hand through, he
could lift the fastening and push back a slab of forty-eight
glass diamonds set in what looked like old silver. He put his
head in and smelled a kitchen. When he was sitting astride
the sill, one leg in and one leg out, all he could think of was
that poster of the Northumbrian coast. He tried asking
himself why he was where he was. He just could not get a
grip of his mind.

He struck a match and in the brief guttering saw
enough of the inside of the kitchen to make him lift his left
leg over the sill. He dropped quietly to the floor and struck
another match. This was how he was going to find Nell:
walking quietly and striking matches. By now he had rid his
mind of the Northumbrian coast and was thinking of Brush
stretched out on the baker's trough. Not at all, he recognized, what he *should* be brooding over. He could not

concentrate. Behind this match-striking in the dark there was some tremendous assumption. He was aware of its existence but not what it was. The plan was to wake Nell up and ask her to explain this gossip he had heard from Toplis. That is what he would have said in court if that policeman had followed him. But there was another explanation just out of reach. The match burned down to his finger and made him grunt. The explanation was always just out of reach.

He imagined the light being switched on and some wise bird he had never seen in his life before getting up out of a chair in the corner and saying, "You have always made a certain assumption about yourself. I'm going to put you right. The false assumption is—"

What? He wondered if the parson he met in the train, the Reverend Warp, was enough of a sage to take a chap behind the scenery of his own mind. He could imagine the Reverend Warp smiling and saying, "By way of preliminary, Hedges, I want you to put out of your head all thought of a God who, so to speak, is not you. I want you to think, very seriously, about the possibilities you discover in your own heart for a really generous love."

Hedges sometimes thought that if only he could spin his mind sharply enough he would catch a glimpse of something just whisking out of sight: part of some metaphysical garment, or a feather or an ankle or even a hoof. He struck another match and saw that he was at the kitchen door and that it had a corroded iron latch that had probably been lifted up and down for three or four hundred years. A low-powered bulb was burning in the passage beyond. When he gently opened the door of what he knew to be Nell's bedroom, enough of this light was thrown across the

bed and sleeping face to give Hedges quite a shadow to
follow when he moved towards her. He held on to the wall
and stood on one foot until the throbbing in the other
began to fade. As his heart beat so his foot throbbed.

The woman had turned her sleeping face towards the
light, and he could see now that she wasn't Nell; momentarily the features were those of a stranger. Then they
swam into a familiar pattern. She became Prudence. Almost
aloud—he checked himself—he wanted to call the imagined
confidant from the kitchen and tell him, "See this? Here?
Not——"

"Yes," this confidant would say, "it's Prudence in
Brush's bed. What d'you reckon you're going to do about
it?"

But Hedges put his slippered foot to the ground. The
slightly different position gave a new angle, and he could
see now that he'd allowed the bad light to play a trick on
him and it really *was* Nell lying there in bed. Her lips were
parted and he could even see her teeth and the way two of
them in the top jaw were slightly crossed. In her hair she
had some kind of curlers. They stuck up like a coronet.
Like a coronet they were gold, and this (he saw now) was
what had mainly persuaded him it was Prudence lying
there. He thought it was yellow hair. He could see the
dampness on Nell's forehead. Her pinched nostrils quivered
as she breathed. Between the curlers, or whatever, the hair
looked black.

In spite of the bad light you had to be Hedges, though,
to make a mistake like that. Hedges knew he was in a
peculiarly personal spot. He was the one man capable of
looking at Nell asleep in bed and thinking it was Prudence
Styles. A finger was being pointed at some unique quality in
his own experience. At first he could only suppose he was

being told he now thought Brush was going to take Prudence away from him just as he had taken Nell. So he closed the door quietly.

He stood in the dark kitchen, thinking about himself. No, he wasn't accepting that rather trivial explanation for the mistake he'd made; it didn't fit the facts. It would have meant assuming his unconscious failed to keep up with life as he lived it, imagining that Prudence and he had some deep understanding, were engaged or married or something; and all that was nonsense, because the last time they had met she more or less accused him of driving Saundersfoot to suicide. She had been really hostile.

He climbed out through the window, closed it carefully behind him, and descended the steps into the black and yeasty yard, remembering that row differently. It became more and more different with every step he took into the moonlight. Prudence, it now seemed to him, wasn't angry. He saw that she had been trying to stir him up. It had taken quite a long time to realize how deep she had gone.

In other words, his unconscious had been functioning superbly. Seeing Prudence apparently in bed meant no more than a wish on his part to climb in with her. With this confession he saw no need to argue at all, and as a tug hooted on the river he looked round for the Triumph Herald only to remember he'd travelled down in Brush's car and the Triumph Herald was still at Brewchester. So he walked home.

He walked home.

He walked.

He.

I.

CHAPTER FOUR

◆◇◆◇◆◇◆◇◆◇◆◇◆◇◆◇◆◇◆◇◆◇◆◇

A Friend in the Treasury

Within a fortnight he was out of his carpet-slipper and wearing a shoe, loosely laced. His foot was that much better. Sometimes he was able to walk about quite normally, not even using a stick. There was a little black mark on top of his foot, and he looked at it every night before getting into bed. He looked at it every morning in the bath. He pressed it with his finger. Quite painless. And yet there were times when he hopped about on one foot grunting with pain. The only relief came from sitting down and putting his leg up. It was when he was sitting in his office with his right foot resting on the *Financial Times*, which was spread over his desk top, that it occurred to him his foot hurt only when he was thinking of nothing in particular. When he thought of Saundersfoot and Prudence and all that wicked scandal there was physical bliss. This worked even when recovering the car from that station yard.

He called at the school one morning early when, as he realized after tapping at Saundersfoot's door, everyone was in assembly. At atmosphere of scholastic hush, of floor polish, chalk, and damp school caps, blew down the corridors. He was, he realized, standing at the open door of the stationery store. His body was not hurting him anywhere. He was so confident about his right foot, in particular, that he wiggled his toes inside the shoe. Nothing, not even a tickle. He breathed in the bitter reek of ink, peering at a complex geological strata of exercise books, stacks of blotting-paper, graph-paper, and brown packages like giant blocks of shop-soiled toffee. This was where the trouble had started. It was quite a dark room, he noticed, with one small window near the ceiling and a door built solidly to keep out the pilferers. Once in there, with the door slammed behind you and the knowledge that the building was deserted—deserted, that is to say, but for you and Saundersfoot, who was there at your elbow, breathing heavily—well, you might easily get the wind up. There was no room between the shelves and the stacks of books for a lot of skirmishing. Then why hadn't she tried the stiletto-heel stab?

He turned his head to find Saundersfoot looking at him and very nearly asked him.

"We're in trouble with the police," said Saundersfoot. "One of the Toplis warehouses has been broken into and a lot of wanton damage done. They think it's boys from here. Well, I've been talking to 'em all in assembly."

Boys were marching past in pairs. In the distance a piano could be heard banging out Shubert's "Marche Militaire."

"I asked young Peacock." Saundersfoot lowered his voice. "I had to challenge somebody, you know. I asked him if he'd been in Toplis's warehouse three nights ago, and d'you know what he said? He said that before answering that question he'd like to consult a lawyer. All these boys

107

see too much telly, in my opinion. And another thing. Your girl-friend's disappeared." Saundersfoot led the way into his study.

Hedges sat down and made no pretence of not understanding who Saundersfoot was referring to. Saundersfoot went on to say that life was hell nowadays. He was going through one of those periods of storm—they come to us all, et cetera—when there was no other course but to turn up your collar against the wind and the rain and press on.

"I'm a stoic at heart," said Saundersfoot. "It's Mrs. Saundersfoot. Look, I can't stay nattering to you for long because I've got to take Standard Four for Divinity, but I don't mind telling you that Mrs. Saundersfoot has turned against me. I sometimes wonder whether she's gone mad. It must be very difficult, living with a person, to know just when they've gone over the edge. She's always been a very active woman, of course. But she wakes me up in the night and reproaches me. And she talks about age and death. Do you know what she said to me last night? 'For God's sake,' she said, 'If ever you stop loving me tell me at once and I will set you free.' But when the postman came this morning she saw there was a letter for me. She just took it and tore it up in its envelope, unopened. Do you think I ought to ask Sherwood to look her over?"

Sherwood was Saundersfoot's family doctor.

"Where are you going for your holiday?"

"Skye. We're going to climb some bloody mountain."

"Once she's on the rock face she'll be all right, Ted."

"But she's crazy. She might kill me."

"Well, at least it'll be because she loves you. Maybe you're not as virile as you used to be. I don't know, Ted——"

"For God's sake, Ian."

"I'm trying to be objective about this. You just going off to your Divinity lesson means it isn't the best time, but what I'm really getting at is not to worry too much. Just go off on your holiday. She'll change. Perhaps she'll have an accident." Hedges's imagination took wing. "I mean, you might push her off a rock, and then if she had a bad sprain you could fuss over her. That's all she wants. She wants you to fuss over her."

Saundersfoot stood up. He put on his academic gown. Divinity was the only lesson he put on his gown for. He looked down at Hedges, his face flaking and flashing (Hedges thought) like pink Mediterranean stucco, and said, "Obviously you don't know much about rock-climbing, Ian. My wife and I are always roped together. I couldn't push her off without running the risk of going myself."

"She says I'm driving *you* to suicide anyway."

"Who does?"

"Prudence."

"Styles? She's missing, I tell you. This is the third day she's not been in. Do you know her landlady?"

"Who does not know the fair Medusa?"

"She went to the trouble of telephoning my wife to say Styles had departed with a packed suitcase on Tuesday. Naturally my wife was surprised. She wanted to know why she was being given this information. She put the question to me. Why should the Headmaster's wife be interested in the movements of women on his staff? Why? Why? See what I mean?" Saundersfoot went out of the door and came back again. "I don't mind telling you that if I'd really had a go at the girl she'd have known all about it. She wouldn't have got off with a peck and a feel, I tell you."

Hedges observed the stiff jaw and glassy grin that had, often more than cane or cuff, disciplined the generations.

But now Saundersfoot softened. He smiled. He lifted his right hand and spread his fingers.

"After all, this is nothing to lose one's head about. Think of the story of the House of Atreus—babies in pies, incest, husband-murder, hitting your mother down with an axe, and all that sort of thing; you don't need a theory of being purged by pity and terror to explain why tragedy like that makes you feel so much better. You just come out of the theatre, saying to yourself, 'I may be having a bad time but not so bad as *that*,' and you go home feeling more cheered than sobered. I'll weather this storm."

"Anyway," said Hedges, "promise me you won't kill yourself."

"Oh, well, if you insist."

Hedges nodded. "If you've got yourself under control I'll go and see Mrs. Kidwelly."

Before pressing the bell, Hedges paused to look at the view. These houses on top of Mythe Hill had the finest site in town. The estuary looked like hammered tin, and there were puffs of vapour going up between the warehouses and the great dockyard cranes, egg-yellow because of the sun. Smoke from a few dirty chimneys drifted westward over the blue roof-tops. The view gave him a quite unexpected pang of happiness which was changed, strangely, into a physical throb in his right foot just as the door opened and Mrs. Kidwelly appeared in her tweeds to stare at Hedges pitilessly with one eyelid hung lower than the other.

"I'm not God, am I?" she asked, as soon as they were sitting side by side on her moquette settee. Everything creaked: the pine floor, the big sash-window as the wind pressed against it, the ceiling under the weight of somebody walking about upstairs, Hedges's shoes (they had never done it before), Mrs. Kidwelly's clothes (or it might be her bones). After her question the very silence seemed to creak. "So I can't tell you why she went. She went on Tuesday."

"She must have gone to her father, surely?"

"Be candid," said Mrs. Kidwelly. "Talk frankly. Why should we lie to one another?"

Hedges was surprised. "I wasn't lying. In fact, I don't think I've said anything much yet, have I?"

"We should always be honest with one another." Mrs. Kidwelly turned her head to look at him, and her neck certainly creaked. "I've always been very direct with people."

"People should look each other squarely in the face, I agree," said Hedges. "I like everyone to know the truth about everybody else."

"Why? There are times when some people would say it was kinder to keep silent."

"But *we* don't?" Hedges spoke to the embroidered fire-screen and made gestures in Mrs. Kidwelly's direction. The bones of his wrist gave little moans. The house was probably damp as a cave. "One winter night. . . ." He paused and almost decided to change the subject. It was not at all what he had come to talk about, but Mrs. Kidwelly brought out the exhibitionist in him.

"Can I get you a cup of tea, Mr. Hedges?"

"No, thanks." Upstairs a door was slowly turning on an unoiled hinge. "That night, I came in from the office—it was four years ago, in the winter—and I just stood knocking snow from my shoulders, and my wife came out (I was married then) and gave me a glass of sherry. And she said— and quite without any preparation or warning or anything—she just said she wanted a divorce."

Mrs. Kidwelly stuck out her legs, and Hedges noticed

111

she was wearing white ankle-socks. Her bare legs were like brown marble.

"We have all been deceived," she said. "Even the shrewdest."

He hesitated. "You discover that someone you love is different."

"Mr. Kidwelly fell into the dock." There was an odd quaver in Mrs. Kidwelly's voice that might even have been laughter. "He was superintendent. A very fine job. You must have a nice job—education."

"It's all right."

"All that power!" she said reflectively.

She had made Hedges brood too. "I just don't want to be deceived any more."

"My colleague would understand that," said Mrs. Kidwelly.

"Which one would that be?"

"At the Red Cross Stores in Peascod Lane where, as a member of the Women's Voluntary Service, I am in attendance every Wednesday afternoon, this colleague said to me, 'Oh, Mrs. Kidwelly, what is all this I hear about Mrs. Saundersfoot divorcing her husband because of misconduct with your lodger?' I said I had no comment to make one way or the other."

"You ought to have told her she was a bloody malicious gossip-monger and there wasn't a word of truth——"

"Perhaps it's true. I can't know everything. I'm not God."

"What was the woman's name?"

"I would never have told you all this," said Mrs. Kidwelly, with a brassy ring to her voice, "if you hadn't told me about coming in out of the snow and all that deception. I could have lied to you, couldn't I? Is it my fault that rumour flies about the town? D'you think *I'm* a gossip? Do you think I take pleasure in all this? You're an official! You have responsibility for these people! Would you rather hear the slander from someone else?"

Hedges stood up. He hated this woman and should never have confided in her. "You've no idea where Miss Styles has gone to?"

"None whatsoever." Mrs. Kidwelly leaned back to look squarely at him. The sound of her leaning back was like the forcing of screws into hard timber.

"Then I'll let myself out," he said—and bolted before she could so much as creak at him.

Just a rush of blood to the head. For some minutes he sat in his car with the window down. The human animal raged, but at last he brought it under control. If the blue front door now opened and Mrs. Kidwelly appeared, he would have been able to say something genial. Her style was impressive. She had made him confess that he minded Nell's leaving him less than he minded the deception involved. And she had a vein of malicious fantasy that must, year in, year out, have poured enough nourishing gossip into Perstowe to have invigorated a far larger community. Why had he not detected the yeasty bubbling before? Perhaps Amos was right. He was out of touch. Saundersfoot had set him on the escalator, and he had risen out of the sweaty press where he would have known all about Mrs. Kidwelly, her creaks, and her enchantments.

Lies, of course. A woman as clever as Mrs. Kidwelly must have known this tale from the W.V.S. was a pack of lies. Being Prudence's landlady and seeing the sort of girl she was, Mrs. K. could have put on her stare and killed the invention stone dead. But she knew a bit of promising gossip when she heard it. She even tested its value on one of the people involved, by telephoning Mrs. Saundersfoot to tell her of Prudence's departure. Hedges saw all this, now that he had stopped being angry, as the behaviour of a woman with an awareness of the tribe she lived in.

He drove off wondering how he could square the findings of this moment of insight with what he had told Brush about the importance of truth. This proving rather difficult, he allowed a period of complete blankness of mind to supervene and drove home to lunch, where he found a message from Gideon Toplis waiting for him: would he go up to London with Toplis the next day to meet somebody in the Treasury?

Well, he might, and he might not. He did not want to think ahead as far even as tomorrow. He had quite enough to deal with already. Directory Inquiries gave him the telephone number of Styles *père* but there was no reply to his call, so he had to send Prudence a telegram at her father's address: "Ring Perstowe 0901 during office hours or 5654 thereafter Hedges."

All this activity led to no result whatsoever.

For starting a university nothing was more important than having a friend in the Treasury. Jacob Bream had been at school with Toplis, and apparently he knew just where the money went. Toplis said that if they could sell Bream the notion of Perstowe having a university, they could advertise for a Vice-Chancellor the next day. Hedges said he thought Toplis was living in a dream world. It was more than likely that major Treasury decisions were no longer taken on an old-boy basis, and indeed he had heard a rumour from one of his own contacts in the Ministry of Education that there were so many applications for universities that the Treasury was thinking of using a computer to deal with them. If that particular story was not true, at least there were other signs that a real attempt was being made to handle the applications rationally.

"It'll never come to that," said Toplis.

"When all physical and intellectual labour is taken over by the machine," said Hedges, "I think we shall see what it truly is to be human. When you've got a machine that'll weed an onion bed, write stories, and even have a nervous breakdown for you, it's my belief we'll wake up to the blood and bone of living. The machines will be able to do everything, but we'll still want to be different from them. I foresee a time in which personality is deliberately cultivated. The hero will be the eccentric. Sex deviants will be on a special eminence of their own——"

Toplis shook his head. "It'll go quite the other way. I'm pretty sure that for as long as civilization lasts the psychological and behavioural patterns of human beings will be set in about the year two thousand. It'll be at that point, I reckon, that machines will reach such a perfection that human beings will be unnecessary. Now, just as dog-owners get to think and actually look like their dogs, so it's my guess that at the beginning of the next century people will be modelled on the machines they've devised. And as the machines have been devised out of the *then* state of knowledge—you see what I mean? From the twenty-first century on, mankind will be completely the prisoners of the twentieth. They'll still be laughing at our kind of joke."

"You said that dog-owners *looked* like their dogs."

"Well," said Toplis, "posterity will be square-headed and dial-eyed. But they'll still be watching Westerns."

They were alone in a first-class compartment smoking

the little Dutch cigars that Toplis had brought back from a
trip to Amsterdam the week before. A countryside of
scoured hay-fields, gravel-pits, and pylons shook past the
window. In ten minutes they were stopping at a junction,
and if Hedges decided to get out and catch the next train
back to Perstowe, so that he could carry on looking for
Prudence, presumably old Toplis would not be able to stop
him. He was wiry, though. Hedges could imagine Toplis
taking an Old-Man-of-the-Sea grip round his neck. However, the junction came and went and they both sat on,
talking about Jacob Bream now and his fondness for charcoal biscuits (though Toplis confessed he hadn't seen him
for ten years and Bream's tastes might have changed), until
Hedges realized he didn't really want to go back and
continue looking for Prudence Styles. He was enjoying his
day out too much for that.

"We'll let our hair down," said Toplis. "Let's see if we
can get old Bream tight."

The arrangement was that they should lunch with
Bream at the Athenæum, where he was a member. They
were barely inside (so it seemed to Hedges) before Toplis
was rolling his eyes like a startled horse and developing a
scorched complexion. Time passed quickly for Hedges because he had never been in the Athenæum before, and he
was impressed by the faded Victorian splendour, the well-
smoked spread of carpet, the rubbed leather upholstery and
the staircase, walls, and pillars, all formed as it might be out
of old and port-impregnated Cheshire cheese, the pink kind.

"Well, I'm damned!" Toplis was saying. As soon as he
had asked for Bream, the porter from behind his glass
screen had pushed an envelope at him. "He's let us down,
the dirty dog." And he handed Hedges the note he had been
reading.

116

Dear Toplis [it went],

I'm most frightfully sorry but I've had a change of secretaries, and in the hand-over I'm afraid I've asked you and Hedges to lunch on a day when I was already booked. I tried to get you on the telephone this morning but you had already left. What is so awful about this is that you've come up specially from Perstowe, and normally it would have been easy to arrange something for this afternoon or dinner this evening, but I've got a job in Glasgow tonight and I'm catching the afternoon plane. I really am most distressed. I'd have put this other chap off (he's the Member for Brewchester), but as it happens the two other guests have actually travelled up from Brewchester for the occasion. You see my dilemma. One of the people I'm to meet is a lady, so we've got to lunch out, at Prunier's, where I shan't be able to resist the lobster, and as lobster always kills me you will have the satisfaction of knowing that I shall fly north frothing at the mouth. I'll be back on Friday and I'll give you a ring then. Indeed, I think I owe it to you and Mr Hedges to come down to Perstowe and save you that appalling journey once more.

> *Your abject*
> *Jacob Bream.*

"I don't know what you want to do," said Toplis, "but I suggest we have a bloody good lunch somewhere and go to a strip-tease."

Hedges read the note twice before handing it back to Toplis, saying, "I agree to the strip-tease, provided you agree to the place I want to go for lunch."

"Where's that?"

"Prunier's."

It was Toplis's turn to read Bream's note for a second time. Already he was back to a more normal colour. He was

showing less of the yellow of his eyes. "Well, it's near," he
conceded, "and I'd dearly love to sit behind Bream and
follow every morsel of lobster to his lips. But he only mentioned Prunier's as a hint to keep away."

"I have never been to Prunier's," said Hedges. "I have
an ambition to eat at Prunier's."

"No, it would only upset old Bream and we've got to
be sly and diplomatic, haven't we, Hedges, my boy? So
we'll go to Scott's. Look, my treat."

They were standing on the steps of the Athenæum
where well-nourished but energetic, tight-jawed, middle-
aged and elderly men in dark suits, the successes of the
nation, were passing them on either side. Hedges responded
to the competitive atmosphere. Insist on Prunier's and, who
knows, one day he might be a member of the Athenæum
himself. "Toplis," he said, "I have a suspicion that there is
much more at stake here than you possibly realize. If you
won't come to Prunier's I shall go there alone."

Here a flabby-faced man with a ragged moustache,
wearing a loose, stained raincoat and carrying a box on the
end of a looped strap, came up and said, "They've not flung
you out, have they?"

Hedges gazed at the man incredulously. It was Brush.

"Hallo, Brush," said Toplis. "There's been a bit of a
misunderstanding, a mix-up in lunch dates, and we were just
debating——"

"Did you know *he* was going to turn up?" Hedges
demanded.

"Not actually to the lunch," said Toplis. "But when it
was over he was going to see if he could record an interview, weren't you, Brush?"

They were walking westward along Pall Mall. "I take
this very ill, I do," said Hedges. "You can't treat blokes in

the Treasury like that. I ask you," he went on, getting angrier, "what you'd think if *you* were in the Treasury and some pip-squeak came up with a recording machine and wanted to milk you after you'd been having a confidential talk. It detracts from the status of a human being as a political animal. It transforms public affairs into a consumer commodity. Issues of national importance are transformed by the gawping journalist and TV reporter into the kind of goods you can sell like any other goods: detergents and tooth-paste, say."

"I'm earning my living," said Brush. "I don't sit on my arse waiting for a monthly salary chit like some people. Besides, I have more respect for democracy than you have. Be careful, Hedges, or I'll smear you."

"I'd never have come if I'd known Brush was in on it."

Even Toplis was looking worried now. "I don't think Bream would have minded. After all, he could always have refused to talk, couldn't he?"

"It's the very thought of the thing: that two men should come to talk to someone in the Treasury about Government support for starting a university, bringing a snooper with a tape recorder under their coat-tails; it's enough to make anybody puke. Now look here, Brush," he concluded, as they turned into St. James's Street, "Toplis and I are going into that restaurant over there. You are not going into that restaurant over there. Neither are you going to wait outside. I warn you. I'll clobber you with your little black box."

"It's B.B.C. property." Brush was unimpressed by all this loud talk. "Lend me five quid, and I'll buzz off and get a sandwich in a pub."

Before Hedges could stop him, Toplis had handed over

a fiver and Brush was legging it up towards Piccadilly. "I couldn't keep it from Nell that we were coming," Toplis explained, "and when she suggested that her husband bring his recorder along I hadn't the heart to say no. It's quite true. He has to make his living. To be honest," he said, as they walked into Prunier's, "I thought we might get old Bream a bit squiffed, and then we could get Brush to record him promising to give us a couple of million quid. He's a gentleman. He'd have never gone back on his word." Toplis looked round him, grinning like a fox. He nodded at one of the waiters in his blue blouse and black apron. "Real French! Well, young Hedges. You got your way after all. Here we are in the Maison Prunier. Wonder if they'll let me drink whisky with the soup."

"Have you got another fiver?" said Hedges, as they waited for the head-waiter.

Toplis produced his wallet and extracted a note as though it was expected of him. Hedges gave it immediately to the head-waiter, saying, "I know that table in the corner is reserved, the one next to the table where the young lady with the fair hair and blue eyes is sitting, but"—Hedges's imagination began to race as he saw the head-waiter's resistance beginning to stiffen in spite of the fiver—"my friend, Major Toplis, and I would particularly appreciate it if we were allowed to sit there." This was cutting no ice with Prunier's, and Hedges entertained the notion of creating the impression they were on some kind of Intelligence work— Do you *know* who that thick-lipped man is, sitting with the fair-haired girl—but his nerve failed and he said into the head-waiter's ear, "Sorry, we ought to have booked a month ago. Terribly important. It's his wedding anniversary, you know, and it was at that *very* table. . . ."

120

"You are mistaken, sir," said the waiter. "The table is not reserved. You are very welcome."

And before showing them to the table next to the one where Prudence Styles, Mr. Styles, her father, the Member for Brewchester, and Jacob Bream of the Treasury were all sitting, he returned the note not—as might have been expected—to Hedges but to Toplis, who stuffed it back in his wallet again and said, "That bald-headed fellow is old Jake. He was like that at school, you know. It's hereditary. Headmaster tried to get him to wear a wig. Wouldn't have it. Never agreed with him. Many an argument we've had. Anyway, Hedges," Toplis said, as they took their places, still without having been observed by any of the people at the other table, "he let us down at the Athenæum, and I'm damned if I know why we shouldn't sit at the next table to him. If he gets shirty I'll tell him straight."

Bream, his large, dark eyes looking out of the polished skull, was now diagonally opposite Hedges; he was like an anatomical model. At the appropriate moment a white-jacketed attendant would appear and open the skull neatly into two halves, like the section of a bloody walnut; then the head would be shut, tapped with a hammer for resonance, and described as Caucasian Brachycephalic, and the whining North Midland voice with its flat, nasal vowels would pick up again, talking, as it was now, of Cultural Crisis. There were no standards, either in the arts or private behaviour; the arts, particularly, were hopelessly corrupt. He would not be at all surprised to learn of some new play that provided for actual rape on the stage. He himself was not so much Square as Cube-like. And so on. He had spotted Toplis and recognized him, but there had been no greeting.

121

"Hallo," said Hedges, catching Prudence's eye. "Fancy seeing you here!"

Prudence stared at him thoughtfully with no more than a nod by way of acknowledgement and said something to her father which made the heavily wrinkled back of the old man's neck go red. He was sitting with his rear to Hedges, who was so put out by Prudence's snub that he studied the back of this neck, carefully, and the tall, thin head of grey hair. Prudence's own head, he reflected, was probably just as thin under the hair-do. The little ears—hairy in Mr. Styles's case, pink in Prudence's—were set like a faun's to hear sounds straight ahead. The Member for Brewchester was one of those men who could listen and talk at the same time, and he was telling Bream about some trivial driving mishap he'd had that morning. Bream didn't so much as falter. He was saying how difficult it was for the police to find someone who would admit to being corrupted by a book; it meant that the days of prosecution for an obscene libel were over. The Member for Brewchester said the upshot was he'd finally decided to sell his car, and Hedges decided he was the sort of chap who, if he couldn't get a university for Brewchester, would settle for a sports ground. There was no doubt that was why Bream was being lunched at Prunier's. The University for Brewchester pressure group was taking action. Hedges was too angry even to eat.

Bream began throwing remarks to Toplis. Toplis replied. The Member for Brewchester told Hedges there was no parking, except for cabs, in St. James's Street. Hedges was so angry he defied Prudence by calling out how glad he was to see her. They'd missed her, been worried, et cetera. He was sensitive to the little currents of feeling that flowed between the two parties. Only the Member for Brewchester and possibly Toplis were unaware of the significance that lay in the presence of the party other than the one to which he himself belonged. Of those who knew, only Bream enjoyed his knowledge. Hedges picked at his Sole Véronique and drank Pouilly Fuisse, thinking what a lot of latent energy was about to be released. It was like sitting over some nuclear reactor and waiting for the atomic pile to go critical.

Bream leaned forward and said (maliciously, Hedges thought), "Toplis, d'you know Jack Guntrip, Member for Brewchester, who's very interested in a university down there? Guntrip, this is Gideon Toplis, who wants a university in Perstowe."

"This is too much of a coincidence," said Jack Guntrip savagely. "You didn't just *chance* to be lunching here, did you?"

And Bream was eating his lobster.

"I like that." Hedges took Guntrip's remark as being addressed to himself. "Anybody would think the British people, by the time they got into the nineteen-sixties, could discuss the siting of new universities in an objective and fair-minded way. But what happens? Lunching influential people in the Treasury. It almost amounts to an attempt at corruption." Immediately he turned to Bream and said, "I'm sorry——"

"Quite all right, my boy. Carry on."

"Precisely the kind of tactics," said Hedges, "that brought in commercial television. The pressure group."

"What are you doing here, anyway?" asked Prudence.

"My God, you're right!" Hedges bundled up his napkin and threw it on the table. "I'm ashamed to be playing such a dirty game."

"A game, yes. Dirty, no." Bream twiddled a lobster's

claw between thumb and forefinger. His thoughts were with the lining of his stomach, but he liked talking. "In the kind of ideal world you wish we were inhabiting, Hedges, all problems could be solved by geometry, and to everybody's satisfaction. And there'd be the one correct answer which the Deity himself would lean over a cloud and tick. In our world there are many correct answers. Take universities. Why was the first one at Oxford and not Banbury? Banbury would have been better for all sorts of reasons. But Oxford it was. And who's the worse for that? Take the siting of new universities. Speaking for myself, I can't think of a more suitable cause for a pressure group to champion. D'you get me, eh?"

"I'll bet you want commercial radio, too," Hedges said to Guntrip.

"So what?"

"And anyway," Bream was saying, "I like pressure groups, particularly when they give me a lunch like this."

"You amaze me," said Hedges coldly.

"How can you sit there"—at last Prudence managed to make herself heard—"hypocritically mouthing this stuff about pressure groups when you yourself are the Secretary of the Perstowe lot, I just can't imagine."

"I do believe in right decisions," Hedges answered her, "and that means the decision that is to the advantage of the greatest number. Provided," he added after a pause, "nobody suffers for it."

The top of Bream's head had a bluish sheen that Hedges had not noticed before. He was eating lobster voraciously. Could it be some kind of phosphorescent effect? "Justice will be done," he said, "as it always is eventually in a bureaucracy such as ours. People who labour in a bureaucracy have one governing thought: the avoidance of work. This is the obsession of Whitehall—not power, as Sir Charles Snow would have you think. We are driven by the fear of paper. In our experience, then, it always pays to be absolutely right on every occasion. Only by impartiality and justice can Government avoid labour into the small hours."

"How do you know when you're absolutely right?" asked Hedges.

"Why," said Bream, surprised by such simplicity, "when we've done something that closes a file."

Toplis lifted his left arm and pointed at Bream. "Your lobster has been obtained under false pretences. You realize that Brewchester and Perstowe can't both have universities. They're too close together. And as Brewchester, being a one-eyed village rather than a town, is out of the running anyway——"

"I don't know who you are, sir," said Mr. Styles, turning on him and showing eyes like two blue buttons, "but I must insist there is a tradition of university learning at Brewchester." Hedges just loved his broad country vowels; this was the lulling voice that Prudence had heard as a child while she watched her father make saddles. "In fourteen eighty-two, there was a disagreement at Oxford and a group of scholars migrated to Brewchester, taking with them one of the bells from Merton College Chapel. That bell is still in Brewchester Parish Church."

"The reason I keep looking at my watch," said Bream, "is quite simply that my chauffeur is calling for me at two-twenty sharp, and of course the police won't let him wait. But I do beg the rest of you to go on with the meal." He got up and shook Guntrip warmly by the hand. "My dear fellow, how can I possibly thank you?"

Toplis whispered in Hedges's ear, "Don't let him get away like this. You're younger than I am."

Bream must have had very sharp hearing, because he said at once, "I was about to observe, Toplis, that as Hedges appears to be the brains of your party he might care to drive with me to London Airport and tell me about Perstowe as we go. Someone—Miss Styles, say, from Brewchester—might like to come along to see fair play. After I've caught my plane the car will be at your disposal, to bring you back to town or even to go for a nice drive in the Chilterns, which are most attractive at this time of year. There now! I must hurry."

He was out of his seat and trotting towards the door, talking as he went, grabbing hat and umbrella from one of the waiters, waving them both in the air, smiling, his skull winking. "I haven't enjoyed a meal or a talk so much for. . . ."

And he was gone. By the time Hedges and Prudence had joined him in the limousine, he was already in amiable conversation with Christopher Brush, who was sitting at his side, plugging a microphone lead into his portable recorder and reeking of beer.

"Will you be able to play it back to me immediately?" Bream was saying. "To be perfectly honest, I just love hearing myself talk."

The Hedges family had been butchers in Perstowe since the end of the eighteenth century, and it was only natural that from time to time the descendant of so many men in striped aprons should consider how he would have made out as a butcher if he'd not gone in for the book-learning. Hedges had nothing against being of butchering stock. He had nothing against butchering. He had never minded the blood. He'd seen his father slaughter beasts and pigs and poultry in the old days when a butcher had his own slaughtering shed and gear, before the government-licensed abattoirs came in. He had never been upset by it. If things had turned out differently, he'd have been able to bid ˙ for the prize ox at the Christmas fair with the rest of them—and put a bullet through the beast's brain and cut him up. On his Egyptian campaign the all-conquering Napoleon wrote to his brother, saying he now dreamed of nothing but retiring to live the simple life of a farmer in the French countryside. Hedges had been much struck by this. Towards the end of the war, which he spent on various anti-aircraft sites in Kent, his thoughts, like Napoleon's, turned to the quiet life. Not farming, though. Butchering. The small businessman was one of the few roles left in which you could play the individual. (It was a mistake to think Napoleon had grown tired of glory. He was momentarily in a situation—plague in Cairo, bad luck in Syria, a faithless wife—when he was no longer the controller but the controlled. As a farmer, a man might at least preserve the illusion of independence.) Well, like Napoleon. . . .

He had no illusions, really, about the future of the small shopkeeper in this chain-store civilization. At least, one existed as an individual; one made one's own terms, even with bankruptcy. As an administrator, it was impossible for him to be the man his father was. At the end of his first month's work his father asked him how he was paid: did they give it to him loose in the hand or was it in an envelope? When he had to confess it was automatically credited to his banking account and that no actual notes or silver passed, the old man was scandalized. "They've got you under their thumb." He was right in a way. From that moment he had been part of the organization—adapting himself, gaining something there but conceding more here, fitting in, deferring, adjusting, trimming. After years of administration he couldn't be really rude to people any more, even to Brush. He tried but it was never really effective. Brush treated it as verbiage. Hedges thought of the cause he served and could never bring himself to believe that he was bigger than any cause. This was an error into which no butcher ever fell. Hedges thought of his red-handed ancestry and knew that not one of those meat-gorged men would, in his position—seeing Brush there in the back of the limousine with his tape recorder, calmly interrogating the great Jacob Bream—nevertheless have climbed in behind Prudence, seated himself on a well-uphol-stered jump seat, and allowed himself to be driven off to London Airport. Well, his grandfather wouldn't, anyway. Perhaps his father would have been so overcome with laughter at Brush's cheek he would not have hit him.

Brush, Bream, and Prudence all sat on the back seat with Bream in the middle; Hedges sat on his folding chair watching the back of the driver's neck and listening.

"I speak anonymously," Bream remarked to the tape recorder, as they all swept round the Ritz into Piccadilly, "because I am a civil servant." His voice floated on a fat pool of self-satisfaction. "But I am glad to give evidence. From time to time people who want to start universities approach me. Why, I don't know. I'm not really influential."

"How do you think people come to make this mistake?" asked Brush.

"A good question. I've already answered it."

"If *you're* not influential, who is?"

"Well, of course, there are the members of the University Grants Committee, there is the Vice-Chancellor's Committee, above all there is the Minister. . . ."

"But Mr. Bream, you yourself serve on the U.G.C."

"Purely in a technical capacity. I am a servant of the committee."

"But you know what goes on."

"Yes, I know what goes on. It is unsensational. . . . Now will you let me hear what I've said?"

As they bowled down Knightsbridge, Bream listened to a minute ear-phone, nodding and smiling, saying, "Good! Good! Wonderful invention. Perfectly splendid! Of course," he said, as he handed the ear-phone back to Brush, the recital having finished, "lunch always dulls my intellect. I'd have been even better before I'd eaten."

Noticing that Brush had placed the microphone with its lead on the floor between his feet, Hedges had contrived to draw it forward until, still without Brush noticing, he was able to pick it up and slip it into his pocket.

"Mr. Bream," he said, "did you have any special reason for asking Miss Styles and myself to come on this trip with you?"

"You interested me. Your enthusiasm and your idealism interested me. Miss Styles interests me. You are unlike the usual university pressure group." Bream seemed to be feeling the heat. He was wiping his head and face with a handkerchief. "The rest of your respective parties were not."

"Not what?"

"Not unlike the usual university pressure group. Even poor old Gideon. True, there wasn't a clergyman. Anyway, I wanted to isolate you and Miss Styles. I felt you were phenomena to be studied. In return I would give you advice."

"Hey! Where's the microphone?" Brush was saying. "Have you pinched the microphone, Hedges?"

"I've got it in my pocket. What advice?" he said to Bream.

Bream produced a flat tin from his jacket pocket and, opening it, revealed that it contained a lot of little black biscuits which he offered round and found no takers.

"Carbon," he explained, "has the invaluable property of absorbing all poisons into itself. If I had my way they'd be available on the National Health Service." He crunched one noisily.

"Give me back that microphone. Don't be a fool."

"What advice?" Hedges repeated, with one hand guarding his pocket.

Bream wiped his lips. "This, really. It's just a feeling I have. You understand that my only wish is to be friendly and helpful? Good. It's about the geographical position of both Perstowe and Brewchester. Here are two towns, both contending for a university. They are only thirty or so miles apart. Now there's nothing we dislike more than two neighbours competing in this way. We have to be impartial. The only way we can be really impartial is to accept the claim of neither. In short, I believe that if both Perstowe and Brewchester launch simultaneous attacks on us it will be the surest way of establishing, say, the University of Carlisle, which is just about as as far away from both as can be decently contrived."

"This is disgraceful," said Prudence.

Hedges turned round and examined Bream's face. "You're joking." Or running a temperature, he thought. Bream's head was glowing and shining. He looked like some ruddy-headed goblin caught at his labours in the gold-mine, sweating, hairless, blubbery; both humorous and dangerous at the same time; as ready to hit you over the head with his pick as give you an ingot to take up into the daylight. Bream popped another charcoal biscuit into his mouth. There was black dust on his lips. It occurred to Hedges that he was deliberately counteracting the effect of the lobster with all this charcoal. Perhaps he meant no more than he said: that lobster was poison to him, but he had been quite unable to resist it. Hedges marvelled that it was necessary for him to go through this experience—travelling down Kensington High Street with a senior Civil Servant who all the time was more and more assuming the colour of the boiled crustachean he had eaten—to realize that the word intoxicated really meant poisoned. Bream's translucent-seeming head was giving out a fungoid light. Hedges looked into the grey eyes and thought of the octopus.

"Are you all right, Mr. Bream?"

"Perhaps we could have the window down just a little, there's a good chap."

"You didn't really mean," said Hedges, "what you just said. You were joking."

"What did I say, Mr. Hedges?" asked Bream, beginning—it seemed—to steam.

"That the siting of new universities was decided not on merit but in ways that gave you the least possible trouble afterwards."

"I said nothing of the sort," said Bream. "It was really most kind of you and Miss Styles and this gentleman with the recording apparatus to offer to drive out to the airport with me. We servants of the public, you know, are unaccustomed to demonstrations of public emotion. And that is what you are, after all, aren't you? Members of the public. It is fine, very fine indeed. How extraordinary to see Toplis after all these years. He's shrunk, you know."

131

"For Chris'sake, Hedges, gimme back that microphone. You don't want me to miss all this, do you? It's worth money."

Hedges slid back the glass panel and spoke to the driver. "Mr. Bream has been taken ill. I think you ought to take him home. He's certainly not fit to fly to Scotland."

The driver didn't even turn his head. "That's all right, sir. He's often like that after lunch."

"No, but——"

Before Hedges could finish, the driver had raised a hand and flipped the panel shut once more.

"Booker," said Bream, "drives me everywhere. He drove my tank in the desert, you know. We're like brothers."

"I want to get out," said Prudence.

Bream looked out. "Not here, my dear, it wouldn't be suitable. This is the Television Centre."

"Will you please ask the driver to stop. I insist on getting out."

"But, Prudence!"

She had to stand up to slide back the glass panel, but this she achieved before Hedges could prevent her. "I want you to stop here," she said to the driver, very coolly. "I'm going to get out."

The car stopped opposite the White City underground station, and Prudence did as she promised. Hedges had had to get out first in order to make Prudence's exit possible, and they stood side by side on the pavement.

"I'm sorry about this," said Bream. "But you'll be all right with Mr. Hedges to look after you. Now that I know he's to be with you I'm easier in my mind. Think over what I've said, won't you? This gentleman will stay with me because I've just thought of something else to say into his recording engine." Bream raised a hand. "Good-bye."

"Good-bye," said Hedges.

Prudence was already starting to walk away.

"Wait!" Bream actually insisted on climbing out of the car. For some moments he stood in silence, cooling in the fresh air. He seemed to crackle like a pan fresh from the oven.

"If only we'd lunched at the Athenæum I'd never have talked like this. They never do lobster like Prunier's. But I don't want you to think from my manner that the essential truth has not been exposed. It has. If Perstowe and Brewchester put forward rival claims to a university—well, I wonder. There's a strong case for an institute of higher education in that part of the world. Join forces, why don't you? You, Mr. Hedges, and you, Miss Styles, why not sink your rivalries and come to the Government with a common proposal? Take that message back to your Promotion Committees. Let us hear you speaking with a single voice. You have my word that the ear of Jacob Bream will not be inattentive."

He smiled greasily, climbed back into the car, and Hedges barely had time to throw the microphone in through the open window before the car shot off in the direction of London Airport.

"Do you think there are any more like him in the Treasury?" Prudence asked.

"It was the lobster. It has that effect on some people. I've heard about it. I dare say he'll be quite all right once he's been sick. I hope it's over Brush."

"I don't think it was the lobster," said Prudence. "I think he's always like that. What's more, I think that there

was quite a point in what he had to say. Well, Perstowe will
have to drop out."

They crossed the road to the tube station, arguing
fiercely. They were still arguing when they reached the
platform.

"And another thing," said Hedges. "You've been away
from school for several days. Without permission. Why?"

There was no one else on the platform. The sunshine
fell like silk on to the steel rails. The White City underground station enjoyed, for some moments, a remote mountain stillness; only a little wind murmuring over the lip of a
hoarding.

Prudence shrugged. "I looked at the expressions on
those kids' faces. I sort of thought, What's the use? I
thought of Saundersfoot and you and all this talk. And I
asked myself, What's the use?"

"You thought of me?"

"Yes."

"It's a nice afternoon. What say we go for a trip on the
river? We could go down to Greenwich and see the Cutty
Sark."

"All right," she said.

Tower Bridge seemed a suitable place to embark, but
no sooner had they walked down to the landing-stage from
the tube station than Prudence began worrying about her
father. She found a telephone kiosk and rang Prunier's, only
to be told that the party of three gentlemen had left about
twenty minutes previously, that a cab had been called for
them, and that no message had been left. Hedges said that
either Toplis had taken them to the Athenæum or Guntrip
had carted them back to the House; but he privately
thought it more likely that Toplis had got his way over the

strip-tease. He had no idea how Prudence would take such a speculation. In the state of uncertainty they now found themselves, they decided not, after all, to set sail for Greenwich. They would visit the Tower instead.

"We were going to catch the six-ten from Paddington," said Prudence. "I expect I shall find him on the platform. We've had a completely wasted journey. Mr. Bream seemed a fool. Guntrip is a fool, too. And I'm a fool or I wouldn't be here talking to you. If there ever is a Brewchester University, it'll be due to the tenacity and imagination of one man."

"Your father?"

"Yes. Do you think Bream was lying—I mean, about Brewchester and Perstowe cancelling each other out?"

"I think he was rather skilful, really. He's said something that, without being actually irrelevant, leaves him uncommitted, and what more could a Civil Servant ask?"

They joined a party being told by a Yeoman Warder that the traditional founder of the Tower of London was none other than Julius Caesar himself. There followed half an hour or so of walking about, up and down stone stairs, emerging from dark chambers into brilliant sunlight; of hearing the names of the illustrious dead; of seeing greys and a certain amount of green and a little scarlet. But Hedges felt that he and Prudence were not quite there. In the Chapel of St. Peter ad Vincula, the guide said, "Thomas More, Anne Boleyn, Katharine Howard, Lady Jane Grey and her husband Dudley, Monmouth"; and when they came out and found a seat looking down over the grass and the trees and the parading ravens and Traitors' Gate to the milky gleam of the river, Prudence said, "It's all very soothing," which was inept comment on such a blood-stained piece of stone and earth; and Hedges thought it was because

they were just floating through the place. She knew very
well it wasn't soothing. But she wasn't thinking. At least,
not about the Tower.

"Did you know your ex-wife came to see me?" she
suddenly asked.

"Nell?"

"Is that man with the tape recorder really her husband?"

"Brush? Yes."

"She wondered if I'd like to collect for Famine Relief."

"Just like Nell."

"What do you mean?"

Hedges was taken aback by the news that Nell had
faked an excuse to call on Prudence, but he didn't want to
hear any more about the meeting. There was something
about Prudence's manner that made him nervous. He suggested they go and look at the Armoury. Prudence
followed meekly, but he was not deceived. Once in the
White Tower, she looked around at the helmets, the breast-
plates, the swords, the maces and spears and said, "Is it true
you still send her birthday cards?"

"Yes. Why not?"

They stood in front of a fifteenth-century suit of
armour mounted realistically on a wooden horse, also in
armour.

"Why she should want to come and spill this bile over
me, I can't think. I said it was nothing to do with me. I tried
to stop her."

"She's all right, really." The painted eyes of the horse
stared at Hedges through the holes in the face-armour; they
had the kind of rage that Prudence seemed to be feeling. He
couldn't think quite what to say to defend Nell. "I suppose

we're all haunted by an irrational and aboriginal remorse, looking for someone to lay it."

"Remorse? I've never seen anyone freer from it."

They wandered around until they came to the Execution block. Prudence said that Mrs. Brush—it was clear that from now on this was to be Prudence's way of referring to Nell—would be quite pleased to get his neck over just such a block. There was no need for Prudence to fill in the details. Hedges could imagine them only too well.

"She said you were still in love with her. I said it was no concern of mine. I tried to stop her. She was boasting. At the end I almost had to push her out."

A squad of soldiers were drilling on the parade-ground, and Hedges made Prudence stop on the White Tower steps to watch them. He hoped she wouldn't try to talk over the clump of boots. The dust and the heat made him thirsty, but it was too early for anything but tea or soft drinks, and although his mouth was dry it wasn't that kind of thirst.

"Hip! Hup! Hip! Hup!" coughed the drill-sergeant.

"Although she was talking about you"—Prudence's mouth was near his ear—"she was looking at me all the time and—and measuring me with her eyes. She was inspecting me. I didn't understand it."

The sergeant told his men to stand easy, and Hedges took Prudence by the arm and urged her down the hill, reminding her of the tradition that in the Wakefield Tower, where the Crown Jewels were kept—it lay straight ahead— somebody or other had been strangled while saying his prayers. Prudence said she could well believe it. That was the sort of world we lived in.

They went out of the Tower altogether and stood on

137

the jetty with the river mud shining black beneath their feet.

"In your shoes I'd find it easy to hate her. She says you're as infatuated as ever. That was the word she used: infatuated. You sent her birthday cards. You lent her husband money. She seemed to think this reflected credit on *her*."

All Hedges could think to say was, "I'm sorry she came and bothered you."

"She's absolutely right, of course." On the third word Prudence's voice began to wobble. Astonished, he looked at her and saw there were tears in her eyes. "I think it's absolutely terrible, the way you let her trample on you. You don't hate her at all, and I think it's absolutely beastly of you."

A launch was leaving for Westminster. Looking at his watch, Hedges said that by the time they arrived the pubs would be open and there'd still be time to get a taxi for Paddington. They sat at the front, full in the sun, the river churning away beerily on either side. Prudence's bitterness against the woman she called Mrs. Brush made Hedges feel half alive; perhaps she was right, perhaps the ability to loathe and vilify Nell was the sign of some essential biological mechanism, and he lacked it. In the same way a man might be physically healthy but unable to feel pain as keenly as he should: the sort of chap who might lose a leg or an arm out of sheer carelessness and not notice. Ordinary mortals were warned of appendicitis because of a bellyache. But not this chap. Hedges looked at Prudence, saw that she wasn't weeping any more, and took her hand in his.

CHAPTER FIVE

◇◇◇◇◇◇◇◇◇◇◇◇◇◇◇◇◇◇◇◇◇◇◇◇◇◇◇◇

Love in August

For the rest of July, a nightly sea mist stole over Perstowe. By noon the sun broke through and the afternoons sparkled. The scheme for the university was afloat. Toplis and Hedges were not the only ones who popped up to Town. Primrose went up on his own and gave Bream another lunch. Arthur Supple, as chairman of the Education Committee, was in Hedges's office daily, quite unable to understand why the Government took so long to make up its mind now that he had bulldozed his way through the Borough Council meeting with the proposal that Lack Park should be the site of the university. Letters had appeared in the *Times*, the *Guardian*, the *Daily Telegraph*, over the names of Arrowsmith, Jimmy Pigge, and Toplis respectively; and the Promotion Committee had considered Bream's view that they had better scotch the Brewchester application before it reached Whitehall.

Hedges was pleased that enthusiasm was building up. Nevertheless he felt there was something wrong. They all wanted a university, yes, but they wanted one for unworthy reasons. Even old Supple had stopped talking about the New Jerusalem and became intoxicated instead with matters he hadn't the remotest understanding of, such as the relationship between the Faculties of Science and Arts and whether there should be a free-access system in the libraries (Minchin had been talking to him). Hedges now saw that Supple, for all his Calvinist guff, wanted a university as a means of giving the town status, just like the rest of them. That act at the dinner about the need for a disinterested belief in the value of a university education had been part of the never-ending role imposed on him by religious bigotry and plain cussedness. Supple, like Toplis, Arrowsmith, Amos, and the rest, wanted a university because they wanted a university. Only one man had a view of what the university was really for—Hedges. He saw it as a social gesture. He saw it as the great statement of Perstowe's self-awareness. Unless the borough really understood what a university was and that theirs could link their own unexamined lives to the world of abstract thinking, then Perstowe was in for just another red-brick institute, like the one Hedges himself had been educated in. Unless the Promotion Committee was, from the beginning, animated by this almost mystic concept, they could never acquire it later. How could they be startled into an awareness of the opportunity that lay before them? How could they be jacked up to the required moral and imaginative height?

Well, there was human sacrifice. This shocked people, filled them with awe, enlarged their understanding of the grotesque possibilities of life; and in this state of receptivity they had it in them to act like gods. Hedges allowed his mind to play around the subject. He had been led to thinking about violent self-immolation by reading in the paper about a Buddhist monk who sat down and ordered his companions to pour petrol over him. They set him alight and he died, apparently without moving or uttering. The monk was making a political protest. The strangeness and the horror of the act made an impression on Hedges; he would have liked to read, the following day, that the story was untrue. The nearest British equivalent he could think if was the suffragette who had herself killed at the Derby. But, to be honest, he couldn't see himself setting out to be *that* kind of martyr.

One reason for hesitation was that his cause was rather hard to explain to people. If it had simply been a question of, say, whether the university concentrated on the biological instead of the physical sciences, Hedges could have driven his point home in the high Indian manner by fasting. A neat problem such as the one over mixed halls of residence could be brought into prominence by climbing on to the parapet of the borough offices and threatening to jump off unless he had his way. But his concept of a university that belonged organically to the town it was situated in could not be presented to the citizens of Perstowe as one of two dramatic alternatives. He couldn't even think of a slogan to shout as he balanced on the parapet. Public opinion was bound to be confused, and in the confusion he might fail to get proper nourishment or actually fall off the ledge.

Secondly, the threat to do something terrible to yourself unless you got your own way was not what one expected from a real sacrificial victim. Just the opposite. The threatener believed in coercing people by violence, even if it did happen to be directed against himself. Perstowe (as Hedges saw it) required a really passive sacrificial victim, one who had to be offered up because of his good qualities but certainly not with his consent. There was no other way of contriving the kind of tension which, when the sacrifice

141

had been made, would drive the mob to make good what they had done away with.

Hedges was still drawn to a real blood-letting but he saw the difficulties. Assuming that he was sufficiently important in the town to qualify as a really potent sacrificial victim, one whose destruction would bring the town to some sense of its own identity, the vital part to be offered up (in squeamish England) was not the body. It was more likely to be a reputation. Where was the scandal to bury rotting in the roots of Perstowe?

Well, not rotting exactly. That would imply a scandal of such a sordid kind that. . . . What he was getting at really, was the need for a scandal that—anyway, a rumpus in which he was shown to be shocking and endearing at the same time: a hullabaloo that showed him up to be a real villain and one who could be done down with a good conscience but, somehow, lingeringly, affectionately, and even respectfully. Like Milton's Satan.

During the second week of August, when the schools were shut, when the Saundersfoots were on a mountain-side in Skye, when Prudence was shut up in Brewchester, writing a novel, and educaton had the scarcely perceptible pulse of a hibernating mole, Hedges was able to talk his idea over with Amos.

"You must be aware," said Amos, "that it is widely supposed you're marrying this school-teacher to cover old Saundersfoot."

"That is Saundersfoot's scandal," said Hedges, "not mine, and, of course, he's not terribly interested in this university idea anyway. Frankly, I'm not at all happy about that particular story. I don't like being thought about in that way. What sort of creature do they think I am?"

"Well——"

"A man who gets his wife pinched and then assumes the paternity of somebody else's bastard. Obviously a figure of fun. It's an image that's got to be changed."

"I never thought you'd get obsessed with yourself like this. Why don't you take a holiday? You need it."

"I have long since ceased to live for myself," Hedges replied, thinking to entertain, "but I suppose that is hard for you to understand."

"We're going pony-trekking in the Lake District. Like to come?"

Hedges put an arm round Amos's shoulders (they were in Hedges's office) and urged him gently towards the door. "Sometimes I just feel like somebody in a never-ending play who's learned only his cues and the sort of thing he's supposed to improvise when those cues come up; but as to what the play's about and what all these other people are doing—I know what I'm improvising but I don't know what effect I'm supposed to be making. And while I'm off stage I suspect that the *real* story is being unfolded. When I appear the audience sees me in the light of something I don't know about."

"Speaking as one of the audience——"

"You're not one of the audience. You're on stage too. You think that if I've a certain view on the way the university should develop, I should put that view as persuasively as I can to the rest of the committee. But what are they thinking in the audience? They can see I stand no chance of persuading anybody with the kind of idea I have about what a university is for. They also know that being the man I am I can best argue with the help of catastrophe. Over and above this they will know something I don't know. What?"

They were standing at the head of the stairs. "Get this

into your head," said Amos. "There *is no audience*. There's only us."

"There's only you and me. Basically there's only me, and I just want to be completely aware of the situation in which 'me' finds himself. I could push you down these stairs, for example. Let's imagine you break your neck. That gives me the unambiguous role of the murderer. Murder is the basic, unambiguous act."

"I still think there are less complicated ways of starting a university." Amos went down the stairs slowly. "The circulation of the *Advertiser* has gone up eight hundred copies since this university lark started. People like the idea. They're interested. They don't need you to murder me in order to whip up excitement."

"I was merely illustrating an argument," said Hedges.

"No you weren't. You were threatening me."

"I was paying you the compliment of being quite honest about myself!" Hedges shouted after him.

Amos was unimaginative, and it had been a mistake to talk to him. He had gone off with the idea that Hedges was becoming odd. Nothing could be more damaging than a reputation for eccentricity. It robbed a man of dignity, and without dignity (Hedges thought) there was no chance of gripping the imagination of Toplis and Primrose and Pigge and the rest. Hedges was certain there was nothing basically dotty about his theory. He might have expressed himself a little more apocalyptically. That was because he was trying not only to convince Amos but to convince himself too. He would have to be less passionate, though.

Within three days he had met Nell for the first time since he had seen her in bed and come to the conclusion his trouble lay in not being passionate enough. Glands leaked giddy secretions into his system. For the first time in years he could feel cold air penetrating to the remotest lobe of his lungs; and he had seen that his theory of a sacrificial victim was nothing like as absurd as Amos made it out to be. Nevertheless, there had been a flaw. He had been wrong to think he could shock the town with anything less than the curved knife and the blood-stained sacrificial stone; the immediate victim, however, was to be not himself but none other than Christopher Brush. The country Hedges tramped through to reach this particular view looked as follows.

Nell Brush was, in spite of a sharp end to her nose and a long upper lip, a strikingly beautiful woman. She was in her mid thirties. From under surprisingly long lashes (they may have been artificial) very dark eyes, slate-coloured but alive, stared without self-consciousness into yours. And around the line of vision the rest of her face seemed to vibrate in some strange, golden way, as it might in candle-light. There was a constant flicker of motion (a complete illusion; it was caused by the muscles of one's own eyes trembling under her stare) that seemed to promise some gasped endearment, or laughter, or cry of wonder. In reality she was as hard as nails, but on Hedges, in spite of everything that had happened, she had this hypnotic effect, and it made his very eyeballs ache.

Since the divorce they had often met, usually in Brush's company; but they had never been alone with one another, not to talk, until this Saturday afternoon, and as the meeting had been deliberately fixed by Nell (she had telephoned: "You by yourself? Mind if I pop round?") Hedges looked out his cheque-book in advance because this kind of approach seemed to indicate that some considerable sum was in question. He saw her get off the bus at the corner and had the front door open and waiting. She was wearing what

Hedges thought a very nice grey suit—wool, *knitted*, he thought—and a quarter of an hour went by, during which she sat and talked and didn't mention money once. He began to think there was some other reason for her visit.

"Where's Brush?" he asked.

She shrugged. "You wouldn't have come across an umbrella of mine?"

"What sort?"

"A green one. I may have left it about." It was two years since she had walked out.

"No. Is that what you've come for?"

She shrugged again. "I just thought I'd like to see you. Would you have me back? I mean, if I left Christopher?"

"No."

She was sitting on a low chair with her knees on a level with her breasts. She ran one hand up and down one shining and hissing calf. "Oh, yes, you would." She smiled and he didn't resent her confidence. He watched the unblinking black eyes and was aware of the way she caressed her legs almost as though she was caressing him. She spoke so quietly he could hardly make out the words. "I think I shall come back to you, Ian."

"Sorry, my dear. I don't know if you're having a game——"

"That would be very cruel. No, Ian, I'm just reporting a state of mind. I was watching Christopher eat some sausages last night. It was the way he was all greasy round the mouth and he went on chewing. I looked at him and thought—well, I thought what I thought." Ending on a sigh. "Here I am."

"So you want to leave Brush. Well, leave him. You can't come back here."

"Yes, I can."

"No, you can't."

She shook off a shoe and extended one stockinged foot towards him, working the toes. This was enough to enable him to look away from her eyes, and when he saw the foot, about a yard in front of his face, it was as much as he could do not to put out a hand to grasp it. His own right foot began to throb under the tension, and Nell spotted his grimace.

"I'd come back to you now, if you like. This minute. If I chose, I could come back to you now and you'd be quite helpless to stop me, Ian. Everything depends on what I choose. What you choose doesn't matter. Does it, Ian?" She put her foot back in the shoe again and watched him with her chin up and her eyelids lowered. "You might offer me a cigarette."

"Sorry." He brought a box over from the writing-table and, after lighting her cigarette, put one between his own lips and mumbled, "What a bitch!"

"You haven't answered my question."

"What's that?" He had not lit his cigarette. He sat squarely in front of her, as he had sat before moving, looking into her eyes and feeling a hot wash of sweat on his throat. He had the box of matches in his hand, but he could not light that cigarette. He was sweating and screaming silently to himself and his right foot throbbed and he wanted her to take off her shoe again and—

"Everything depends on what I choose. Doesn't it?"

He jumped up. "Look, clear out, will you, Nell? I don't bear you any ill will, Christ knows, but clear out, will you? If you leave Brush I don't want to know anything about it. You understand?"

"But what if I've nowhere to go?"

"Well, I'd help you, of course. But you can't come here. What about your mother? How's your mother?"

"She's all right. Asks about you."

"Will you go now?"

"All right," she said. She had smoked so little of her cigarette that when she stubbed it out it broke in two. "Actually, if Christopher knew I was here he'd kill me."

"Would he?" The blood was still roaring round Hedges's head. The room was too small, suddenly, for all the furniture in it. If he moved he would collide with a chair or a table. He hung on to Nell's eyes as it might be for support and asked her to repeat what she had just said.

"If Christopher knew I was here he'd kill me," she said, laughing; and Hedges thought, Oh no, he's the one to be killed. He's the victim. He's the one to bury in the tangled roots.

"I hear you're getting married," she said.

He didn't want to go into this at all and just grunted.

"And without even asking my permission. I'm not going to let you marry *anybody*. I mean, I'm not going to let you *marry*. I shall probably need you myself. No probably either. I'm *sure* I shall. As for you, let's face it, these last two years have been a dead loss for you. You've crumbled. It shows in you physically. Notice those little chalky knobs in the lobes of your ears? I can see your scalp through your hair. The flesh is beginning to hang on the bones of your face. You've got broken blood vessels in the right side of your nose."

"I'm all right."

"You don't get enough exercise."

He studied her to see whether she too showed any signs of wear and tear, but, so far as his sexual excitement permitted him to focus at all clearly, he had to admit she looked the same as always, just marvellous. The thought of Brush even touching this woman made him feel he was looking down from a great height, dizzy and sick. How the hell *could* she? It must be like copulating with an ape.

"The emotional mess you're in," she said, "you're just ready to marry anybody. But you don't deceive me. It's pitiable, really."

He wasn't serious about killing Brush, but if those murderous thoughts had been anything more than part of the general flexing of the imagination he gave himself from time to time Nell's complaint about the way he ate sausages would have clinched it. He'd have been ready to go straight out and—well, he would have . . . made it seem like an accident. Walk on the cliffs. Slippery patch of clay. A woman who loved a man would never complain about sausage grease round his mouth. It followed that Nell's infatuation with Brush was genuinely over. Hedges reflected that he could never have put paid to the man if there was any danger of its bringing her even a spasm of grief. It was marvellous that, even now, he didn't want to hurt her.

"Look," he said, after they had been looking at each other in silence for about a minute. "I don't want to seem inhospitable, but what did you want to see me about?"

She gasped and showed a lot of eye white. "This! What we've been talking about."

He was disappointed. "I thought you wanted to say something about the university idea. You ought to go before my father comes in."

"But I *like* your father."

"O.K., O.K. But you must have done something, because he's turned against you."

Finally she stood up and looked round for her handbag.

He helped her hunt, and, his head being near hers, he could not draw back in time to avoid the kiss she planted on his cheek. "When you've had a little time to think over what I've said, Ian, you'll just come screaming after me; and I just wanted you to know I wouldn't shut the door in your face. Good-bye, darling—for the present, that is."

Although that kiss had been the only physical contact between them, he felt, after she had gone, as though they had been making love. He could smell her skin, vanilla and salt. Very slowly he went upstairs and flung himself, face down, on his bed, where, at once, he was asleep and water rushed before his eyes.

In his dream, he was painfully caught by his right foot, under water and fighting for breath. The peaked-capped policeman who appeared and charged him with murder said it was useless for him to deny that he didn't even know the man, because a photograph had already appeared in the *Perstowe Advertiser* showing the two of them together, sitting on a harbour wall. Hedges woke and lifted his head. Outside, the wind boiled in the trees. His foot hurt, and it worried him to know what sort of crime it was, to allow yourself to be raped and sucked dry by a woman who used to be your wife. It wasn't just ordinary adultery.

Waking a bit more and sitting up, he remembered that in actual fact she had kissed him and nothing more, so he had nothing to boast of when he saw Brush next. If he so much as mentioned it, Brush would only guffaw and say a kiss would never have satisfied him. Brush still had his heel on his neck.

"What d'you do for a woman these days?" Brush had once asked him.

A man like that could be taken for a walk on the cliff

path, knocked on the head like a rabbit, and dropped on to the rocks below. Nobody would believe it was an accident, but that was as near a criminal charge as anyone would get. Hedges would walk about the town cocking his ear for the talk. "That's the fellow who went for a walk with his ex-wife's husband, only the husband didn't come back." He remembered the hard peck of her breasts as he stroked her naked flank. If he weren't so prim and prissy, she'd be right there on the bed with him. He would have phoned the flat and asked her to come back, but he was sure it would be Brush's voice he'd hear at the other end of the line. Well, what if it was?

"Send Nell back to me," he would instruct.

No, he didn't want to talk to Brush. He wanted to kill him. Just before the despatching blow he might talk to him.

"You've asked for this, haven't you, Brush?" he would say.

"Yes," Brush would answer. "I'm glad you see it that way."

"Then you co-operate?"

"Certainly I co-operate."

But he couldn't telephone Nell with the risk of talking to Brush himself. She was not a fast walker. Maybe there was still time to catch her up. He looked at his watch and saw that it was all of two hours since she left. He had been asleep for two hours.

He went downstairs, made himself a cup of tea, and read Amos's editorial and saw that his name was mentioned in the second paragraph.

Hedges couldn't think what the university had to do with him. He washed his face under the cold tap.

* * *

August 25 that year fell on a Sunday. At three o'clock in the afternoon Hedges, wearing one of his office suits, and his father, Harris tweed in angry auburn and highly polished brown boots, were leaving the house together when a no-longer-young Sunbeam Talbot with rusty fenders drew up and a little grey-headed man jumped out. Instead of walking round to the pavement, he stood in the middle of the road, looking at Hedges and apparently talking to himself, for Hedges could see his lips moving.

"It *is* Mr. Styles?"

"Ah! I've called at a bad moment. It's about these anonymous letters."

Hedges introduced his father and the two men nodded at each other, but as Mr. Styles stayed out in the road conversation was not easy.

"Just going up to the cemet'ry," said Mr. Hedges.

"Sorry to intrude!" shouted Mr. Styles.

"My wife's birthday." He displayed the large club he had been holding in his right hand, and it turned out to be red roses in brown paper. "McGredy's Sunset. Her favourite. You just driven over from Brewchester? Lot of traffic about, I make no doubt of that. 'Ow many miles to the gallon d'you get out of her? You do? Well, there's some'at wrong there! Lunacy these days, running a car, if you can't service it yourself. Take my advice. Never trust a garage. Bloody robbers! Well, if you'd like to come with us for the ride," said Mr. Hedges, as he searched for his car-key first in one waistcoat pocket and then in another, "you're welcome. A clear day like today you can see twenty miles down the estuary. Still, what's the use of a good view from the cemet'ry? It's too late then."

"I wouldn't want to intrude."

"Leave your car. Nobody'll pinch *that*, not people in

these parts won't. Room for us all in the Mini. From my wife's grave," said Mr. Hedges, "there's a fine view of the moors. Mrs. Styles still living?"

"I'm a widower too."

"Ah!" Mr. Hedges sighed baritone.

"But I'm not a Christian," said Mr. Styles. "Indeed I have no religious belief at all, and certainly I don't believe in the immortality of the soul or the resurrection of the body." By this time he was seated by Mr. Hedges's side in the Mini. Ian, at the back, leaned forward to hear. "So that the visiting of graves means nothing to me. As a matter of fact my wife was cremated and her ashes scattered in the garden."

"You vote Labour too," said Mr. Hedges, "no doubt."

"I hope I've not said anything to hurt your feelings."

"Not at all," said Mr. Hedges. "See that row of cottages? I could've bought those for six hundred quid. I was offered them! Six hundred! That was twenty years ago. I was a fool, of course. Ian, you remember Percy Lambert? Six hundred! That's what 'e wanted. I said no! Cor! Six 'undred bloody quid, I ask you!"

"Worth a couple of thousand now," said Mr. Styles, as they shot past.

"What are you saying?" Mr. Hedges cried out as though he might be in pain. "In that situation? Six thousand if they're a penny. I was at school with Percy Lambert. Tell you what, I could've had 'em for *five* hundred. I could've beat 'im down."

Mr. Styles looked straight ahead. "I feel very privileged to come with you on this journey. I respect other people's beliefs, even if I can't share them myself."

There was a pine-tree, clear air blowing off the sea, and warm sun. While his father talked to Mr. Styles about

153

someone they had both known in the Perstowe tannery, when there had been a tannery, Hedges filled the stained-glass vase at the tap behind the shed where the lawn-mowers and spades were kept. The old man was so lost in reminiscence that he was unaware the roses had been gently taken from him. Hedges arranged them in the vase and set it on the gravel chips.

ELIZABETH MARIA HEDGES

1900–1940

beloved wife of EDGAR GEORGE
HEDGES *and mother of* IAN

"Caught Up in the Chariot"

Hedges tried not to think of his mother, but he could not manage it, not even by counting the roses and multiplying the answer by the number of graves between the seat and the pine-tree. One year she had a whitlow in the index finger of her right hand, and he remembered the peculiarity of holding that hand—he must have been about six—as they walked into somebody's front door together, out of white sun into shadow, working away with the tip of his little finger at the black leather sheath. He had hurt her. He remembered her snatching her hand away and hissing. She sounded, now he came to think of it, rather like the wind in the pine-tree. Thoughts like that just stopped the clock. He stood up and looked across the grave at the two men, who had fallen silent and were looking at the roses, his father frowning, Mr. Styles with his lips apart to show dentures crooked in his mouth.

The clock had stopped. The pine-tree hissed. Hedges put the fingers of his right hand up to his nose and smelled the stems of the roses. Light was sifted over the cemetery as it might be out of some cloud-high easter. The light fell, it flaked, it broke this way and that. Hedges knocked his hands together because they seemed dusty, and he did not want to walk all the way back to the tap behind the shed to wash them.

Mr. Styles began talking about the anonymous letters once more, and when Hedges said he knew nothing about them—what was this about anonymous letters?—the old fellow took a black wallet out of his inside pocket, opened it, and produced a single sheet of paper no bigger than a postcard which he would have handed to Hedges actually across the grave if Hedges had not walked round to take it on the other side. It was typed.

Dear Miss Styles:

I am a fool to warn you in this way because I know it will not be any good. But your behaviour is being watched by people who are in no way so well disposed towards you as Ian Hedges, fool that he is. I wish to inform you that it is very distasteful to see a young woman exploiting the frustrated sexuality of older men, not Ian Hedges only (though he is old enough to be your uncle).

Hedges returned the piece of paper, and Mr. Styles put it back in his wallet. "This is the third note she's had, and they are all typed in the same way. They come in envelopes with a Perstowe postmark. As anonymous letters go I've seen worse. She put the first two in the fire, but I got hold of this one because it occurred to me you might be interested, Mr. Hedges."

"Is she upset?"

"Yes. Very."

"Let me 'ave a look," said Mr. Hedges. Styles apologized for the oversight, produced the note once more, and Mr. Hedges pushed his spectacles to the end of his nose to read it.

"I should 'and that straight to the police," he advised. "They'll trace the typewriter, I shouldn't wonder."

"Pru won't go to the police."

"Then it'll get worse," said Mr. Hedges. "You mark my words."

"What lies behind all this?"

The mood he was in, Hedges might have had a shot at answering this comprehensively: behind the dream is the dreamer, or there are the everlasting arms, or the never-ending dark swell that breaks intermittently into a fine fire of mind. Behind all *this*, he wanted to say—meaning the grave, the pine, and the hissing air—there is something that doesn't bear thinking of. Let's try something easier.

"Does Prudence know you've come over?"

"As a matter of fact, she doesn't."

"She's very fond of you."

Mr. Hedges put his hat on and they walked in single file, Mr. Hedges leading, Styles in the middle, to make room for the dark-suited men and their women who strayed up and down, heads turning from left to right. Hedges examined the red, wrinkled back of Styles's neck. Brittle as a carrot. They turned a corner full into the wind and saw women holding their hats on and their skirts down. The wind blew straight up the estuary. Mr. Hedges and Styles had to put hands on top of their trilbies. Hedges had to shout to make himself heard.

"The Robbins Report won't be out until well into the autumn, I hear."

"I gave evidence to them," said Styles. "At least, I

wrote a letter to Lord Robbins. I've no doubt it will be published as an appendix."

Hedges put his mouth to Styles's ear. "What did you say?"

"Being as it's a report on the future of universities and higher education in this country, I said it was bound to touch on a lot of vested interests."

"Is that all?"

"It'll have helped to put Robbins on his guard."

Just outside the main gates, they were able to stand in the shelter of a wall. Styles said urgently, "I dare say you think I'm making too much of these letters. They ought to be thrown in the fire and forgotten. But it's what lies behind them that I want to get at. I just want to know, you see?"

"I don't suppose there is anything, much."

"Until these letters started arriving, she'd quite made up her mind she wasn't coming back to the school here after the holidays. I don't entirely know why. Perhaps you do. But now she says she *is* coming back. She says it's all nothing. But you see my position. She's my daughter. She's upset, and she's going to come back to Perstowe and be upset some more. Why? What's it all about? Is there any reason you can think of why your name is mentioned in that letter?"

Hedges shook his head. There was no need for Mr. Styles to worry. Prudence was in no kind of trouble, personal or professional, and if she really was upset by these letters she ought to destroy any new ones unopened.

Mr. Styles screwed up his eyes in the bright sun and said that in his view the letters were written by a woman, some unhappy woman who needed treatment.

"The ducking-stool," said Mr. Hedges. "I'm against all

this doctoring of criminals. Take murderers. Hang 'em, I
say. It's more capital punishment we want, not less."

"If I thought you were right——"

"Of course I'm right."

In the car park, a man wearing a hat made out of the
Sunday *Express* was selling ice-cream from a stall, and Mr.
Hedges insisted on buying cornets all round. They stood in
the shade of a dust-choked hawthorn, curling their tongues
along the rim of the cornets and grunting appreciatively.

"If I thought you were right," said Hedges, "and that
the human animal was a creature like you think he is, I'd go
in for religion a bit more, because that would be the only
way to control the kind of brute you say I am."

"I've killed a man and you haven't," said Mr. Hedges,
"and that's the difference between you and me. In the
Kaiser's war," he explained to Mr. Styles. "What mob was
you in then?"

"I was in the siege of Kut," said Mr. Styles, "so I
finished up P.O.W. in Turkey."

"Ah! You 'ad no ice-cream there."

Hedges felt sorry for the writer of the anonymous
letters and he felt sorry for Mr. Styles, who had put so
much steam into the Brewchester University campaign,
because it would certainly come to nothing and he would
go defeated to his grave and Prudence would weep over
him. He had survived the siege of Kut and marched
through the sands of Mespot, sweated it out in a P.O.W.
camp, come home, waited a number of years, and married
cautiously (in 1935 maybe), reacted to the coming of
another war by begetting Prudence, all the time reading
Darwin, and no doubt Ruskin and Morris too, seen his wife
die, thought of Brewchester University, had his bit of fun,
and now it had all come to this: anxiety over anonymous

letters and the university (if he did but know it) out of the question.

"Hope you don't think there's anything personal in this local university scheme, Mr. Styles."

"No, nothing personal," agreed Mr. Styles. "It is the cause."

Impulsively Hedges shook him by the hand.

The front door opened a couple of inches and then stuck. The aperture was not wide enough for Hedges even to slide his arm through and so grope for whatever it was lying wedged against the door. His father and Styles were still at the gate, talking about some elephant harness Styles had once made.

"I can't open it," said Hedges. "There's something heavy on the other side. I'll go round the back."

The back door would be locked from the inside. There was a way, though, of opening the kitchen window, and he was about to climb over the coal-bunker and do this when he thought he'd try the back door, just for luck; and sure enough it opened. There's someone still in the house, he thought.

The kitchen table was on its side; the drawers of a china and cutlery cabinet had been pulled out so that the floor was littered with broken china, knives, forks, spoons. Someone had merrily thrown frying-pan, saucepans, and the electric kettle into a heap in the corner.

Hedges rushed into the hall. "Hi! Hi! Hi! Is there anybody there?"

"What the hell's going on?" his father was shouting through the letter-box.

The wrought-iron Victorian hall-stand which had always been a bit top-heavy anyway now lay on its back with its black antlers lowered in dismal mock hostility against the door. Hedges took hold of it, umbrellas and walking-sticks rattling, and dragged it on a cushion of overcoats over the linoleum.

Mr. Hedges could now push the front door open, walk into the hall, and start swearing. He saw a smashed picture propped against the wall, looked at it unbelievingly, and said, "I bought that one of a batch of twelve at the Lack 'All sale, and that's the one I kept because it was the only one I liked. It's flowers."

Hedges raced up the stairs. His father's room and the spare bedroom were untouched. But Hedges's own room was laid waste. The bed had been stripped to the mattress, and the loose bedding—the sheets, blanket, and bedspread—thrown through the window into the branches of an apple-tree. Drawers had been pulled out and turned upside down. The dressing-table mirror was intact—possibly out of superstition. The Lear water-colour of a banana-tree (the first present Nell had given him), the seventeenth-century map of the county, and the photograph of his mother on the beach at Weymouth holding an enormous teapot were lying under smashed glass, face upwards, as though they had been danced on. Not a book was left on the shelves. They had been thrown madly about the room, everything from the *Shorter Oxford Dictionary* to his *A. A. Handbook*, really weighty books, some of them. Whoever it was had been putting in some work, he thought. The nausea and slight giddiness passed after a few moments, and he went upstairs to the attic rooms. They had been untouched and there was nobody there. His father's every oath rang through the house; the very click of his dentures could be heard in the attic.

When Hedges returned to the front hall, his father was

standing with one foot on the prostrate hall-stand, red-faced, shouting laughter at Styles, who was looking at him with the lower lids of his watering eyes trembling nervously. Mr. Hedges then fell silent. Noticing how pale he had gone, Hedges took him by the arm and led him into the sitting room.

"I'll be seventy-five next month," Mr. Hedges told Styles. He stretched himself out on the settee. Hedges undid his collar and slackened his tie. "See if the safe's all right, Ian."

Hedges went and looked in the cupboard under the stairs. "The safe hasn't been touched." He went into the dining-room and poured half an inch of brandy into a tumbler. At first his father said he didn't want it. Then he took a sip and his colour came back.

"Your mother's birthday! Cor! Oo'd believe it? I'd phone the police if I thought they'd be sober."

"*Certainly* you must phone the police," said Mr. Styles.

"On a Sunday afternoon? You wouldn't get 'em out for a murder."

Hedges came back from another tour of inspection. "It's just the kitchen, the hall-stand, and my room. My room's the worst. I don't think anything's been taken. It's just wanton destructiveness. They must have got in through the kitchen window and left by the kitchen door. The key was in the lock, on the inside. It's just bloody-minded malice."

He went to the front door and looked up and down the street. Behind him, the house held its silence like the stunned. Before him, empty pavements, the parked Mini, the parked Sunbeam Talbot, two or three other cars parked a bit higher up. Nobody stirred. The curtains of the lower windows of the houses opposite were drawn to shut out the sun. Behind them families were taking tea. Laurel-leaves turned and winked in the wind. Hedges looked at his watch. It was quarter to five. They had been away from the house for just under two hours. He went indoors and picked up the telephone.

"Somebody's got it in for you," said Mr. Styles. "You know that?" He looked more upset than you would expect in a survivor of Kut. He would have needed to be much cleverer to think of a remark that would not make Hedges even savager, and Hedges replied coldly that the more universities there were the more smashing up of furniture and private belongings there would be. It was in the Oxbridge tradition.

"Students might do this in Oxford and Cambridge," said Mr. Styles. "I've read of them breaking into each other's rooms. But this wouldn't happen in a new university."

"It will happen in any university where students own their own furniture. As the affluent society becomes more affluent, so there will be more vandalism."

"I'm against private property," said Mr. Styles, "though I'm far from being a Communist. I'm all for the small shopkeeper. Perhaps I'm a Poujadist. I don't know." This house-wrecking, coming on top of the business of the anonymous letters, made him querulous.

"Ian." Hedges heard his father calling from the sitting-room. "Whoever it was must have known we were out. They must have watched us go out."

"Mark my words," Mr. Styles answered, "the writer of the anonymous letters and your intruder are one and the same person."

This was enough to make Hedges put the receiver back on its cradle.

Mr. Styles drew in his breath sharply. "Aren't you going to call the police?"

"I don't think so."

He went out of the house again, down the steps to the pavement. The rough-cast detached house with the net curtains on one side was where the Willetts lived, and he knew they were away on holiday. On the other side was old Mr. Ogdon, who lived by himself and rarely emerged. Hedges was looking to see if the edge of a curtain lifted. Not a flicker of life. Hedges thought it was scarcely worth worrying the old chap with any questions about suspicious characters.

He climbed the steps again and walked through to the kitchen, where he began tidying up the mess. They would all have a cup of tea. No, he was not calling the police in. He did not say so, but Nell mightn't have fixed an alibi.

Again Mr. Hedges told Styles he would be seventy-five next month. This was the first sign that he was feeling old. He did not talk about his age normally, and Hedges himself never thought of the old chap having passed his three-score years and ten: he climbed ladders, dug the garden, drove the Mini faster than was safe. The vandalism, though, broke a spring. Odd that it should have had such an effect. If it had been any day but August 27, he might not have been struck so hard. In some sore and unscratchable part of the mind, the old man was struggling with the thought that while they had actually been at the cemetery. . . .

We've all got sore and unscratchable parts of the mind. Hedges took the Mini after lunch some days later and drove up the hill towards Brewchester thinking about the un-get-at-able part of his own awareness. It was like trying to turn the eyeballs in his head. All the winds had dropped. There was heat, stillness, a haze over the sea. Cows stood on iron ruts under the black shadow of trees, whisking the flies from their khaki-plastered rears. There were thin dribbles of white cloud over this particular group of trees. Through the open window he momentarily caught the sweetness of milk and excrement: this blue sky, as it might be, dripping milk.

Hedges was in Brewchester by three. The *Floreat Brewchester* banner had disappeared from the Styles's front gate, but Hedges thought it would be wrong to read too much into that; maybe the bean poles had snapped off in the wind.

"Is this business?"

He ran the Mini on to the grass verge, and he had no sooner climbed out than he heard this question through the hedge. He could see what looked like a white shirt and the sun gleaming on some kind of gardening implement. It startled him to come on Prudence as suddenly as this.

"I'm not putting it down to official mileage." He bent down and peered through a gap in the hawthorn. "Thought you might be at the typewriter."

"Look, I take this writing seriously. I use a goose quill."

"Your father in?"

"No."

He left his jacket in the Mini. So he was now wearing biscuit-coloured slacks, and when he walked through the gate and round to the other side of the hedge he found that Prudence was wearing biscuit-coloured slacks too, though tighter-fitting than his, and the coincidence struck him with such force that it was as though he could not stop walking towards her; he *collided* with her frontally. He saw her mouth fly open. He grabbed her, thinking he might be knocking her down. It was a confused encounter. His right thigh went forward and somehow got lodged between her two thighs. He had her in close grapple, kissing her. The secateurs dropped from her right hand and struck the ground with a clink. He was surprised how soft and fleshy she was. After all, she wasn't big. He had expected her to be harder and, indeed, from what he remembered of last time she was harder. Of course she might have been wearing roll-ons, or whatever they called the things, on that occasion. He had to hold her to stop her falling to the ground. He put one hand on her buttocks; quite enormous, he thought, for such a little woman. And once again, how fleshy.

"Do you mind?" she said, once he had withdrawn his face a few inches so that he could look at her.

"You fill me with lust."

When she began pushing at him, he knew it was time to give up. She stood there with her legs still planted apart, stuffing her shirt back into the top of her slacks and staring at him with her head on one side, the tip of her tongue showing, hair gummed to her wet forehead, and so much colour she looked a schoolgirl. Just how angry she was he didn't know. She hadn't kissed him back, that was certain. Her lips had been tight.

"Look, if you're cross with me I'm sorry. If you're not cross with me, let's go into the house."

"No, I'm not cross with you." She picked up the secateurs. "I was just cutting these dogrose briars out of the hedge. If you come at me again I'll stick this in your throat."

"The ground's so uneven. I more or less stumbled."

"What do you want, if I can be so blunt?"

"Whisky, for preference."

She laughed and stuck the secateurs, points down, into the hip pocket of her slacks, and he watched their curious circular swing all the way to the front door. She was on the edge of the hall darkness when he noticed that the tail of her shirt had worked up to reveal a sliver of bare back over the top of her slacks. Impossible not to touch. She stood with her back to him in the darkness of the hall, and he slid his hand gently over the dry skin. She gasped and began to turn. He ran his hand round under the shirt until it was flat, precisely, over her stomach and the secateurs were pressing rather painfully against his right thigh.

"I wasn't very honest about the whisky," he said. "It happened to be mentionable."

"I'd hate to think you drove over with thoughts like that in your head."

"I started out with the very best of intentions. The sight and the touch of you, they did it."

"Your wife let you come?"

He knew this was provocation and clasped her small right breast—or, rather, some container with a surgical and therefore rather disagreeable feel to it, certainly less stirring than the belly, to which with nostalgia he now returned. Anyway, he lost a telling grip and she revolved in his arms. They were jammed so tight and she revolved so rapidly he could feel the point of the secateurs scoring his thigh, but as she now had her lips clapped against his he could not even yell; that was another thing—he would never have thought she had such a big mouth, but he supposed women had some erotic way of distending their lips. It was alarming to hear her crying out and know all the time that she was still kissing him. She had turned so neatly that he needed to drop his right hand a mere three inches to pluck out the secateurs and drop them to the floor.

"Look, Pru, I've got to have you, see? It's no good. . . ."

She pushed him off at that and made for a door which opened into a room where the sunlight fell through six-inch gaps in the not-properly-drawn curtains and there was an impression of Edwardian rugs, cushions, glass cabinets, and framed photographs. When he shut the door he saw that Prudence, of all things, was dabbing at her face with a lace-edged handkerchief, her eyes shut. He felt as though he had run a hundred yards, and she looked puffed too.

"I've never been in this room with gardening boots on before."

"Take 'em off."

Thinking back on it later, he supposed they must have been crazed; there was no reason why old Styles shouldn't have come back to the house at any moment. What she called gardening boots were actually heavy shoes, and he tried to remove them without untying the laces; this turned out to be the most tantalizing part of the preparation because one of them stuck painfully on her heel and he had to go back into the hall to find the secateurs to nip the tightly knotted lace. As for the rest, though, he couldn't imagine how lovers managed before the invention of zip-fasteners, if they wished—as he and Prudence plainly did—to cover the embarrassment of taking their pants off by kissing all the time.

"It isn't me, is it?" she said, looking rather brazenly, he thought, straight up into his eyes. They stared into each other, these two pairs of eyes, one lot blue and the other brown, for quite some time.

"What do you mean?" Absurd to talk, absurd to ask

questions, absurd to think, absurd to do anything but feel. He should have told her to shut up. He didn't even want to feel. He wanted to lose himself.

"I'm just a substitute for Mrs. Brush."

It would have made a satyr impotent, and Hedges was at once struggling between the requirements of common politeness on the one hand and the weakness of the flesh on the other. The struggle was absurd and yet heroic.

"Don't be so foul." He tried to cover her mouth with his own, mainly to stop her talking, but she caught his lower lip between her teeth and gave such a savage nip that he yelped and drew his head back. He was not a sadist, and she wasn't at all heightening his desire if that were her intention, just the opposite; and he wondered if she were calculating enough to know this too and had some deep plan.

He jerked his head back far enough for her to see the expression on it. This made her laugh. Perhaps she wanted to humiliate him. She might have guessed he couldn't both make love and talk and so had drawn him into talk as a way of cutting him down to something less than size. The annoying thing was he couldn't keep his mouth shut, either. She was provoking him too much.

"You're not there." When she gasped these words out, for they were writhing like snakes, he thought they might have some awful physiological connotation; but when she went on to say, "You're not here, you're not with *me*," he had wit enough to cry, "Don't be such a bloody fool," and try once more to stop her mouth.

"You're not thinking of me," she said, "you're not thinking even of yourself——"

"I'm not thinking, full stop."

"You're not in this house. You're not in this room. And

you never are," she said. "Because you never do anything for itself alone——"

"Don't be such a bore, darling."

"I don't get the words right, but you know what I mean."

"You flaming bluestocking."

"Everything you do is done to distract you from the fact of being alive."

"Let's stop and think, shall we, my sweet?" By now he was desperate.

"O.K. Let's stop and think."

He could have clapped his hand across her mouth, but it was more honourable to ask for a truce. They lay and listened to the heartbeats. He had, even, a grudging admiration for the clever—though, perhaps, not very *nice*—tactics she had adopted. It argued a shrewder understanding of the differences between men and women than he was comfortable with, not when it shone out of the face of this dewy girl.

He would have liked to say that from now on he could not bear to contemplate the possibility of being separated from her even for ten minutes at a time. This, though, was untrue. And if it was untrue, what the hell was he up to? He wasn't a lecher. His pride wouldn't let him be one. Then if he was neither lover nor lecher, might not this confounded girl be right after all and that not only making love but everything he did, his work, his campaigning for a university, was a drug to keep him from thinking and seeing?

Thinking and seeing what? He was dazed and shaken.

CHAPTER SIX

◈◈◈◈◈◈◈◈◈◈◈◈◈◈◈◈◈◈◈◈◈◈◈◈◈

The Fight at Lack Hall

One result of the Perstowe University idea was that Peacock changed his ideas about the kind of education appropriate for a young Communist. Walter was to go to the Grammar School after all, and it didn't even matter what the boy's mates said. He wanted Walter to be a dentist. He explained to Hedges that he had always fancied the dentistry himself, sitting blokes in a chair and working on them with instruments. You wore this white smock and you had all the instruments locked up in a cabinet, right up until the last minute, so that the bloke couldn't actually see just what you were using and had to trust you. There wasn't a lot of pain, not with all these different drugs, or so he was told, though he couldn't speak from experience, him, Peacock, because he'd had false 'uns since he was twenty-four. The dental-mechanical side didn't appeal, not all that messing about with casts and plates. The real satisfaction, as Peacock saw it, came from pulling teeth out and drilling. It was science.

By the time Walter had been through the Grammar School, Perstowe University would be there to make a

dentist of him. Walter could live at home. Peacock himself
and Mrs. Peacock attached a lot of importance to that.
They wouldn't have approved of him going off to Oxford
or Cambridge to be a dentist. At universities like that a
young chap lost his working-class values. A school of
dentistry on the doorstep was a different matter, and, said
Peacock, Walter would become one of the scientific ar-
biters of the new society without losing solidarity with the
masses.

Hedges said he had to be honest about this. He didn't
think Oxford or Cambridge turned out any dentists, and so
far as he knew there was no plan for Perstowe to show
them up in this respect. Peacock swept all this aside. He said
that one of the finest schools of dentistry in the world was
in the University of Moscow, and that it was well known
that the British Government was using the Russian university system as a model for the new universities in this
country. Hedges may think Perstowe was not having a
school of dentistry, but history was against him.

Peacock's firm was on contract work for the borough.
This meant he was always in and out of Council offices, and
he made a point of having a few words with Hedges
whenever he had the chance. He liked Hedges and said so.
Peacock said he was not a man to hide his feelings. Hedges
could borrow ten quid from him any time he liked. Peacock
didn't believe all this filthy gossip he heard, either. More
than once he'd had to ask Mrs. Peacock not to tell him
about it. The Peacocks and the Hedges had lived in Perstowe for hundreds of years. The most precious possession a
man could have was the sense of history. Hedges and
Peacock were Perstovians. They ought to stand up for each
other. Probably they were related. Their names were in the
parish registers of the seventeenth century. But you

wouldn't find Saundersfoot there. Where did the Saundersfoots come from? In 1643 Perstowe declared for Parliament, but where were the Saundersfoots in 1643? Fighting
for the bloody King, no doubt.

Peacock was a fresh-faced, smiling, blue-eyed man of
about forty who wore rope-soled canvas shoes, dungarees,
and a dirty cricketing pull-over. He was the only man to
whom Hedges confessed his loyalty to Newcastle United.
Peacock was very interested. He asked as many questions as
an analyst and came back the next day with the theory that
it all sprang from the 1927 Cup Final when Newcastle had
been playing Arsenal and everybody in Perstowe had put
their money on Arsenal. "But you, of course," said Peacock,
"had to be awkward. Everybody said Newcastle would lose,
so you decided to support Newcastle. It was sentimental
defeatism. You're never so happy as when you've got a lost
cause. That's why history is going to roll over you and
people like you."

"Newcastle did in fact win."

"They'd fixed the linesmen. Everybody knows the ball
went over the goal-line before somebody hooked it back
and banged it into the net. There was a photograph to
prove it! How reactionary can you get?"

The October day Peacock came in to point out that
Newcastle had sunk to the Second Division of the Football
League whereas Arsenal were in the top half of the first was
the most frightening of Hedges's life. It changed him. Not
because Peacock spelled out the ideological implications of
his irrational loyalty ("You can't deny you still want them
to win"), though he found time to brood even about that;
but because it was when he fianlly realized the daze he fell
into when making love to Prudence had been no quirk of an

172

erotically inflamed mind. It was a holy stupor. It was revelation.

Prudence was pregnant. He had known this for some time, but it was only today that he learned she would continue teaching in Perstowe and that she would not marry him. She did not believe that marriage should be based on an accidental conception. Besides, marrying Hedges would only appear to give substance to the rumour that Saundersfoot was the real father. This ridiculous point of view was put in a letter he read shortly before nine, by which time it was too late to get her on the phone at Mrs. Kidwelly's. There was no question of contacting her at the school, because the only telephone there was in Saundersfoot's room. He thought of going along to the school at lunchtime, but at twelve-thirty he found a postscript that he hadn't noticed before, saying, "I have no intention of doing anything to procure a miscarriage, so if you have been thinking along these lines, don't." He went over to the pub instead and had whisky, beer, and a cheese sandwich for lunch. At three o'clock that afternoon, Arthur Supple was throwing a tea-party at Lack Park and launching an appeal for university funds which Brush (Hedges suspected) would record on his machine. As secretary, Hedges was down to make a speech too.

After lunch he had a way of sitting in his office chair that allowed him to doze but be instantly (well, not too instantly) alert if Beryl came in or the phone rang: the chin sunk into the chest could be guaranteed to lift, the eyes open and focus, deceiving the best. The more annoying, then, that when Peacock walked in and accused him of being asleep he had in fact been wide awake; how could a man sleep when he was in love? That was the effect Prudence's letter had on him. Her idotic reason for not marrying him made her seem more admirable and desirable than ever. He yearned for her. He wanted to pay tribute to her independence. He was stirred by her defiance. He wanted to be near her and stirred by her loopy courage. Temper! Spirit! Blood! Sweat! Battle! Victory!

Hedges listened for some time to Peacock explaining why his support of Newcastle United was a sign of a reactionary disposition. He stopped him by saying he didn't believe a word in all Peacock's talk about young Walter becoming a dentist. He didn't even believe that Peacock himself had ever wanted to be a dentist. The reason for Walter's going to the Grammar School was Mrs. Peacock's insistence that he should.

"She's been difficult," agreed Peacock.

"She's twice as intelligent as you are."

"To think of the way I stick up for you!" said Peacock, and he went, still grinning.

Hedges was still brooding over Prudence with what, to him, seemed a maddening inability to focus her clearly when Amos walked in and said it was gone two-thirty and they ought to be on their way if they were to get to Lack Park in time for the opening festivities: Supple's speech.

"I feel doped," said Hedges. He didn't want to go to Lack Park.

"What's the matter? You had some bad news?"

"No, I'm fine. I just feel I need forgiving, that's all."

"What for?"

"Nothing in particular. Everything."

"You're tight," Amos accused.

"Wish I were." Who would forgive him for what? The canals on Mars, that's what. He had read in a book that if you looked at Mars through a low-powered telescope and used a bit of imagination you could see those canals easily. If you used a really high-powered telescope, they resolved themselves into patches and blemishes. What he needed was a telescope that was just the right power to reveal, without the need for any imagination, his heart's desire. It was for his heart's desire he stood in need of forgiveness. He looked at Amos but he didn't even put the question; the Martian canal in his mind needed excusing and possibly justifying (forgiveness was a big word); that was no excuse, though, for involving Amos who had worries of his own—circulation, for example, of blood and the *Advertiser*. Even in summer he went to bed with a hot-water bottle.

"I was once," said Hedges, "in a non-smoking compartment with a parson who was smoking a pipe. I couldn't get anything out of him. You'd think a parson would be glad to talk."

"Thought you were a nut, I expect."

"Well. . . ." Hedges hesitated. "It occurred to me afterwards he might have been on his way to do some mischief. There hasn't been a fire at Lambeth Palace, has there?"

"Not that I've heard of."

"He was going to Lambeth Palace."

"Look," said Amos, "the fact that he was smoking a pipe in non-smoking compartment didn't mean——"

"Cuthbert set a barn on fire. I expect that's what I was thinking of." Hedges was wondering whether he'd tell Amos about Prudence but he decided not to, because wrong though he'd been to seduce her somebody might forgive him for that one day. Even Prudence might. In the unscratchable part of Hedges's mind festered that which

175

nobody he knew or had heard of could forgive. He wasn't absolutely sure it was there, his heart's desire. He feared it was, though. His liver's lust! His spleen's content! His kidneys' delight!

"I haven't been sleeping. I lie awake in the still night. D'you know what I hear? The plop, plop, plop of the human animal dropping from the branches of the forest trees and loping with his knuckles just clear of the ground out into the moonlight. That's how one or two of our fellow citizens arrived on the scene. Jimmy Pigge, for one. Brush, the bastard, for another. These men weren't born. They fell out of the trees. Another thing is this. The human animal needs numbing with holy dread. I lie in my room in the quiet night and hear the beasts dropping out of the foliage and go scuttering into the world. Where are the magic fires to drive them back? I like to think of them coming out of the darkness and looking at fire with eyes that light up like jewels. I like to think of them that way, but it's all a dream. There are no fires. D'you know what I mean?"

No," said Amos.

"Hell fire," said Hedges, "it was a great mistake to put it out."

"If this means," said Amos, "you're rooting for a School of Divinity in the university, I'm not on your side. Why don't we get started?"

"How do you deal with people?" Hedges had to plead with someone, and Amos was the only listener he had. "You can't reason with them. No, I don't mean them. I mean us. You can't reason with us because we're not open to reason. What's the alternative? Whips and scorpions have no prestige these days."

"You know perfectly well," said Amos, trying to shepherd him towards the door, "that the answer is for men to become like gods: to eat, drink, and fornicate like gods."

"Lack Park might be the place to begin," said Hedges.

Hedges had neither seen nor heard from Gideon Toplis for ten days, and as he immediately broke off any conversation in which Toplis's name came up he had no idea what the latest developments in *that* particular affair might be. They would meet at Lack Park, no doubt. It was unlikely that Toplis would cut him. He had no intention of cutting Toplis—unless it was confirmed that Toplis was easing him out of the Promotion Committee. At best, their relationship could never be the same again: Toplis the moneyed wirepuller and Hedges the policy-maker. It had been a good partnership. Perstowe had been well served. But if it came to choosing between Toplis and him, Hedges had no doubt this would prove the very moment the committee would discover the impropriety of having the Borough Education Officer as Secretary. You couldn't have a Council employee lending his support to a pressure group.

If someone said this to him at the Lack Park party, he would know Toplis had been talking. The thought of such a possibility lay behind his remarks to Amos about the human animal dropping out of trees and loping into the moonlight. Put out on his ear by Supple, Pigge, Primrose, and the others, he really would have the horrors. He saw himself in a frenzy setting the dirty old mock-Tudor mansion on fire.

The news that Nell Brush had been up to London with her employer, Gideon Toplis, presumably to take notes in that little black book, was followed by the information there was so much stenography piling up they were working all hours of the day and night. Mrs. Brush's post became residential, and there was no one to lock Brush out of the flat at the bakehouse when he came home late. Toplis's housekeeper gave in her notice. At the factory, the men in one of the shops came out on strike in protest against the language used by the foreman when he discovered that the safety shield had been removed from a press: Toplis appeared and addressed them with such a flow of swearing that the men began to laugh and cheer. They'd heard, of course, what the old man was doing with his secretary, and they were, in reality, applauding him not only as a master of cussing but for his green vigour in age.

Hedges had seen him over the preparations for the Lack Hall party and been immediately struck by his alertness. He looked straight out of his small black eyes. He did not blink or raise his voice. But he was not giving his attention exclusively to his visitor. He was keeping himself under careful observation too, rather as though, having surprised himself once, he wanted to miss nothing of any further phenomena. If his brain caught fire, he wanted to rush to the mirror and see the smoke come out of his ears.

They settled whatever it was they had to settle. After small talk, Toplis began talking about Nell. Hedges tried to stop him, but Toplis said that as the woman's first husband he ought to be interested. What's more, if it hadn't been for the remark Hedges had once made about their both being as sterile as mules—it had made an enormous impression on him—he would never have realized how much he wanted an heir to whom he could pass on the 51 per cent of the Toplis equity. Sex—well, he'd spoken on that subject and didn't wish to repeat himself. He'd tried it when young and not liked it much. Nell was a clever girl, though. She had awakened him. She was to be Mrs. Toplis.

For the first time in weeks Hedges's foot began to

throb. The pain made him gasp. After that he felt very cold, although it was a warm autumn afternoon and the big-windowed room was looking straight out at a yellow sun. The skin tightened over his jaw. His stomach seemed to contract. After the nausea he could feel the sweat on his face, quite cold. As he waited for his body to recover from the shock, Hedges stared into Toplis's eyes as though looking for tadpoles. Who was Toplis to put a claw into his guts?

"There are a lot of rumours swilling round the town," he'd said. "She raped you for your money, you old clown. What's more, I stick to that mule theory. Have you thought what gossip will do to the University Promotion Committee of which, may I remind you, you are Vice-Chairman and chief corruptor of the University Grants Committee? You've discredited the lot of us."

"You're a fine one to talk."

"That scandal involving Saundersfoot is an absolute bloody lie. I deny flatly that there was anything between Saundersfoot and Miss Styles. What I do not deny, of course, is that there is a rumour about my supposed role in this disgusting affair. The town is entitled to one scandal a year to tone up the body local-politic. It makes the place fizz. The virtuous are made to feel more virtuous, and the wicked watch their paces. Scandal is an important social cohesive. But it's got to be kept under control. One scandal at a time. That's what I'm bitter about. The smelly egg you've laid is just going to do no good at all."

"Are you crazy?"

"Listen, Adonis, do you know what you've done? You've brought the whole idea of Perstowe University into disrepute."

"Oh!"

179

"My little shot of civet sweetened the whole town. But when you come along with a dose, the whole place begins to reek. It's a question of degree. 'The Promotion Committee? Ah, they're a randy lot.' Can't you hear 'em in the pubs? 'A lot of pushers talking big about the good of Perstowe,' that's what they'll call us. Toplis, you've opened a gulf between the committee and public opinion. I wish to God you'd resign, emigrate, and take that blasted woman with you."

"Let me give you a drink."

"Thank God Saundersfoot isn't on the committee! The reputation he's got, the committee and Perstowe would be in a state of mutual alienation."

Toplis's tone was surprisingly mild. "Your ideas on society, Hedges, are old-fashioned. People don't want to live in each other's minds. They want money. They want to keep themselves to themselves. Look at the houses with big fences round the little yards so the neighbours can't see in. The working man likes to drive his little family in his little car down to a parking-lot at the seaside and just sit there watching the sea through the wind-screen, listening to the Light Programme. As near as dammit he's taken his sitting-room with him. He doesn't want to share it with other people. The British aren't like that. If you want to be happy you'd better go and live in some African tribe."

"I wouldn't, if I were you."

"Wouldn't what?"

"Talk about things you don't understand. The family as a social unit is on the way out——"

"This is not what we were discussing."

"And don't underestimate the forces of joyless Puritanism. In your own eyes you're a fertility god, but in the eyes of Perstowe you're a dirty old man, and it gives me a pain at the lower end to have been associated with you."

"Old? I'm fifty-seven. How old are you?"

"You look much older than that. You look a good seventy-five, varnished over to keep the worm out. And it's appearances that count."

"How old are you?"

"Young enough to be a father. I'm going to be a father. The feeling's absolutely bloody marvellous."

They were standing on either side of the table, waving their arms. An invisible table-tennis ball was flying backwards and forwards.

"Saundersfoot's bastard, you mean?"

"No, my own bastard. Saundersfoot's had nothing to do with it. But I'm a young man. I'm not an old goat like you. Can't you see how disgusting you are? People don't like lewdness in the old. It'll cut ten thousand quid off the first week's takings."

Toplis made him drink a big whisky before he left, but Hedges was not deceived. Nor was he worried. His stomach had long since stopped churning, and the candour with which he had expressed himself was a tonic. He rode a wild sea, and the only real fear was of fetching up on some shoal where there was nothing to distract him, nothing to think about, nothing to do. On the way back to the office, he would have called on Supple and written out his resignation from the committee on a paper bag and handed it over the counter. More dignified than waiting to be slung out. But he needed the uncertainty now, he needed it badly and, addict that he was, could do nothing to interfere with the supply. His dreams at this time were not at all striking. On waking he had difficulty in remembering them. When he did it was of fragments; pruning a lime-tree with a broken saw, a dog barking, a stained-glass window, that sort of thing.

* * *

The Robbins Report to the Government on the future of higher education in the United Kingdom happened to be published on the very day the Perstowe committee launched its appeal for funds. It was quite fortuitous. Hedges knew that the report was coming, of course, but Supple almost certainly didn't. This did not stop him, at four o'clock in the afternoon of Wednesday, October 23, claiming there was more in this coincidence than met the eye and if you didn't believe him what did the presence of Jacob Treasury Bream in the Long Gallery of Lack Park signify? A witches' sabbath? With the exception of Bream, nobody had read the report, and all he was prepared to talk about was pelicans. The pelican was in the town coat of arms, and Bream remarked that "a Pelican in its Piety" and nourishing its young with its blood would be a happy badge for a seat of learning.

"An institute of corrective training, perhaps," he said to Mrs. Supple, slumped and sweating in her sapphire mink, "because of course we must never forget that the story of the pelican is the story of discipline. The pelican's children got very unruly, you remember, and flapped their wings in their parents' face. So the parents struck back and killed them. Three days later, mark you, the mother pierced its breast and poured her blood over the dead bodies, bringing them back to life."

"How horrible!" said Mrs. Supple.

"Out of keeping with modern theories of education," agreed Bream, "but if I were the governor of a Borstal I'd work it into every address I gave to the boys. What a very nice Borstal institution Lack Park would make, now one comes to consider it. That splendid pillar over there: can't you just see some young brute naked to the waist and tied to it while the governor flogs him? Perhaps this is not what

they do in Borstals. I'm not well up in it. One has to special-
ize these days. Did you know Robbins wants colleges of
advanced technology to have university status? I shall have
to get to know about them now, I suppose."

"This was my family seat," said Jimmy Pigge, "and the
old family coat is the twenty-teated sow under a harp."

"I see the Aristotelian reference."

"Don't know about that," said Pigge, "but I'm glad
Robbins has given the O.K. for the university here, because
we've set our heart on it and it might make old Beeching
change his mind about cutting off the railway."

It was widely supposed in Perstowe that the Robbins
Report was exclusively concerned with advocating their
university. This was why Pigge blinked when Bream spoke
of colleges of advanced technology, because this seemed
the most extraordinary irrelevancy and quite enough to
justify his mention of the Beeching Report, which had,
after all, referred to Perstowe six times.

Ever since his arrival, Hedges had been walking about
shaking hands with as many people as was convenient and
trying to think what he would say in the speech Supple
would ask him to make.

The Long Gallery was the finest feature of the house,
though the pictures that had once hung there had long ago
been sold to pay death-duties. The Pigges had been great
hunters and travellers; they had placed the usual antlers,
tusks, horns, heads, and weapons on the walls, and, as they
had little market value, there the relics still hung—tiger,
eland, buffalo, boar—gazing down at the silver urns, the
china, the white table-cloths. There were huge, stuffed pike
in glass cases, crossed spears, rosettes of scimitars and axes.
Once there had been a scheme for partitioning the Gallery
and causing the Borough Treasurer, the Borough Surveyor,

and the Registrar of Births and Deaths to establish their
offices there, but they would have been inconveniently far
from the town, and, in any case, John Betjeman got wind of
the scheme and pointed out it was as good a piece of Eliza-
bethan pastiche as you'd find anywhere—it was built in
1867—so the Surveyor went into the stables, the Treasurer
into the ground floor on north of the house, and, for the
rest, it was a museum (if the heads and horns and weapons
made it a museum), a home for Jimmy Pigge (he had a flat
with free heating and no rates as part of the deal), a white-
elephant, and a temptation to any town to start a university.
Supple said that if the university came to nothing they'd
have to burn Lack Park down.

Hedges walked from one end of the Long Gallery to
another, shaking hands and grinning. He found that he was
not immediately recognizing people he knew perfectly well.
To discipline his mind, he thought of the history of the
Pigge family and how their living representative was re-
duced to a few rooms in one corner of the ancestral seat,
but this only reminded Hedges how the world was slipping
away from him too. Once he had been ambitious. Once he
had dreamed of a statue in the Market Square. He looked at
the buffalo to the right of the great fire-place and saw from
a brass notice that he had been shot in 1903. Well, sixty
years after its death the creature was now being thought
about. Who would think of Hedges sixty years after he was
dead? Who would think even of old Bream after sixty
years? If it was posthumous attention you were after, a
stuffed fish would beat you every time.

Saundersfoot's head would look well on a wooden
shield peering down from the wall of some twenty-first-
century sitting-room, always assuming current propensities
had worked themselves into the open by that time. The old

chap was standing with his hands thrust deep into his trousers pockets and *it* thrust forward at roughly the right angle.

"I suppose the do was fixed for this time of the afternoon," he said, when Hedges walked up to him, "to economize on the drinks. I must say I could do with one. There's one chap who must have a flask in his pocket, judging by the state he's in."

"You mean somebody's tight? Who?"

"Fellow fixing up the microphones. Tight as a boot. You and I shouldn't be talking here like this. Can't you feel the eyes of Perstowe on us?"

"As a matter of fact," said Hedges, "this is something I'd been meaning to bring up. Prudence is expecting. I mean this. In actual fact, she is pregnant. This is not rumour. I know."

Saundersfoot let his face go dead.

"I thought it only fair to let you know," said Hedges.

By his appearance of lifelessness, Saundersfoot was indicating that out of shame and embarrassment he had spiritually withdrawn from Lack Hall. He was even considering whether he should pretend not to have heard Hedges and walk away to join some other group. But anger got the better of him.

"She's told you officially?" he asked in a hoarse voice.

"I don't know about that. She told me. And she's going to have this baby. And she's not going to marry anybody. And she's going to carry on teaching at St. John's Road."

"What are you looking at me like that for?"

"Look, Ted." Hedges put a hand reassuringly on Saundersfoot's arm. "You know me. I'm not the censorious type. There but for the grace of God, and so on."

Saundersfoot began to whisper. "This has nothing to

do with me. My wife would kill me. Why do you begin talking about this dreadful business here? First of all she stays away from school for no good reason. Then I hear she's writing a novel. Now this."

"You ought to respect her for her independence."

"But Ian!" The relaxed, dead lines on Saundersfoot's face changed direction. They turned down at the ends. Saundersfoot had returned to his body and was now trying to rouse it from the nightmare in which he found it. "This has nothing to do with me. Besides, I won't have a pregnant, unmarried woman on my staff."

"This," said Hedges, "is a situation in which I'd thought to hear you speak as a man, not a headmaster."

"I swear——"

"The world we live in," said Hedges, "at this moment of history—well, we're realistic about some things but not about others. The belief that everybody is equal. Democracy goes farther than that. It says everybody's the same. Why don't you give up your seat on a bus to some woman? Because women are emancipated and they think they're the same as men and we think they're the same as men. But they're not, Ted. *You* know that, don't you?"

"Shut up," said Saundersfoot. He was six inches taller than Hedges and had to lower his head in order to hiss into Hedges's ear. "For God's sake, shut up. You don't think I've had anything to do with this young woman, do you? I'm fifty-eight. I'm retiring in a couple of years. I've got grandchildren."

Hedges took Saundersfoot by the elbow and steered him into a windowed alcove from where they could look straight down the main drive. Cars were still arriving. A policeman had propped his motor bike against a tree and, still wearing his crash-helmet, was directing the traffic into the car park. Near the house the grass had been cropped and was shining like paint. Farther off it had seeded and was giving tawny shudders under the dry wind.

Hedges could hear the incredulity in his own voice. "Do you mean to tell me, as a man of the world, that you've never been attracted by Prudence Styles?"

"Well. . . ."

"This story about the stationery room. You're not telling me——"

"Hell, I tried to kiss her——"

"You what?"

"I tried to kiss her. Once or twice, perhaps. But that's as far as it's got."

"Then how do you explain her present condition?"

All around were people talking about the Robbins Report; the twenty per cent of science Ph.D.s who went to the States, never to return; the possibility of raising money by Flag Days; the weather; holidays; even, perhaps, whether or not Toplis would put in an appearance; and Saundersfoot and Hedges, ignoring it all, stood side by side looking out of the great window at the autumnal sycamores on the other side of the unmown grass. Saundersfoot's was a baritone groan, Hedges's a tenor murmur.

"There's nothing to explain," said Saundersfoot. "I don't believe it. It's imagination. It's a false pregnancy like Mary Tudor's."

"Why are you so vehement, Ted? Take it from me it's real. There are such things as doctor's certificates. Why don't you trust me? You know I'll stand by you."

"Somebody will hear us. You must be out of your mind, bringing a subject like that up in this place. I tell you it's all lies or imagination. It has nothing whatsoever to do with me. If anyone says it has I'll sue him."

He would have marched off but Hedges stopped him. "You tried to kiss her. What happened?"

"Nothing. It was just fooling about. I wish to God I'd never appointed her. The vacancy was really for a geography specialist."

"You swear you're not the father of her unborn child?"

"I swear," said Saundersfoot and disappeared into the crowd.

Hedges glimpsed him on several occasions after that, and he seemed to be enjoying himself, talking, waving his arms, taking gentle bites at a sandwich like a caterpillar at a cabbage leaf. His eyes were bright. He was excited. Hedges could see perfectly well that his imagination had already moved forward to occupy the new territory that had been opened up for him; he was Casanova. Hedges wondered what would happen when he went home and confronted Mrs. Saundersfoot over the supper-table. To her the fancy dress would be invisible. Perhaps she would ask him if he'd been drinking again. Perhaps she'd observe him for a while and then, judging the moment nicely, say something on another wave length, something depressing, and bring him down like a partridge.

In bed Mrs. Saundersfoot would go to sleep first. Ted would lie there for a long time, looking into the blackness. He would grow more and more alarmed. Hedges could even imagine him going downstairs again and trying to beat his insomnia with a book. All the time, though, he would be thinking of the rumour linking himself and Prudence Styles and Hedges. Up to that day it had been wicked and absurd. Now it had become dangerous. He would have to do this. He would have to do that. He wasn't Casanova any longer. He was the respected citizen struggling against calumny—as indeed he had been for some weeks—but if the girl really was in the family way, there was a prospect of really dizzy work immediately ahead. Once he had his breath back he would play his role with almost as much relish as he was playing the fancy-dress Casanova at that very moment.

Hedges envied him.

"Ian! After all these years!"

Hedges turned and found a man in a dog-collar smiling and holding out his hand. The face was pink and brown, unnaturally clean; it might have been fresh from a Turkish bath. The closeness of the grey, watering eyes seemed vaguely familiar, but Hedges could not think of any parson who knew him well enough to call him by his Christian name.

"Cuthbert Simms," said the stranger. "My mother's still alive, you know. I was making one of my little visits. Eighty-four. Marvellous old lady. So I hear about this function and——"

"Hallo, Cuthbert. I expect you're a bishop or something."

"A bachelor country parson, that's all. You don't seem to have changed a bit, Ian."

"You're joking."

"I mean, not changed more than one would expect. We haven't met since before the war."

Hedges piloted him out of the throng, because once he had got used to the idea that it really was Cuthbert he wanted to talk to the man. There was some shouting coming from one of the small rooms leading off the Long Gallery and people were looking in that direction, but the Reverend Mr. Simms and Hedges were quickly absorbed in their conversation about old times. Hedges found he was sud-

denly remembering surprising details about their school-
days together; once they had borrowed some golf-clubs
belonging to Cuthbert's elder brother and on a summer
night at the full moon played round the links down at St.
Elmo's. The extraordinary thing was that they didn't lose
any balls. The moon itself was bright, and quite a lot of
reflected light came off the sea. The balls stood out clearly.

"I often think of that," said Cuthbert.

"Funny, it had gone clean out of my head."

"It was one of the great things in my boyhood. All
those stars and the sea and the click of the club as it struck
the ball."

"Don't think I've thought about it from that day to
this. But I can see it quite clearly."

"What's happened to you, Ian?"

"Oh, nothing much, you know." Hedges was still
searching those watery grey eyes. "I was a gunner. Ack-
ack. Nothing extraordinary."

"I went out to Korea."

"What?"

"Yes. I was a padre until 'forty-six, and I thought I'd
volunteer again."

"It's almost a quarter of a century since we clapped
eyes on one another. You realize that?"

"We ought to have kept in touch."

"D'you know what? You've broken my dream. Some
months ago I was playing croquet in the dark. I mean, we
had car headlights. But all the time I felt I was going
through some ritual I'd experienced before."

"It was the midnight golf."

"Extraordinary, isn't it?"

"You pointed out Orion to me, remember that? It's the
only constellation, apart from the Plough, I've ever been

able to remember. Whenever I see it, I think of that night and the waves breaking."

"Don't go out at night much now, not to see the stars anyway."

"The older you get, you don't go out to see the stars."

"A bachelor parson in the country," said Hedges. "Don't you ever get bored, I mean?"

"No."

To hear one another in the general roar of conversation, they had to put their heads close together; anyway, near enough for Hedges to detect that Cuthbert was wearing a lemony-sweet perfume. He could swear it came from Cuthbert, though people were pressing around so closely he couldn't be sure. The heat was making them both sweat. Cuthbert seemed to be waiting for him to say something. For all his well-scrubbed countenance and the schoolboy eagerness, Cuthbert clearly had his moods. A bachelor parson who wore scent was bound to have his moods.

"I got married, then I got divorced," said Hedges. "You know I'm Education Officer in this borough? Well, my father's still alive too. You remember him in his boater? That midnight golf was twenty-five years ago."

"I'm sorry," said Cuthbert. "About your marriage, I mean."

"Here I stand in the middle of the journey, in the middle of my life, a slightly thyroid, incipient manic-depressive, heterosexual, and—if I may say so without offence —lapsed Anglican. That is my formula."

"That night on the golf-course," said Cuthbert, "was the finest moment of my boyhood."

"Finer than when you set Fenner's barn on fire?"

"I didn't set Fenner's barn on fire."

"You didn't?" Hedges noticed for the first time that

Cuthbert's dark-grey suit was an expensive one: even his inexperienced eye could see that it was well cut. The material was a silky light-weight—tropical, probably—and he wondered where Cuthbert could possibly wear it when he wasn't at crowded receptions in the Long Gallery at Lack Park. "You must have set Fenner's barn on fire, because that's what made you a Christian."

Cuthbert laughed. "What nonsense! I know nothing about——"

"Amos told me. You remember Amos. He said it convinced you there was something that really could be called original sin and it was the first——"

"Absolutely not, old chap." Cuthbert shook his head. "It's a mistake."

"You weren't a young savage at all?"

Cuthbert hesitated. "Not really."

"Then I don't know what's pushed you. There can't be any urgency or sense of importance behind your beliefs. Cuthbert, you're a bloody fraud, d'you know that?"

"Yes," said Cuthbert calmly.

"What? You know it?"

"Every man with a conscience knows he's a bit of a fraud."

"I'm bitterly disappointed in you," said Hedges. "Did you or did you not commit arson in your youth? I know you've answered me once, but I'd like you to answer me again, now that I've put it into different language? Did you?"

"No."

"You don't see that it matters very much?"

"On the contrary, I'm very glad I didn't commit arson—or any other crime, for that matter."

"You're a whited sepulchre! You, a priest, saying

you're very glad you've never committed a crime. Isn't it what makes a priest, a crime? Why else should a man be driven to it?"

"Don't shout, old chap. This isn't the place——"

"Why don't you answer me? Why should a man become a priest?"

"We'll get together after the party. I want to persuade you that these ideas about religion and guilt are based upon a complete misunderstanding."

Angry male shouting was still coming from the far end of the Long Gallery, and Hedges thought the time had come for him to investigate. It wouldn't surprise him to discover Toplis in one of his libidinous moods creating a scene.

Hedges's parting words for Cuthbert had to be shouted above the rumpus. "I'd never have raised the subject if I'd known you were going to look at it in that way. Who d'you think I am? Calvin? Do I sound like Calvin? Do I behave like Calvin?"

In a panelled anteroom, Christopher Brush was slashing the air with a cavalry sword and saying that the idea of having a university at Perstowe was beneath his contempt. It made him angry. He was drunk, unshaven, dressed in dirty brown cotton slacks and a blue turtle-neck sweater. The room, which was about thirty feet square, had been cleared well before Hedges came up and joined the tight knot of protesting men around the door.

"He was going to tape the speeches."

"Get the police."

"Disgraceful."

"How did he get in?"

"I was in the army with an Irishman like that."

"*Somebody* must know who he is."

Hedges shouted at him, "Don't be a fool! Put that thing down."

Brush stopped at this, looked about him like some baited animal until he picked Hedges's face out of the mob, when he aimed his sword at it with a shout and a ferocious expression that took Hedges straight back to a steel-engraved nineteenth-century cavalry charge. He could see the splayed nostrils and rolling eyes of the terrified horse. There was the fireman's helmet and the nodding plume and streaking for his throat the shining steel!

"In the name of culture," Brush yelled, "I protest against the barbarians! Down with Perstowe University! Citizens of Perstowe, know your place, you Philistine dogs!"

Swish! The crowd retreated another couple of feet. Hedges's idea was to choose the right moment and rush the fellow. He would wrest the sword from him. Together, they would go out into the park, Brush would put his head in the lake for a few minutes, and the pair of them would sit under a tree and talk about Nell. Hedges would tell him she was a whore. "Take it easy," he'd say, "and look on the bright side. You ought to get smacking damages from Toplis."

On the wall to the right of the doorway was a sword identical with the one Brush was waving about, and Hedges lifted it off the hook with the idea of using it to get to close quarters. If he was not quick enough, he could use it to parry any blow that Brush aimed at him; but he really wanted to jump so close to Brush that this would not be necessary.

"He's a friend of mine," said Hedges. "Let me talk to him."

194

"There's another of 'em!" somebody shouted.

"I tell you," Brush was yelling, "that your university will be a baboo university! Your intellectual pretensions disgust me. You are cockroaches. You are cockroaches in the house of knowledge. I will crush you like cockroaches!"

Brush and Hedges were now facing each other like duellists, one in the anteroom, one in the gallery, with an open doorway in between.

"Drop that thing, Brush, and let's get out of here."

"Do you or do you not agree with me that a university in Perstowe is a grotesque idea?"

Hedges walked through the doorway and the two men were alone in the panelled room, circling, Brush laughing and slashing, Hedges wary and a bit frightened by now.

He could not remember ever before having handled a real sword. He had seen swords in junk-shops and museums, but they were relics of the romantic past and about as much to do with him as three-cornered hats. The weapons Brush and he were grasping seemed too long and heavy for spectacular sword-play, jumping on tables and battling up and down flights of stairs, and Hedges supposed they really needed administering with the full weight of a horse travelling at about forty miles an hour. They had ornate guards and seemed to be about a yard and a half long, special swords for use with a tall animal—camel, possibly—and not the weapon for spitting the foe in an anteroom.

Hedges had to remind himself he was not there to fight Brush, whatever the omens might be. The fellow had drunk himself silly, was dangerous, and ought to be disarmed. He looked as though he had been on the bottle for days. Why, didn't matter. That their lives had tangled, this didn't matter. Hedges wanted to make the next five minutes as impersonal as possible.

The sodden Brush said that if there was anything he couldn't stand it was education. Education was a bloody bore. Universities were centres of life-hating discipline. He was against systematization of any kind. He wanted to be left alone to cultivate his lusts and appetites but, come the university, they'd be wanting to find him a job teaching in the extramural department and he wouldn't stand for it; he wanted his freedom. He drove his sword past Hedge's ear into the wainscot but pulled it out again and was away so quickly that Hedges didn't have time even to prick him. Tight he might be, but nimble with it.

"If you don't put that thing down," said Hedges, frightened no longer, "I swear I'll run you through the guts."

The two men were so intent on one another they forgot they had spectators. Hedges could not recollect how he had got caught up in this sword-play. Brush and he were circling each other on one of the lower reaches of Hell. They had been there through centuries. There would be no end to their torment. Hedges was sweating. "For God's sake," he wanted to say to Brush, "at least let's open a window and kill each other in the fresh air." He wasn't frightened, he was certainly tormented, but he would not have escaped from the room even if he had been able to. And if that crash-helmeted copper appear behind Brush and grabbed his sword-arm, Hedges would have resented it. Brush and he were playing a totally absorbing game.

"Who am I?"

"Eh?" Brush stopped, lowered his sword for a moment, and peered at Hedges as though through fog. "Did somebody say something? Hedges, you tit, Hedges, she's cuckold —cuck——"

He flicked forward with the sword, summer lightning

flashed in the dark room, there was a gasp from the men in the doorway, and Hedges could feel a sticky welling of blood down into his right eye. He immediately jabbed for Brush's sword wrist, missed, and Brush, roaring out of a wide, black mouth, stood glancing along the blade like a bullfighter, taking aim.

"I never wanted her in the first place."

Brush was resting the blade on his raised left wrist and aiming at Hedges's throat. Hedges looked at the point but could see none of his blood on it. He felt vaguely sorry for Brush in the way he might feel sorry for a hurt animal that was about to be put out of its misery. This pity was swallowed up, though, by excitement. He remembered, now, Cuthbert's perfume and the same sweetness hung in the air of this panelled room, the smell of flowering lime-trees, though it was autumn, as sharp in its sweetness as the unstained point of steel in line with his throat.

He could not see out of his right eye. He tried to rub some of the blood away with the back of his left hand, but it made no difference. Brush lunged forward slackly and Hedges knocked away his sword. He didn't want to hurt Brush. He bore him no malice. To his excited mind, though, it was as though opening up the right artery in Brush's body would release a fountain of life. He could see himself bathing in and drinking the blood of the magic animal.

Their shoes shrieked on the block floor.

He didn't hate Brush, but he wasn't going to let the fellow escape. Not letting Brush escape had been—he saw it now—his unacknowledged obsession. No matter what he had said or done during the past two or three years, whether it was building the New Jerusalem, starting a university, or loving Prudence, *this* was what he had been really thinking of and working towards. Ironically, Brush

197

had struck the attitude of a bullfighter, an imaginary cape over his left arm and the sword poised in the right. Hedges was in such transports he saw no danger. Indeed, he now perceived Brush as the bull-headed monster and supposed that Theseus must have felt very much as he did before knocking off the Minotaur.

And yet, excited though he was, he suspected he was being a bit absurd. He didn't want to be a fool. Only a fool would go in for wanton blood-letting. He could think of nothing more to say to Brush, and Brush, now silent but breathing heavily, appeared incapable of saying anything to him; so Hedges supposed they were both in that ultimate state of folly when they could only act.

This is important, Hedges was thinking. Something going on here is important. What?

Brush cut at him; Hedges parried and lunged to see the point of his sword disappear into Brush's throat. The black mouth gaped. The head shot back on its hinge.

The party went on as planned. The Lord Lieutenant made a speech, Supple made a speech, Primrose made a speech, and even Pigge made a speech. Now and again they were all blanched and frozen by the photographers. Someone even got Brush's recorder working, so all this rigmarole was perpetuated on tape; and the failure of Hedges to make a speech, and the absence of Brush himself, and the two swords which were wrapped up in newspaper and in the care of the crash-helmeted policeman, and the absence of Dr. Slocombe, the borough M.O.H., were little noticed. It was surprising, really, what small impact the battle in the anteroom had on the reptilian gaiety of the proceedings, which now bumbled on with an air of not knowing what had been digested. Sitting up in the back of a car and supported by Slocombe and the policeman, Brush coughed and snored in his own blood. Hedges thought he would be dead before he reached the hospital. So, after following to the outskirts of the town, he turned off towards the Market Square, parked against the clock tower, and walked up to his office. The plaster above his right eye concealed a slit he was supposed to get stitched; but the blood seemed to have stopped seeping through, and he thought he wouldn't bother. He hoped he wasn't inhuman, but all this university business, and Brush and Nell, and pretty well everything that had happened during the past two or three years, no longer had meaning or importance. Brush was dead. That meant a lot of other things were dead too, dead as though they had never existed. Perhaps he would be able to get on with a little real work, just for a change.

He tried to reach the Borough Surveyor on the phone, but his secretary said he was at the University party, and Hedges had to say, Yes, of course, he'd forgotten, but would she get Mr. Green to ring him in the morning because there was a point about the plans for the new Junior School at Swan End.

"What's the matter?" said Beryl. Hedges had rushed through her outer office so quickly she hadn't time to open her mouth. She now came and cross-examined him. "What have you come back for so soon? What's that patch? You've got a big stain on your jacket."

"It's blood, I expect. I just killed a man."

"You had me worried. I thought it might be coffee. You'd never get a coffee stain out of that colour material."

"I'm not joking."

"Sure, that would be very bad taste, wouldn't it?" She took the jacket off to the wash-room and came back some minutes later, saying, "It really was blood, too. See, it's come out clean. I won't give evidence against you, Mr. Hedges, because you know of my devotion."

What he had to say to Green about the new Junior School was not trivial. On the way back to the office, Hedges had driven through this Swan End development area and been struck by the fact that the main road was carrying heavy traffic even at that time of day and that the new school would be on one side of it and most of the children's homes on the other. You could have a man in a white coat holding up the traffic while the kids crossed, but Hedges did not remember the issue being discussed. Now he really wanted to know about it. Maybe the Surveyor was taking what the County Architect prescribed. Perhaps a controlled pedestrian crossing was as far as their imaginations took them. At the very least you wanted a foot-bridge. Better still—and at this point Hedges got out the Swan End map and put a call in to the County Architect.

The great thing in local Government work was really to sting one's fellow bureaucrats with this word "local." Refuse to accept general solutions at the expense of local amenity. Get the detail right. Wasn't that why he was in the racket? Then why hadn't he noticed this potential death-trap before? He, the warrior for the New Jerusalem, had not properly examined the location of one of his new schools. He blamed everything on to the break-up of his marriage. But for that he would never have been a visionary.

The County Architect was a man called Trewin, who seemed a bit annoyed at being called out of a meeting. He said he did not know what Hedges was talking about. Yes, of course he knew about the new school at Swan End, but he couldn't be expected to discuss siting problems over the telephone. In any case they had to grab what sites they could.

"You've got a sports ground on the other side of the road. Why not build the school there and put the sports ground where the school's planned for?"

"If it was as simple as that it would have been done. There must be some——"

"No, there's no reason. It just hasn't been thought about."

"O.K., O.K.," said Trewin, "but you're talking to the wrong man. You've got your own Architect and Surveyor's Department."

"They're all out at some bloody party."

"I'd go and join them if I were you."

"Some people have work to do. And look——"

"Do you mind?" said Trewin, putting his receiver down.

Hedges could see from the map that the site of the sports ground occupied five acres and the school three. The switch was not impossible. In fact it was staring you in the face. Why hadn't he seen it before?

He was wondering whether he ought to drive out and examine this sports ground when the phone rang and it was Amos. "What d'you mean, you're working? I've been looking all over for you. D'you know what? You're about to be visited by the police. From my window I can see across the Square, and there's a police car stopped just outside the Council offices. Don't talk to them without a lawyer. Hold on, I'll pop over myself."

Beryl came in, looking worried. "What's this about the police, Mr. Hedges?"

"I just killed a man, just as I told you. Now, when the gentlemen arrive, show them straight in."

"And Mr. Amos?"

"Why not?"

"I thought you were joking. I washed the blood off! What about a lawyer? Shall I look one up in the book?"

"Just show the gentlemen in."

The gentlemen were a sergeant in uniform and a man in a brown suit with a flattened boxer's nose who said he was a Detective-Inspector Pollock. Hedges asked them to sit down, but he himself remained standing. He offered them cigarettes. They were friendly but refused. Hedges wondered whether he was suffering from shock because he couldn't take their visit seriously. He couldn't even answer their questions as precisely as he would have liked.

"Certainly I killed him," he said, after they had tried the usual verbal grips on him.

"You didn't, you know," said Detective-Inspector Pollock, "because he was still alive when we left the hospital ten minutes ago."

"I don't think he'll get over it," said Hedges. "It's just a matter of time. What are the extent of his injuries?"

"Didn't see it myself," said Pollock, "but I understand there's a nasty gaping wound just below the Adam's apple, and his windpipe has been pierced, so he was, in a manner of speaking, in some danger of drowning in his own blood. That looks like a nasty gash on your forehead, Mr. Hedges. How did you get that?"

Hedges was explaining when Fred Amos walked in. He knew the two policemen and immediately told them that Brush had been pissed and running amok. Hedges ought to have a medal. It was a bloody marvellous story. Hedges was a hero. Amos said he'd phoned the story through to London. It would catch the late editions of the evening papers.

202

Hedges ought to be given the medal of the Royal Humane Society.

"When you divorced your wife, Mr. Hedges, she married this man Brush, is that right?"

"Look, Inspector, I killed this man. I lashed out at him."

"He's not dead, sir."

"Of course he's not dead," said Amos, "but somebody would have been if Mr. Hedges hadn't stopped him."

"He'll die, all right. It's the sort of case in which pneumonia develops and you can't do anything about it, not with a drunk like Brush."

Detective-Inspector Pollock shrugged. "Well, perhaps you'd come round to the station and make a statement, Mr. Hedges?" The sergeant in uniform nodded, anticipating Hedges's reply. He did not take his eyes from Hedges's face and seemed under mild hypnosis.

"Ian, you mustn't make a statement without seeing a solicitor," said Amos. "We can pick up Troughton on the way. I'll tell your Beryl to get him on the phone."

"I'd dictate it to my secretary here and now, if you like," Hedges said to Pollock.

"Tidier round at the station. If there is a charge against you, anything you say in this statement may be used in evidence. You understand that?"

"I jabbed at him deliberately," said Hedges.

Hedges would not hear of calling a solicitor in at this stage, and as he and Amos decided to walk to the police-station—it was only a few minutes—they argued all the way. Pollock walked slightly behind them, saying nothing. The sergeant drove the car off in the direction of the railway-station, a journey of about a mile through one-way

streets in front of him; and indeed Hedges, Amos, and the
Detective-Inspector arrived at the station before he did.
They walked through a couple of acres where old property
was being swept away to make room for a new shopping
centre, a hotel, and a three-storey car park: all this was
announced on a hoarding that stood at the entrance to the
smashed townscape, the scoured patches of tawny earth that
had been cleared so recently the weeds had not had time to
grow. A curving row of red-brick dwellings, shops downstairs and living accommodation over, stood tenantless, be-
grimed, windows smashed, waiting for the demolition men.
One house had been sliced away from its neighbour, leaving
wood panelling downstairs, flowered wallpaper up, and a
hanging fire-place, exposed to the afternoon. The air was
gritty. A bonfire of rafters sent up a little flame and a lot of
black smoke.

"Few years' time we shan't recognize this place," said
Pollock.

"You're not a Perstowe man?"

"No, sir, I'm not a Perstowe man, but I'll still not
recognize it."

"They're not even keeping to the old street plan.
They've grubbed up the cobbles, look. I don't like that. I
think they ought to have stuck to the street plan. There'll
be no continuity. There won't be even the old street
names."

Hedges didn't know whether he was pleased or sorry.
Pleased, perhaps, on the whole. If the wind veered, the
sparks from that bonfire might carry as far as the Old
Plough, set fire to the thatch, and the whole town would be
ablaze. They could build afresh on the ruins. Hedges looked
at the flaming rafters and thought that was how he too
would like to flare up, big bright eyes staring out of his cal-

cined skull. The men must have been burning something
other than wood—old sacks, perhaps—because Hedges could
certainly smell the combustion of something that had once
been alive, even if it was only in a jute-field. He peered at
the burning ghat of Perstowe with—yes, quite unmistakable
pleasure.

In a back office of the police-station, he dictated while
Pollock wrote in longhand. The sergeant had joined them
once more, and he kept his round eyes on Hedges's face
while Amos stood at the window, smoking a small cigar.
When it came to formal statement, Hedges found he could
not claim he deliberately jabbed at Brush's throat. All he
could be certain of, now that he stood in this office, dicta-
ing to a policeman, was that a man called Brush had been
drunk, that he had a sword and was acting dangerously, and
that he, Hedges, had picked up another sword to stop him
and been gashed on the forehead. He had been forced to
parry another thrust. And then?

"Course it was an accident." Amos spoke without
turning. "A real jab would've cut his head off, very nearly."

"Then I saw that his throat was pierced," Hedges
wound up. "I saw that his throat was pierced with my
sword. I can't say any more."

"A real jab would have killed him outright," said
Amos, when Hedges had read his statement over.

"Surgeon put a silver tube in the chap's gullet, just as
though he was a racehorse." Unexpectedly the sergeant
gave tongue. "I knew they did it to horses but not to human
beings."

Hedges signed the statement. Pollock said he now had
some more witnesses to see. He asked if those present were
aware that duelling—and the present affray was clearly not
a duel—was illegal. A man killed in a duel was by the law

regarded as murdered. "And even if it is not a duel," said
Pollock, "but just an engagement with naked swords, this is
an offence."

Amos didn't even bother to take the cigar out of his
mouth. "You mean the law makes a distinction between
duelling and just sword-fighting?" The eyes of all four men
were watering in his smoke.

"I'm not a lawyer," said Pollock. "I looked this up in a
book."

"Can I go now?" Hedges asked.

"Sure. I'll pop round some time and see you. O.K.?"

Hedges and Amos walked out into the street.

"What are you up to?" said Amos. "Are you confused?
Why don't you let me drive you up to the hospital to get
that gash seen to?"

Hedges shook his head. "I've got work to do."

"Look, if you don't——"

"Leave me now, will you, Fred?"

He turned his coat collar up and set off across the
building site, which had now darkened so much that the
bonfire seemed the huger and more brilliant. The men had
knocked off work, and Hedges walked towards the Market
Square behind a group of them. He would have taken them
into the George if he'd had the time. It would have given
him real pleasure to buy them a pint apiece.

During the previous half hour the blue sky had
thickened, first of all milky and now to a real dark military
porridge that let down rain in cold flurries. The clock in the
Square said ten past five. He sat in the car watching the
wind-screen wiper gain momentum. The town was switching on its lights. He eased out into the flow of traffic and
caught in the driving mirror a glimpse of his own face

pulsing red and white in time with the indicator of the car in front. At the High Street traffic lights he turned right up to the station-yard, cut under the bridge, and within a matter of minutes was climbing above the Memorial Garden trees to Mythe Hill. Out over the estuary the grey cloud broke, and a lot of thin yellow light hung in clusters along the horizon. Parked outside Mrs. Kidwelly's, he sat looking at this light for some time. Then he found a plastic mac in the dashboard pocket and draped it over his head and shoulders while he made a dash for the door.

Far away in some recess he could hear a bell vibrating like a nerve. Footsteps approached with the kind of deliberation that said the bell had certainly been rung for some trivial reason, and then Mrs. Kidwelly herself, wearing black brogues, knitted stockings, a pleated skirt, and a great goalkeeper's sweater, but knitted in Fair Isle, stood framed in the doorway.

"Mr. Hedges?" She sounded pleased, and then he understood why. "You're hurt. You've got a big piece of blood-stained sticking-plaster over your right eye." She pointed. "Just there."

"Is Miss Styles in? I'd like to speak to her."

"She's just finished her tea."

Hedges did not wait for an invitation. He stepped past Mrs. Kidwelly into the hall and would not allow her to pilot him into the sitting-room. He would wait just where he was, in front of the big gong on the bamboo stand.

Mrs. Kidwelly hesitated, but Hedges went on smiling at her, because he saw that if the Archangel Gabriel appeared and asked Mrs. Kidwelly if he could go up to her first-floor balcony to blow the Last Trump she would have hesitated over him too. And Hedges, though he had lived

through much in the last few hours, been purged, transfigured, and lifted up by his experiences, knew he was no
archangel; he was a mortal man in a hurry precisely because
of his mortality. He had lowered the plastic mac to his
shoulders, and the water dripped from it on to Mrs. Kidwelly's red and blue linoleum. His black, mud-splashed
shoes apparently rested on the red and blue linoleum too.
But this was only what Mrs. Kidwelly saw. Hedges knew
that he was standing on the naked rock of life. He meant
real life. He was supported by a sense of having arrived at a
basic truth about himself. What a lot of people gave up
money and months on the analyst's couch to achieve had
descended on him, undeserved and unlooked for, like old-
fashioned grace. But it was no good trying to explain this to
Mrs. Kidwelly. It would have been no good trying to
explain it to the Reverend Mr. Warp, even; though Hedges
was beginning to think other men in his position would
have been quick to see what was religious in the sweet
liberation he bathed in.

"What do you want?" It was Prudence, at the other
end of the passage, looking as though she had been there
some time. Hedges was surprised that her appearance was as
he remembered it: cool, precise, with an eagerness in the
blue eyes. "You've hurt yourself. Has there been an accident?"

"I want your advice, really. I had your letter. I've got
the car outside."

She walked up to him and looked more closely at the
plaster. She took a raincoat off the hall-stand and, without a
word, opened the front door and stepped out into the wind.
Hedges, who felt like kissing Mrs. Kidwelly's iron cheek,
simply shook her by the hand. He thought that he would

always remember her just as she stood now, in her Fair Isle sweater, arms folded, mouth square; as a man might remember a rock or some other natural object that had kept him company at a moment of crisis.

"Where are you taking me?" It was some time before Prudence broke the silence, and during that time Hedges had been savouring the silence and the way the yellow wound over the sunset was gaping wider and shooting light through the murk of rain. There was a moment when he actually glimpsed a sea horizon and a remote dot of a ship, perched on it like a bird on a telegraph wire. He would have liked to say that it didn't matter in the slightest where he was taking her. They would never be happier than they were at that moment. If life was the pursuit of happiness, they had arrived. He gave her a rag and asked her to wipe the steamed-up wind-screen.

At Swan End he turned left into a jungle of jerry-built semi-detached houses. There were lights in the sports pavilion. Half a dozen cars stood in the park, but the rain was still coming down so heavily that Hedges stopped against the main entrance. Even so, Prudence and he knew they had been out in the wet. Her hair stuck to her forehead like sodden hay. The bar was open, and although Prudence said at first that she wouldn't drink anything the sight of Hedges putting back a double whisky persuaded her she was thirsty, and they sat at a table for some time, he with his whisky and she with tomato juice and a shot of vodka. There were two couples and half a dozen youths in the bar, everyone talking quietly. The plaster on Hedges's forehead aroused a certain amount of attention, but for the most part the talk was scarcely above a whisper. There was no heat. Hedges caught Prudence in a shudder.

"I want to take you up to the first floor. There's something I want to show you."

It was even colder up there. The club-house had been open only a few months, and the first floor was neither furnished nor equipped. Hedges and Prudence found themselves in a large, empty, unlit, chill room overlooking what seemed to be lakes with curtains round them; in reality, hard tennis-courts under the rain with a primrose light falling from the right.

"You see," said Hedges. "Beyond those tennis-courts there's the hockey pitch and the soccer pitch. Don't you think it's crazy to have this sports ground here? There's room for the new school. I spoke to Trewin about it. If the school were here, the kids wouldn't have to cross that road."

"You got my letter then?"

"Yes."

Overhead, the rain drummed on a flat roof. On the far side of the sports ground, lights came on in the little houses, and Hedges felt as though he and Prudence were at sea on a ghost ship looking at shore lights, lights to mark the harbour entrance, lights on buoys; the readiness with which Prudence had accompanied him on this particular voyage he found very touching. She was more lovable than ever. She even thought he had brought her down to the sports club to give her a tomato juice with a shot of vodka and talk about the letter.

"Does it hurt?" she said. "Your forehead?"

"I've got a bit of a headache. But it doesn't hurt really. Smarts and itches. But it doesn't really hurt, if you know what I mean."

"How did you do it?"

"Brush did it. He's dead by now."

"Dead?"

"Yes. I killed him." He interrupted whatever it was she intended to say. "I want to tell you, my dear little girl," he said, "that you are the first human being I feel I've ever really communicated with."

"Don't talk to me like this," she said. "I don't want to be communicated with! Are you joking or something?" The light idealized her face. He could not see the detail— not an eyelash, not a wrinkle—just dark eyes in a pale mask. "It comes to something when communication is just another word for sex."

"Not in my vocabulary."

"And you shouldn't make jokes about killing people."

"The record-player, all bass and no top, started up in the bar, and Hedges could feel the blues rhythm tickling the soles of his feet. He put an arm round her waist but she had her hands up, pushing against him, not very powerfully. "When I'm with you I don't feel by myself," he said. "That's not a little thing. Everybody else, they've just been other people."

"What about your wife?"

"She was so much one of the other people she sort of called attention to them in a way nobody else did. She's one of those bloody-selfish people who show up, quite shamelessly, her own loneliness and everybody else's loneliness. Are you cold?"

"It's cold in here."

"You know, I'm not tight, or out of my mind, or just talking for effect. I've never seen more clearly in my life. You didn't mean what you put in that letter, did you?"

"Yes."

"No," he said. "You didn't mean a word of it, and

we're going to live happily ever after—unless I'm hanged, that is."

"Hanged?"

"As a murderer."

She came back from the window at this and said, "What's this talk about murder?"

Hedges gave her a concise account of the fight at Lack Hall. It was now so dark that he could only dimly make out the shape of her face. He too was beginning to feel the cold. Just enough light hung over the flooded tennis-courts to make the air look greasy.

"He's in the hospital now with a tube in his windpipe."

Hedges stopped talking and listened instead. Yes, she had distinctly sobbed. She did it again. Remembering what she had said about the cold, he slipped off his jacket and covered her shoulders with it. He put his arms round her and tried to warm her with his own body. He ought to have been saying something to cheer her up, but he was marvelling at the weirdness of the situation. In his fortieth year, he stood with a weeping and pregnant woman in his arms under a cascade of water that fell on the flat roof like an immensely protracted explosion; and it was as though, all his life, he had been hunting for just this: the rhythm from the record-player down below, the thought of Brush whistling through his tube like a broken nag, and a little picture of Nell in a lighted room with that old monkey Toplis and a curtain being drawn across their window. He had been brought to all this like some long-tongued and excitable hound who is at long last thrown what he has been hunting and finds it is a bundle of old sacking soaked in aniseed.

"I'm all right." Prudence moved away from him and blew her nose. "Sorry about that! It's just that you talk in such an extravagant way, and you don't seem to know what kind of impression it makes. Even if this man does die, they couldn't possibly arrest you for murder. It was obviously an accident."

"It didn't feel like it at the time, I must say."

"Of course it was an accident, you fool. Or is an accident to undignified for you?"

He thought about this. "On the whole, yes."

CHAPTER SEVEN

Pride and the River

It was six weeks before Brush was well enough to appear before a magistrate, and by this time the police had dropped the idea of charging Hedges, though they had toyed with the idea of giving him a run under Section 18 of the Offences against the Person Act, 1861, in that he unlawfully and maliciously wounded the said Brush with intention to maim, disfigure, disable, or inflict grievous bodily harm. Brush, on the other hand, was charged with wounding Hedges under Section 20 of that Act, a much less serious matter. The difference, so far as Hedges could see, was that whereas Section 20 (Brush's section) envisaged a certain degree of recklessness in the accused, Section 18 (the one Hedges nearly made) was brought into play only when there was evidence of real bloody-mindedness. Hedges saw the police hesitancy over charging him under Section 18 as some concession to his acknowledged readiness to confess to attempted murder. "We think," they seemed to say, "you're suffering from an exaggerated sense of guilt, but to show we don't consider it amounts to mental disorder we'll now reveal we've considered the possibility of charging you with a felony punishable with imprisonment for life. Never for one moment did we think you were merely in the Section 20 category. Brush, not being a senior local Government official, is. He will be charged, rather contemptuously, with a mere misdemeanour."

Brush gave evidence in a hoarse whisper because of the damage to his vocal chords. He said he could remember nothing of the incident, was deeply ashamed of himself, and hoped the court would consider that he had been sufficiently punished. A policeman had to stand in the box with him, listen to what he was saying, and then sing it out for the benefit of the magistrate. Brush looked younger and thinner. He had a red spot in the middle of each sallow cheek and had developed the trick of keeping his head still but switching his eyes about. Hedges gave evidence. He said he had known Brush for some time and had continued to see him, quite amicably, even after Brush had been co-respondent in his divorce. At Lack Park, Brush seemed not to know what he was doing. Hedges knew from experience that Brush was intoxicated by comparatively little alcohol. A policeman, when questioned, said that Brush was living on his own now that his wife had left him. The magistrate wrote for some time with what looked like a silver pencil and then announced that the offence was such that he would send Brush for trial at the next Assizes.

Troughton, the solicitor, popped up and asked for bail. The magistrate said five hundred pounds, and Hedges, who had heard no one could be found to stand surety, attested that he would answer for Brush's appearance before judge and jury at the Spring Sessions. The damp, cold weather made Hedges's foot ache. For this reason, he did not follow Brush when he left the court with Troughton but went and sat with his leg up in the Town Clerk's office for half an hour. He fingered the white scar on his forehead. Theoretically he understood the responsibility he had assumed, but he suspected that it was less real to him than it was to the magistrate, to Troughton, or even to Brush himself. They all assumed Brush was still alive.

To Hedges, as he sat and observed the polished toe of his right shoe, the point was more obscure. The story of the life and death of Christopher Brush seemed to have entered a stage more mysterious than anyone but Hedges seemed to suspect. He brooded over the different views—depending on who you were and where you stood—that it was possible to take of the present state of Brush's existence. The Lack Hall battle had been widely reported in the press, and Hedges was aware, for example, that he and Brush had acquired the reputation of being jolly, extrovert sluggers who shot from the hip and didn't talk for a long time after. Easy to spot that for the fantasy it was! But what about less simple views? How could Hedges justify this feeling that everyone else was wrong, that he alone was right, and that, whatever Brush had once been, now he was a harmless phantom, and that the Assize Court judge and jury would look down at an empty dock?

To be honest, he liked to think that Brush was dead and that he had killed him. He felt no remorse. On the contrary, he was quite chirpy.

Hedges senior was by this time referring to most people, alive or dead, in the past tense. He worked for no more than thirty minutes at a time in the garden. He had his dizzy spells. He would come and sit in the shadow, and Hedges could almost fancy he had all the cohorts of the dead sitting there with him: his mother, Captain Charles who went round buying horses in 1915, Arthur Weeks who farmed where St. John's School now was, Fred Amos's

father who stepped off the top of a horse-bus on to Buz-
zard's sun-blind, and Bert Rivers, one of whose pigs developed swine fever. The police sergeant had to do the
slaughtering in those days.

"Bert," said Mr. Hedges, "wouldn't let the sergeant
come nigh. He had this scythe. He kept swinging it and
swearing, and the sergeant kept jumping like a ballet-
dancer. Bert would've had his legs off. That sergeant went
to Canada and came back with the Canadians in nineteen-
sixteen. He walked about wearing one of those big hats. He
got killed. Police was more respected then. They took the
law into their own hands. If this sergeant, 'is name was
Edwards, caught a kid up to any mischief 'e smacked his
head. Once 'e gave a poacher the choice of a bloody good
hiding or going to court. *An'* he took his pheasants off him,
and no more was said about it. Well, if Bert Rivers'd caught
him with that scythe, it'd 've been grievous bodily harm.
You've only got to break a man's skin for it to be grievous
bodily harm. But he kept missing him. Because you see, Sergeant Edwards kept 'opping. You was cut over the 'ead, Ian,
that's why it was grievous bodily harm. But for that it
wouldn't have been so serious. Brush was drunk and that
was mitigation. Well, it's an ambition, to die drunk."

Sitting in his chair, he would fall asleep and then wake
up and go on talking as though nothing had happened.

"Brush, that's a bloody funny name to 'ave. There was
a man kept bees over at Harridge called Sweep, Tom
Sweep, and 'e tried to sell me a couple of hives. Couldn't
pay his bill, wanted to give me a couple of hives of bees
instead, but I'd rather keep tigers. You know the dew-pond
up at Harridge? He drowned 'isself in that dew-pond. Very
good water. Sweep is a funnier sort of name than Brush,
but they was very different men. Sweep was a quiet little

217

man who never smoke nor drank nor swore, and yet he
went out and drowned 'isself one night in that dew-pond.
Brush was not the suicidal type. He squatted in life like a
sow squats in muck. Some women like that."

Mr. Hedges allowed his hair to grow, and it fell forward over his eyes and over his collar, more of a nimbus
than ordinary white hair, but it made his red face seem
smaller and his chin pointed like a Cornish spade.

The new daily was a Mrs. Rogers who said little but
cooked well and listened to Mr. Hedges for hours on end,
without complaining. Hedges heard him tell her that capital
punishment should never be done away with. "You won't
stop the killings any other way. All the killer understands is
the threat of death. There was a man called Brush—ooh, 'e
was a nice one. 'E went off with my daughter-in-law. If I
was a dog I wouldn'a lifted a leg at him, but even *his* end
should have been respected. The hangman is the guardian of
society."

Mr. Hedges now made little distinction between the
quick and the dead.

As for Nell—

"Surprised to see me, I expect," she said one day.

It was Saturday afternoon, his father was asleep upstairs, and Hedges had been watching racing on television.
Nell was wearing a fur coat and what looked like a Phry-
gian cap in brown sail-cloth. He didn't recognize her for a
moment, and when he did he nearly groaned. She was as
dead as Brush himself. She was irrelevant. She had nothing
to say to him any more, not even with those slinky hips.
And her face didn't vibrate in the old way. She was just a
woman in a fur coat who had a cold in the nose, and he
wished she would go away so that he could pretend she had
never called.

They stood in the hall to talk. "It's about Christopher. Well, I feel a bit responsible myself, but you know how it is. What I mean is, don't you think you ought to do something for him? He's so helpless. Poor lamb! And you've got an interest, too. I mean, if you stand surety for somebody it means you've some kind of responsibility—financial, to put it no higher. If Christopher disappeared you'd lose five hundred pounds. I don't know what the position is if he commits suicide. Not that five hundred quid is either here or there. Anyway, it's your *fault* that he's like he is. He's been ill and can't work. He's got no voice and he can't broadcast. A man can't be expected to take money from his wife, knowing where it's come from. But he's often taken it from you. What he needs more than anything else is friendship. He needs good advice. He says he won't divorce me and he must, mustn't he?"

Hedges was incredulous that he had married this woman. There she was, with her red-winged nose and flat forehead, like a stranger he might have caught sight of sitting opposite him in a bus. The fog seeped through the ill-fitting front door, and the racing commentary whined out of the living-room. Hedges looked at her and hoped she would evaporate.

"Of course, if he won't divorce me I shall change my name to Toplis by deed-poll. But it's all so unnecessary. After all, you divorced me, why shouldn't he? Go and talk to him, Ian."

"No."

"I don't see what you've got to grumble about. You've got this school-teacher, and she's fifteen years younger than you even if she is a bit fly-blown. You can't expect much more at your age. Men usually wear better than women, but you don't, Ian. You're getting to look like old Saundersfoot." She gave a tinny laugh. "My God, it'll have to be a wise child."

"You'd better go now."

"Pop down to the flat and see him."

"Would you come?"

"It wouldn't look well. After all, what can I do to help him? If he won't take money, I mean. Well, they say Pride is a deadly sin, and he's on National Assistance." She looked very unhappy and said she supposed that if Christopher had died after his accident she wouldn't have had all this trouble.

Hedges interrupted by suggesting they both go down on their knees and confess to one another.

"I don't know what you mean," she said suspiciously.

"Let us confess our sins to one another. You confess to me what happened on the afternoon of August twenty-fifth, and then you'll say how you wrote those letters to Prudence. And I will confess I murdered your lover. Then I will absolve you and you will absolve me."

"Are you raving or something?" But she wouldn't meet his eyes, and he knew damn well he would get the truth out of her if he only frightened her enough. He grabbed her by the wrists and after a struggle managed to force her to her knees. He kneeled too.

"I think you gave my father the last little killing shock. He's dying."

Her face really wobbled now, about eighteen inches from his, and there were tears sliding over the make-up. "Let me go, Ian."

"Absolve me! Come on!"

"You're hurting me."

"Give me absolution or I'll break your bloody wrists."

"I don't know what you mean. I forgive you. Of course I forgive you."

"Say, 'I absolve you.'"

"I absolve you."

"And I absolve you. This is as near a priestly blessing as either you or I will get. I forgive you the letters even if Pru wouldn't, and I forgive you the sheets in the apple-tree and my mother's smashed photograph. And my father's death. You needn't have any of this on your conscience. Now get out."

Hedges waited for ten minutes or so after she had gone. He ought to have felt better but didn't. She had not made much of a fight of it. After all, she was thirty-six, and her batteries ran down more easily than they used to.

He had no intention of allowing Nell's wishes to interfere with the visits he paid to Brush.

"Keeping your eye on your five hundred quid?" This was Brush's habitual remark whenever Hedges looked in, as he did now, lifting the latch and stepping straight into the kitchen, where, surrounded by unwashed crockery, pots, pans, empty tins, Brush sat at a typewriter. Heat came from a paraffin stove. The place reeked of the stove and boiled fish. This time, however, Brush went on to say something else.

"Who's this man," he whispered to himself, turning his head away, "who keeps coming into my dream?"

He was wearing a grey pull-over with a high neck. Round his throat he wore a wide flannelette bandage secured by a red safety-pin, and Hedges, noticing it, thought he had never seen a red safety-pin before.

"As if he'd got five hundred quid anyway." The voice came from Brush's chest. It was a toneless whisper, very

221

quiet, like talk on a badly tuned radio. "Hedges, your great mistake, and why you're so dangerous, is because you ask for total explanations whereas the rational mind, like mine, is content to improvise."

Hedges opened the sash-window a couple of inches, removed a pair of shoes from a chair, and sat down. He was content to listen and watch with clinical interest. To him Brush was more dead than, say, Captain Charles was to his father. Captain Charles had been blown up by a Turkish mine in Gallipoli, but so far as Hedges senior was concerned he was still buying horses outside Colchester; and Hedges could think of Brush in no such bright limbo, even though he was sitting on the other side of the table and words flowed from him. It was the clay giving tongue.

"I'm going to Italy after Christmas. I can't stand this climate with a cut throat. I've got an advance from a publisher. Seven-fifty. When February comes round, the majesty of the law will despoil you of your five hundred quid. So why don't you ring up the sodding police-station and suggest they take my passport away? You'd be within your rights."

If Nell had been there, she would have told this zombie he ought to have a shave and that he was absurd to hope she would ever go back to him. Hedges could imagine her turning to him and saying, "Why don't you make him see that he's got to divorce me?" As if a corpse could divorce anyone.

When a zombie stopped talking and dancing, you put him in a box until the next ceremony. But could you imagine Brush in a box in that top-floor bedroom, right over his father's head, placed on top, perhaps, of that single divan bed with built-in bookshelves on two sides full of old

Strand magazines and *Argosy* magazines and a complete history of the 1914–18 war in pictures? Better let him stay here.

Hedges took a half bottle of whisky out of his pocket and laid it on the table; Bell's Extra-Special 70 Proof Scotch. His father had a story about one of the Irish labourers who built the loop railway. A rock fell on his head, killed him, and as the family wanted the body back in Ireland his mates washed it in whisky for the journey; and at that the man sat up and was never better in his life. But that was Irish whisky. Hedges pushed the bottle of Bell's Extra-Special Scotch with his index finger.

"There isn't a publisher in the country would give you seven hundred and fifty brass farthings."

Brush said he still couldn't get used to the idea that Hedges really would have stuck him like a pig, him a man in his cups, a harmless tosspot if ever there was one. But he wasn't a man to bear a grudge.

Hedges shrugged. All the time he was watching Brush narrowly, as though for the first sign of some corporeal change. "It's an extraordinary situation for you to be in, sitting there and talking to your murderer."

"As I say, I'm not one to bear a grudge. I was never a dangerous man. I lived from one opportunity to the next. I am of an essentially easy-going and luxurious nature. You are different. You force things into a pattern. You are too much taken up with truth and explanations. You are like the religious persecutors, and the cruel men in history, and the mad, wet, floundering monsters who rise up and devour everybody. You'd have castrated me if only you could have got your pals to hold me down. That's what you really wanted. You've a cold and vindictive mind. If a man does

223

me an injury, I forget it. But you—" Brush picked up the bottle of whisky and hurled it against the wall, where it exploded aromatically.

Hedges looked at the broken glass and the wet and spoke reflectively "To be quite honest, the idea of emasculating you never occurred to me."

"Get out!"

"I'll look in next Wednesday. And if you should want me——"

"You put Toplis up to this!"

Brush moved so that the light fell across his face from a different angle. He had not shaved for a week. Hedges told him his name now fitted his face and that, on the whole, it was a good thing he was dead because, really, standing there like a wounded orang-outang with a flannelette bandage round his throat and the knowledge that he had no income but National Assistance, it would have been hard to see what he had to live for. As for putting Toplis up to anything, this was rubbish. And if Brush really wanted to know, Nell had been so sickened by the way he ate sausages that she had decided to leave him anyway, and her real ambition had been to come back to him, Ian Hedges, the man she had first married. But he'd told her to go to hell.

There was no need to tell Brush to go to hell. Judging by the expression on his face, he was already in it. It would have been terrible to talk like this to the living.

The weekly meeting of the Education Committee ended early and Supple, the Chairman, asked Hedges whether they could have a private word. Would Hedges like to go up to the house and have a drink? There was enough light in the mild December afternoon for the vapour to be seen rising from the spongy earth, the laurels and cypresses, the drifts of chestnut-leaves lying like so much sodden breakfast cereal where the wind had blown them under the privet hedge in Supple's front garden.

"Hedges!" Supple began hammering the arms of his chair as soon as they were seated in front of the Magicoal electric fire in a sitting-room where the two dominant pictures were of cardinals boisterously feasting and drinking. "Have you ever thought of promotion, my boy? How many years have you been doing this job—and doing it very well, if I may say so—in this town? I know the temptation to stay in one spot. But the world is not what it was. Take Northumberland, for example. This Government development scheme for the north-east will make this one of the most dynamic parts of the country. Or what about Australia?"

"I'm not really an ambitious man, Mr. Supple."

"Well, what'll you have to drink, my boy?" He pressed a button on what appeared to be an upright piano, and the front shot up to reveal the bottles and glasses within. "And how's your dad? A splendid old gentleman! I saw in the paper that a man of ninety-four had emigrated to New Zealand. Soda or water?"

"I've no intention of leaving Perstowe. What I will do, if you like, is resign from the University Committee."

"Ah, dear boy!" Supple began shaking his head and gobbling. "This is the least of it! This is the least of it! Look at it from the official point of view. You're not a young man! You're not in your twenties. You're at years of discretion."

"In any case, the university wasn't my idea. I pinched it from old Styles. He's the father of Miss Styles who teaches at St. John's. Know her?"

Supple gobbled, clucked, and bounced up and down

behind his big, stuffed Bayeux-tapestry-decorated chair. *"Do I know*—but that's what. . . ."

Hedges drank his whisky off at a draught and held his glass out for more. "I can see now that I'm not really committed to this university idea in the way I should be. At the time it served its purpose."

"Purpose?"

"Do you know what a herring-gull does when it's interrupted at its feed by another herring-gull from another colony?"

"What? You mean on the telly?"

"Well, what happens?"

"I don't watch these bird films."

"There are various possibilities. The first herring-gull can either attack the second herring-gull. Or it can run away."

"Yes, but I'm not really interested in nature, old chap."

"I'm trying to make a point. Sometimes the first gull doesn't either attack or run away. The two impulses seem to cancel each other out. But he's got to do something, you see? Do you know what the first herring-gull does?"

"No, I bloody well don't."

"He pulls up bits of grass just as though he's making a nest. He's not really making a nest. It isn't a genuine activity at all, it's a kind of nervous reaction, because the only genuine activity a herring-gull goes in for is eating and copulating."

"And flying," said Supple.

"This bogus nest-building is what naturalists call a displacement-activity, and my view of the Committee for the Promotion of Perstowe University is that very largely it was Hedges's displacement-activity. So, it's time for me to pull out. Or take rats."

"Look, Hedges, I thought we'd get together in a friendly, unofficial sort of way—that's why I brought you here—to talk about your position. I don't know how we got on to this talk about birds and rats. How d'you mean, *take* rats?"

"When a rat is feeding and it's disturbed by a strange rat, it's quite likely to stop feeding and wash its face with its little paws. This is a substitute for actually chasing after the strange rat. See what I mean?"

"Yes, yes, yes, yes, of course I see what you mean. But we're not herring-gulls or rats."

"Yes, we are, Mr. Supple. Art, religion, founding universities—everything that is not directly to do with eating and breathing and sex is one big displacement-activity. The concept of God the Loving Father is the human equivalent of the rat grooming its face with its forepaws——"

"That's what I'd call a bit blasphemous."

"And another thing." Hedges realized he could not talk seriously when sitting. He stood up and walked about, looking at the cardinal pictures, touching them and finding they were real knobbly oil paint, inspecting a plaster duck in full flight across one of the walls. "If you remove the eggs from the nest of a black-headed gull, it preens itself like mad. That's what I was doing. This talk about Perstowe University as a means of building the New Jerusalem was a way of preening myself, just like the black-headed gull. But what, you might ask, are my eggs and who took them away. Who took away my full clutch?"

"No," said Supple. "As Chairman of——"

"Mr. Supple, did you know I'd had to divorce my wife?"

"All right, all right." Supple was getting very angry. "You're telling me you interested yourself in the university as a way of making up for your wife. It's all rubbish. Let's get back to what you were saying about religion. Man is not a bird or a rat. Man is a religious animal. I don't believe his religion is some kind of mechanical response. Are you trying to tell me that, eh? It's all clockwork, eh? Who made the clockwork, eh? Tell me that!"

"I'm trying to explain why I'm resigning from the committee. I don't want to get into a religious argument."

"Tell me who made the clockwork!"

"Supple was on his feet, shouting. The door flew open, and a woman with an expression of alarm on her face appeared. "Get out!" Supple howled at her. She disappeared. He turned to Hedges, his upper lip coiling like a serpent. "You the Education Officer in charge of the young minds of this town, and you believe that man's vision of his destiny is just no more than a scratching of his behind because it itches. You're not fit for your office."

"Look, I do not believe in mechanist explanations, and I am making no attack whatsoever on religion."

"Oh!" Mr. Supple calmed down very quickly because he suspected he had made a fool of himself. "Then what *was* you attacking?"

Hedges smiled, lifted his empty glass. "D'you mind?"

"Help yourself, my boy," said Supple gruffly.

"If you take the gut of a lug-worm and put it in a saucer of sea-water, you'll see it goes on working even if the rest of the body is not attached and telling it what to do. It goes on working without any external stimulus. Built into it there must be some innate disposition to work. In the human animal it may well be there is an innate disposition to worship."

"That's all right, then," said Supple.

"But I didn't want to talk about religion. I was explaining why I didn't feel entitled to go on with the University Committee thing. I thought I wanted to start a university, but all the time I really wanted to kill the man who had seduced my wife."

At heart Mr. Supple was a generous, eager puppy-dog of a man, and he was now wagging his tail vigorously. He wanted to show he had overstepped the mark when saying Hedges wasn't fit for his job; he wanted, too, to show appreciation of the information about the lug-worm. "As a matter of fact, it isn't——"

"I'd even got to the point," said Hedges, "of believing that what the university wanted was a human sacrifice. I did not realize this was a rationalization of my wanting to kill Brush."

Mr. Supple nodded and walked seriously up and down with his hands behind his back. "I didn't want to talk to you about the university at all, as a matter of fact, Hedges."

"Indeed! You should have stopped me——"

"Supple raised a hand. "It's this Miss Styles, the teacher who is going to have a baby. Do you think this is a case where we can insist on Saundersfoot's early retirement? He's nearly fifty-eight. Not much pension loss there."

"What d'you mean, early retirement? Why should Saundersfoot retire?"

"Well, I mean, there's this baby and he can't marry her and there's Mrs. Saundersfoot to think of, poor dear. I mean, I wouldn't at this stage of his pensionable service like to ask for a man's dismissal on moral grounds, would you?"

"No."

"Perhaps *they* could go to Northumberland. They're climbers, aren't they? They'd be nearer the mountains."

"I am the father of Miss Styles's baby."

Supple looked at him sharply. "You? I don't believe it.

Must be a married man. No other explanation for her behaviour possible. If you was her paramour why don't she marry you? I've heard all that gossip, too. Saundersfoot must go! If an older man can give advice, never father another man's by-blow." Supple reached up—he was some nine inches shorter than Hedges—and placed his hands on his shoulders. He looked very cunning. "Going back to what you were saying earlier, about birds and rats and that, wouldn't marrying this girl be a very good example of what you were explaining to me?"

"Displacement-activity? Not at all. Miss Styles and I took to each other quite violently one afternoon last August, and if there's one thing the natural scientists are agreed on it is that sex itself is not a displacement-activity. It is what is displaced. Sex is what is known as a consummatory situation. That is what we did last August. We consummated."

"Why won't she marry you?"

"I don't know. I don't understand her. I love her."

"Perhaps I shall be able to think of an explanation," said Supple. He took his hands away from Hedges's shoulders and massaged them for rheumatism, cracking the joints painfully.

"Since I did Brush's business for him at Lack Hall, I've been through a real process of purgation. I've got to get out of this university thing."

Supple opened and closed his hands rhythmically. "You still ought to think of applying for those jobs in Northumberland. Perstowe will miss you, but they tell me the air is very bracing up there. There's the Roman Wall to walk along, you with your interest in birds. Or there's Australia. A man with your range of knowledge and ability owes it to himself to get on, I say, and he should never turn his back on advancement."

A smell of roast meat drifted from the kitchen, and Hedges, who had drunk six ounces of whisky to no effect, now felt hungry. Supple offered to run him back in the car, but he said no, he would like to take the air. He liked being alone these days, just thinking. At long last he had arrived at the basic truth about himself, and he liked exploring it, as he might explore the surface of some mass of granite on the shore when the tide swilled round it and the occasional bigger wave dashed spray into the air.

Every time he saw Prudence, she seemed more and more dignified and sure of herself. They had become a bit formal with one another. Their relationship was of the utmost respectability. They never went so far as to shake hands, but they certainly sat in front of a coal fire with a tray of tea between them, talking about serious subjects like the education of women. The only emotional outbursts came when Prudence read him chapters from the novel she was writing. It was about a girl called Lorna Grandison who lived her life with the kind of ruthlessness she imagined most men were capable of (Prudence said) but rarely lived up to. What Hedges noticed was that she seemed to be a great seducer of young men. He said she sounded like a nymphomaniac to him. This made Prudence angry. She said a publisher had given her a hundred pounds' advance on the strength of four chapters and a synopsis, and Hedges said he was not surprised. It irked him to realize that after all his soul-cleansing he still had the sneaking belief that life was a system of trials and rewards; and that Prudence, who was the Great Reward in his eyes, should not only go on refusing to marry him but actually bore herself as though she might go away from Perstowe and set herself up as the George Sand of the nineteen-seventies when all the time she had his child in her womb. He could never have led a really promiscuous life. He wasn't generous enough. All the time he would have been haunted by the thought of not being able to claim possession of the children.

Hedges went straight to Mythe Hill from the conversation with Supple. He caught a bus from the station-yard because his legs felt wobbly after the mile and a half of hard trotting he had given himself; and the bus rose like a bumble-bee in the blackness, so that Hedges, looking out through a little panel he had cleared in the steamed-up window, could see the lights of the town fall back. He hadn't been fooled by Supple. The next step by the Education Committee would be to instruct him to dismiss this pregnant schoolmistress, and Hedges wanted to warn her of it. For one thing she might want to write to the National Union of Teachers, and, for another, he had to make it clear that if she said she objected to being dismissed he, as the executive officer of the Committee, would refuse to take action, and the national press, he supposed, would put their photographs on the front page.

As on many a previous occasion, Mrs. Kidwelly stood at her front door like an idol in its niche, implacably awaiting tribute. This time she looked at him for up to half a minute before speaking. "Miss Styles is not here." She turned her head slightly to the right to show that if she was an artifact at least the model worked. "She has gone. She departed the day before yesterday with all her belongings, such as they were. I had to ask her to leave."

"Why?"

"Do you really want me to be explicit, Mr. Hedges?"

"Yes."

"Don't you play games with me, Mr. Hedges. You know better than I do. It was a tremendous shock to me to be told of her condition."

"Who told you?"

"That's just the point. She told me herself. If I had been allowed to discover the truth for myself, it would have been easier to bear. She was quite without shame."

"Where has she gone to?"

"I am surprised you should need to ask me that, Mr. Hedges," she said, closing the door in his face.

At the end of the road was a call-box with the light on, a kiosk of light and (so it seemed) warmth where Hedges stood and examined his small change. His first thought was to ring Brewchester. But if she wasn't there her father would be worried, possibly unnecessarily. In the end Hedges phoned Saundersfoot to ask if Prudence had been at school that day; and Saundersfoot, once he realized who he was talking to, said, Yes, by God she was, and Hedges was the very man he himself now wanted to interview, and would it be convenient if he came up to the house straight away? He sounded angry, in a bitter sort of way.

"Sure you wouldn't like me to come down to you?"

"I'll come to you."

Saundersfoot must have jumped into his car immediately, because when Hedges reached home he was already there, talking in the kitchen to Hedges *père*, who was wearing his old straw boater, dark with the blood of animals eaten long ago, and not really listening to Saundersfoot but stroking a raw steak with the back of his hand. Saundersfoot sprang up as soon as Hedges walked in. He was still wearing his overcoat, a grey, hairy garment that hung below his knees, steaming in the heat thrown out by the old-fashioned cooking-range. Hedges had never seen him so angry, not even in one of those caning sessions which Hedges remembered from his school-days but which Saundersfoot had, on his own confession, now grown out of. "It's no longer the idiom of the times," he was once heard to say. "Besides, the parents take you to court."

"Ian," he now said, "don't you lie to me! I know the truth! You think I'm a grotesque old fool who can be mocked with impunity. Perhaps I am, who knows? But don't you ever think, you in your lusty green youth, that what I and your father are today you will be tomorrow? You'll think of this when some young blade has tied a can to your tail. Or perhaps you won't!"

"What's up, Ted? I'm not a lusty green youth. I'm thirty-nine."

"That young woman"—Saundersfoot was making great gestures, waving his arms, knocking cards off the shelf and a tin of salt off the table—"has told me the truth. It's like being cuckolded."

Mr. Hedges, who was now drawing beer from a barrel in the corner, said, "I'm not like you, Saundersfoot. What d'you mean, as you and me are today, Ian will be tomorrow? My sap doesn't run any more." He lifted the mug to his lips. "I'm drying out at the top."

Saundersfoot said that during the mid-afternoon break he had been going through some papers in his study when he had noticed that Prudence Styles had changed her private address. At that moment she had happened to walk in and, in the conversation that followed, she had told him— she had told him——

"At the Lack Park party," said Saundersfoot, "the

University Appeal party, you accused me of being the father of Miss Styles's child. I shall never forgive you for that. Never! Never!"

"Well, what did she tell you?"

"It isn't me, it's you!"

"Didn't you know?"

"No. I mean, I knew that for my part——"

"I wasn't mocking you, Ted."

"What does it matter? I don't matter in the slightest. It is something to make an old man marvel, but I marvel, Ian, I marvel at the Machiavellian relish with which you have been spreading this report of my sexual prowess—and I would not be ashamed to be as you described me—when all the time you were hugging yourself in cruel glee. You have humiliated me."

"I'm eighteen years older'n you," Mr. Hedges said to Saundersfoot. "That's more'n half a generation. We're not in the same case. Tomorrow, Ian can be like you or he can be like me, but he can't be like both of us. But he's not a boy. He's not a green youth, as you called him."

Saundersfoot ignored all this. "You've got to marry her," he said to Hedges.

"She won't. It's her decision, not mine."

He was sorry he had pulled Saundersfoot's leg, but he could not understand why it had enraged him. Annoyance, yes. But this wounded buffalo was excited to the point of being dangerous. Hedges saw him with blood on his horns, head down, eyes rolling. A false move and he'd toss you!

"I don't believe it."

"She's going to have her baby, she'll be away from school for a couple of months, then she'll put the kid in a day-nursery and go back to teaching. And in your school. She'll fight you, me, the Borough Education Committee, the

County Council, the Ministry of Education, and, if need be, the National Union of Teachers. She is a militant feminist. God help us all, I say!"

"I don't believe it."

"She thinks that but for certain physiological arrangements men and women are much the same."

"I don't believe it."

"That's what her novel is about, and I expect both you and I are in it."

"Ian," said Saundersfoot, with a lonely, self-pitying clank in his voice, "if it had fallen to me—as I won't deny it might—to stand in the same relationship to this woman as you confess you enjoy, I could not, in that role, find it in my heart to jest. She must be aware of the law of libel."

"I doubt it."

"Well, it'll be all lies, lies, lies. I shall deny it and sue her."

"It's made you twenty years younger," said Hedges, "and you've enjoyed every minute of it. You're O.K. I've been scoured, brain-washed, purged, broken, raped, exorcized, given the whole bloody treatment. Of the few natural, good, and meaningful acts of my life, there is one only that still has a glow on it, and that is what Prudence and I did on the floor of her father's sitting room last August. Everything else in my life is a farce and a mockery. This one act is what my life has been for. If this idiot of a girl would marry me, I should know why God created heaven and earth, and the child would be a boy—well, he'll be a boy anyway, that's not what I mean—but she doesn't even take her maternity vitamins, or whatever it is, and get herself examined. Last time I saw her we talked about Ghana. If she goes on rejecting me——"

"She's a nice girl, really," said Saundersfoot, who had

drunk the half pint Mr. Hedges had handed him. "But she doesn't realize the damage she's doing."

"My God, you're right about that!" said Hedges.

Saundersfoot had been damped down by the gush of words and by the beer. "I saw this girl," he said, "like a flower in my wilderness, and all I did—not much more, anyway—was give her toffees, and we talked, you know. It was a great shock when she told me. If I hadn't known the man, it wouldn't have hit me so hard." He turned to the old man who sat in the corner, looking into the fire. "You're quite right, Mr. Hedges. You're older but I feel older—and defeated."

At this, Hedges realized why he had been thinking of Saundersfoot as a buffalo, for now, as he watched the wounded face, he saw a beast retire painfully from the battle that had been raging in its imagination.

"Why don't you take your coat off?"

"No, I must be going."

He drank another half pint, and the sweat came out on his face in rivulets. "When I was a young man, I had an idea for writing a book to prove some theory about history and poetry and the climate of north-west Europe. But now I can't even remember what the theory was. I've still got notes. I could look it up. I could have been somebody, not just a provincial schoolmaster."

"What was the address she went to?" asked Hedges.

"Eh?"

"Prudence. You say she gave you her new address. Do you remember what it was?"

"That's another thing," said Saundersfoot. "She's taken a room with the Peacock family, so I suppose the next we'll learn is that she's turned Communist."

* * *

237

As soon as he saw the Peacocks' house, Hedges thought
he knew why Pru had moved there; it was so small and
overcrowded there was no possibility of seeing her in any
privacy. Little did she know him. He had no secrets. His
mind was open to all, a good, clean mind with no false
reticence—and a happy mind, too, now that it was steri-
lized. They all sat in the living-room of the gaunt, three-
storey red-brick house down by the quay, with a disused
flour-mill on one side and the Saracen's Head on the other,
talking through the December evening about the Perstowe
Silver Band which no longer existed, whether science would
be able to reduce a human being to his chemical constitu-
ents and then restore him again (Peacock said yes), and the
university, which Hedges said held no personal interest for
him because he had now withdrawn from the Promotion
Committee; and, in any case, the idea hadn't been his in the
first place but Mr. Styles's over at Brewchester.

"It's too late now," said Prudence.

The Peacocks were firmly on Prudence's side over
marrying Hedges: Mrs. Peacock because, as she said, there
were the seeds of humiliation in marrying a man who'd
already been tried by one woman and found wanting; and
Peacock said that if Miss Styles didn't want to marry
Hedges that was good enough for him, a woman's independence should be recognized, and if there was any
thought of the child being adopted Mrs. Peacock and he
would be glad to take it into their own family.

They were sitting in a room about ten feet by fifteen
with a television set that was putting out a programme
about the nomads of the Gobi desert, a big coal fire, a
straight-back settee covered in red damask, two armchairs in
the same material, three Windsor chairs, an old-fashioned
treadle sewing-machine and a sideboard with a box of

Christmas crackers on it. Hedges looked about him. Everyone was pinker than normal because of the heat. Prudence had a pile of exercise books on her knee. She was patiently marking them and taking no part in the general conversation, though now and again she detected something in Hedges's remarks which she thought had some personal application and threw it back at him.

Hedges was relaxed and at home. In a sense he had arrived where he had always wanted to arrive: a sense that some disaster had struck, the company of people who knew all about you, even the discreditable bits, and all the time in the world to talk. They could confess to one another. More particularly, he could confess to them. England was not a country that provided many opportunities to confess. Ever since the Reformation, Englishmen had been forced to live with this suppressed need to unburden themselves; as for example, he, Hedges, now unburdened himself by saying that it was a good thing he'd withdrawn from the University Committee because it now struck him that Peacock had been right to expect a School of Dentistry there (what the hell was wrong with a vocational university?): culture and the arts were by-products of people actually earning their livings. But he wouldn't have known how to reconcile this shift with what he'd been preaching about the New Jerusalem.

"I really think," he said, after a commercial for a shampoo which they all, even Prudence, watched attentively, "that if Prudence doesn't marry me it'll be like looking in a mirror and not seeing my own face look back at me. Just the room behind me. But myself not there. Transparent. Evaporated."

"Don't make bids for pity," said Mrs. Peacock. "Don't wallow."

"I've a right. When I think of Prudence it makes me—well, I can bear people lying to me, like the girl in that shampoo ad. I can accept you and the town and the Bomb without squirming. That means I love her."

"Do we make you squirm?" asked Peacock.

"Everything that isn't a perfect geometry makes me squirm. Everything that is not holy makes me squirm. The geometry and the holiness are just something that don't exist. If Prudence would marry me and love me as I love her, then I think—I really do—I should need no other doctrine or vision or secret sign, pattern in the tea-leaves, no drug, no dope, no other consolation until the day I die." He stretched out a hand and put it on a page of fractions. "For God's sake, or the kid's sake, be human."

"No," she said.

"Then what are your plans?"

"I shall go on teaching here until the middle of April. Then I'll go to Brewchester and the baby will be born there. I shall be perfectly all right, don't you worry."

"What are you trying to prove?"

Mrs. Peacock got out the glasses and a bottle of Australian red wine which, she said, had more iron in it than French wine, and her husband rapped at her that she ought to have mulled it with a red-hot poker, wine at this time of the year, and put a pinch of nutmeg in it. However, Peacock took his glass like the rest. Prudence didn't answer Hedges's question, and this caused Hedges to say that whatever she did would seem right in his eyes. When she went to Brewchester he would bring a little ridge tent and camp in the garden. In forty years' time he would still be living in this ridge tent, an unwashed eccentric with a wiry grey beard down to his navel, watching his grandchildren through the runner-beans. He would be found dead in a barrel of apples, with red cheeks themselves like dried January apples, and he would leave a message to be buried in a cave sitting up and facing the sunrise. By that time (he'd be seventy-nine), he'd be wise enough to justify this kind of internment. It was the way kings and seers were buried. Perhaps he was wise enough already. The next scales to fall from his eyes would let him see more than mortal can bear.

"Daddy wouldn't agree to your camping in the garden," said Prudence. "When I go to Daddy's that's the last you'll see of me, I'm afraid."

"You're going to marry this airman."

"I'm not going to marry anyone."

"I've got rights."

"You've got no rights at all, no moral rights, no legal rights. You couldn't *prove* your paternity."

"I thought women were legally insane *after* childbirth, not before," said Hedges, as Prudence went on scrutinizing a succession of maps to show the rivers and mountains of Europe and periodically, with her blue pencil, putting crosses and question-marks and ticks that, Hedges felt, ought to be fed into a computer and wired for electronic sound—when what would emerge but the music of the spheres? She was crazy but she was adorable.

He had to make some show of anger.

"It'll make an interesting case, that, me trying to enforce my paternity rights. I'd take it right up to the House of Lords."

Peacock followed Hedges out into the street, pulling on his army greatcoat. They walked downhill, towards the water, smelling the night air.

"The nearest you can get to a virgin birth," said Hedges, "is with the help of a test-tube, but I must say this lark runs it pretty close."

"Don't talk like that," Peacock begged.

"She really wants to marry her dad. Once she gets settled at Brewchester with her dad and the nipper, that's what it'll seem like."

"Thought you might like to go out in my boat," said Peacock.

"That just about makes her old man God the Father."

Peacock led the way down some steps, and Hedges did not come to—he was wrapped up in theology—until Peacock began pulling on a rope and a small rowing-boat swam towards them out of the gloom. The tide was at the full, and bits of orange peel, straw, and a couple of bottles bobbed in the light of a gas-lamp that bubbled on a bracket at the head of the stairs.

"Always had a boat in the family," said Peacock. "Earliest thing I remember was going out in a boat with my grandfather. He pulled up a bloody great box from the river-bed, and when he opened it it was full of elvers. That's my first memory. I was three. That was up-stream, a way in the sweet water, above the tidal flow and the salt. I take this boat out on summer evenings and just think."

"You don't mean that we're going out in that boat?"

"The point is," said Peacock, "that nobody's looking over your shoulder. There are no microphones out in the estuary, d'you know?"

Hedges shrugged. He clambered down and sat in the stern. What great secret was Peacock going to tell him? Vapour rose from the oily water, and a couple of minutes later, as Peacock rowed out into the night, the gas-light on the shore yellowed, turned amber, and was finally extinguished behind the curtains of mist. The town was a vague glow. Peacock let the boat glide, the blades of his oars spluttering in the water. Hedges did up the top button of his overcoat.

"She's all right," said Peacock.

"Who?"

"You've got nothing to worry about."

Hedges sat tight and said nothing. Now that Peacock had stopped rowing, the boat was pitching in a way that Hedges found very disagreeable, the more so as he could not see the surface of the water and couldn't anticipate the movement. There was, he supposed, a good chance of their being run down.

"I think she's very fond of you, really," said Peacock.

"You've brought me out here to tell me that?"

"I didn't want my wife to hear."

"I ought to be getting home."

"O.K." said Peacock, and he began plying his oars again. He turned the boat in its own length. "My wife would be very cross if she knew I was telling you this, but my view is that Miss Styles is very fond of you indeed."

"Why should your wife be cross about you telling me that?"

"Because Miss Styles would be cross. This solidarity I can both understand and respect. They've made up their minds that you're not going to exploit the fact that Miss Styles is a woman, with all the bodily processes of a woman."

"I don't know what you're talking about."

"I quite agree," said Peacock. "Women can be bloody funny."

"I don't want to exploit anyone."

243

"She's crazy about you, and if it wasn't for this baby she'd marry you tomorrow."

Peacock went on rowing until he asked Hedges whether he could see a light, and Hedges said no, he'd never seen anything so black. Peacock said that meant there was a tide running, though they hadn't been able to feel it, and maybe they were on their way to the open sea. Or they might fetch up on those mud banks below the gas-works. Hedges offered to take a turn at the oars, but Peacock said there was a good chance of their going overboard if they tried changing places now. So Hedges said it was all very like life—Peacock rowing away without too many thoughts in his head, because the physical effort didn't give him time for them, whereas he, Hedges, sat and meditated. All around was blackness, and they didn't know whether they were coming or going.

Peacock became so interested in this that he stopped rowing and said he was ready to accept this description of life. Anybody who sat on his arse and just meditated was something less than human. That's how a lot of this neurosis started.

"Unless you sit and think, how do you know what it all means?"

"What?"

"Life."

"It don't have any meaning, does it, unless you're acting and doing? I'm a socially minded electrician. What my life means is being a good socialist and a good electrician. And a good father and husband. All that."

"If you were deaf, dumb, blind, paralysed from the waist down, and fed by tubes, life would be meaningless?"

Peacock thought for a few moments. "I couldn't stand that."

"What you've said is that a man only exists by virtue of the part he plays in life. But what if he plays no part?"

"I'd want to be put out of my misery."

"But human beings aren't just functional."

"Look, Mr. Hedges. I thought I'd row you out here and do you a good turn. I didn't know you wanted to get into a political argument. We could have done that at home. Anyway, you've got to be practical. You've got to look at the real world."

"I wouldn't know it if I saw it."

"O.K. I'd go part of the way with you in that. There is no reality. There's only the way we respond to the different conditions we find ourselves in."

"I don't believe that," said Hedges.

"That's the way I look at it. I don't want to look up my own backside and I don't want to try."

The oars squeaked in the rowlocks again, and after some minutes of rowing Peacock asked once more whether Hedges could see any lights. Hedges said no. Peacock began swearing and said that by now he didn't know whether he was rowing north, south, east, or west.

"What's it matter to you, so long as you're rowing?" said Hedges unfairly.

If Prudence married him, he'd go along with Peacock to the extent of agreeing he wanted to be a good husband and father; but if she went on saying no he would turn fakir and stand on one leg for forty years gazing at the sun. Was this what lay at the middle of the onion?

He gripped the side of the boat and shouted, "Put your back into it!"

For a moment Peacock looked up at the black mass that seemed about to fall on them. Then he dragged abruptly at the oars. He scrabbled about with his feet for something firm to press against. He found one of Hedges's feet, the one Prudence had pierced with her stiletto heel, and tensed the whole weight of his body against it. Hedges snarled with pain. The tug charged past, reeking of oil and boiled blankets, men shouting, a blur of lights, and belatedly a blast on the siren. The rowing-boat twirled in its wake.

"If only I knew whether she was going upstream or downstream," said Peacock, "I'd know which bank to row for."

"Downstream."

"You think so?"

Peacock released Hedges's foot and rowed into the blackness once more. "I'm sorry about this. Wouldn't've come if I'd realized it was so thick."

Hedges's foot throbbed and seemed to be bleeding into his shoe, but he knew that it was impossible; it must be some trick of the nervous system. He wasn't going to complain. If he walked home paddling in blood he wouldn't complain. The main thing was to stand on dry land and be in a position to walk home.

"There's a light straight ahead."

"I owe you an apology," said Peacock.

"As long as you don't row me up the town sewer."

The boat stopped suddenly and Peacock went on, finishing on his back with his legs in the air. There was a smell of coal-gas. As soon as Peacock had picked himself up, Hedges said they were all right now because he was pretty sure they were near the gas-works; but Peacock was groaning and swearing. He said they'd run aground and, what the hell, he'd had enough of rowing and now they could get out and walk.

He was as good as his word and plopped overboard.

"O.K. She's wedged on the old quay. It's always a

couple of feet under high water. You'll have to get out and walk, Mr. Hedges. Watch it, now! Steady!"

They were, both of them, standing up to their thighs in water, and so far as Hedges was concerned he might have been standing on his stumps on an ice floe. There was no feeling from a point six inches above the knee, not even from the mauled foot. It already seemed that Peacock and he had been standing in this freezing brine for hours. They were trying to lift the boat. The boat was wedged in some way and they were trying to lift it. Which circle of hell was this? What were they doing there? Why had Peacock taken him on the river? Sheer bloody vanity!

"Just drag her on to the quay and we can leave her," said Peacock. "Together, now!"

Hedges had bent to get a grip of the boat. He heaved, and it rose so easily that his feet must have skidded. Anyway, they took the lead in a shallow dive that took him actually under the boat, because in the numbing black brine that he was now breathing instead of air its restraining weight lay on his chest. Peacock must have grabbed a leg, for he came uphead last.

"She's O.K. She's afloat," said Peacock. "You all right?"

Hedges didn't answer, and Peacock said he'd paid eighteen pounds ten for the boat, which wasn't bad considering it was only three years old and tight as a drum—not a drop of water had he ever seen in her, except what came over the gunwale. It would have been a pity to lose her.

A few minutes later they had found a bollard to sling a rope over and were walking, sodden and numb, through the gas-works. Hedges paused to allow a half a pint of salt water to pour out of his mouth and nose. Lamps hung above their heads like amber footballs, and by their light pyramids of coal and coke could be seen steaming.

"It's my belief there's still salmon in the river, and one night you and me's going out with a good torch and a net to see."

"That's poaching."

"Them laws," said Peacock, "have fallen into desuetude."

Peacock tried to persuade Hedges to go back to his house for a change of clothes, and this time he'd get his wife to put a hot poker into that Australian wine. But Hedges said he was warmer now. He'd go straight home.

Peacock examined him in the light of a street lamp. "You look like the Old Man of the Sea. Come and have a rub-down in front of the kitchen fire."

"I'm fine."

"Miss Styles was to see you like that, it'd bring out a bit of human feeling, I reckon. Nice, but proud. See what I mean? She's a woman, though, and she's going to be a mother. It would bring out the concern in her, to see you."

Hedges was so numb and wretched he could not even utter.

"If you like," said Peacock, "I'll say you tried to commit suicide."

Hedges would not even pass Peacock's front door with him but kept steadily on up Silver Street, having told Peacock that he would pick up a taxi at the station. It was still quite early and there were lots of people about. Although the shops were shut, some of them—the radio and TV shops, the furniture stores, the chain grocers—still had their lights on, and there were the usual buses and cars. Hedges was wearing a dark overcoat, buttoned at the throat, dark trousers, and black shoes. The fact that they were sodden went unnoticed. A policeman, looking like a bat in his cape, glanced at him and walked off into the neon-irradiated mist.

Hedges watched him go and thought what a lot you had to do to provoke a policeman these days. How would it be if he started singing and held out his cap? He hadn't a cap. He'd nothing to beg with. There was a certain caste in India. At the sort of age he, Hedges, had now arrived at, and irrespective of wealth and importance, a member of this caste might abandon everything: family, possessions, position. He would go out with his begging bowl. He would consult with himself and the gods what it was to be human.

He was pleasantly warm. That was odd. Even his foot wasn't hurting. He walked through the Market Square with such a glow on him that he didn't make for the station and the taxi rank. Instead, he found himself putting one foot before the other and giving out such a heat that his clothes steamed and stank like a laundry.

Marvellous. He was either developing pneumonia or having an Experience. That is to say, there was either a physical explanation for the way he went along without quite touching the ground, or his psyche was breaking loose. He saw these alternatives clearly. He plumped for the abnormal because he couldn't see how any bug could have got a hold on him in the short time since he fell in the river. Or was it the static lightning? Peacock talking about the elvers had reminded him of it. When Peacock's grandfather was dragging up that box from the river-bed, Hedges was gazing from his bedroom window at the electric storm; he saw the ball of shining fog float ever so slowly along the other side of the street. His mother was excited and said it was a ball of static lightning. It was so rare most people hadn't even heard of it, much less seen it. But her little boy had seen it. If it hit you it would kill you. This particular ball of fire touched a lamp post about three feet from the ground and rose slowly until it balanced on the very top of the lamp itself. Silently, it vanished. Now, at the age of thirty-nine, the lightning had caught up with him. He walked in the ball of fire. The feeling was that at last he could stop fighting. He surrendered. He gave. He had no anxiety any more. He gave. He couldn't be hurt. He floated and gave, like a cloud breathing out light.

Lights in upstairs windows and the face of the town clock looked back at him. A surprise. The town clock was not a face; it was an eye and it winked. Hedges turned and retraced his steps. He walked exactly as he had walked before, and the clock winked for a second time as a chimney came between. The town, with its lights, chimneys, roof-tops running this way and that in the smoking night; all the three spires of St. Mary's, St. Michael's on the Hill, and St. Winifrede's–Without; the two cupolas of the Station Hotel and Magg's Bazaar; the shadow in the valley, and the air so thin on Mythe Hill you could see the moon and the fleeces lying over the river and the marshes—all this man-, woman-, and child-infested interlacing of brick, metal, and air spread itself. It gathered round his heart.

The town that has been so boring becomes interesting just at the moment you clear out in your train or your fast car. The man digging in his allotment, the window-cleaner with his yellow ladder, the schoolmaster in the playground with his whistle and children rush after you. They are alive in a way they were not alive before. Hedges wasn't leaving, though. It was just a manner of speaking. He was ready to take them all in his arms.

The colours were extraordinarily eloquent. The green of the traffic signals shone out like a fiery green bush. Faces had vermilion lamps behind them. This was what you saw if you took mescalin, so maybe, he thought, he was ill after all. Maybe all this heat meant he had a temperature of a hundred and four. He wasn't concerned. He walked on, relaxed, saying good night to a few people, none of whom he knew, and thinking this was not just an experience to go though: he ought to act on it. He couldn't bear any more revelation.

CHAPTER EIGHT

◈◈◈◈◈◈◈◈◈◈◈◈◈◈◈◈◈◈◈◈

The Blessing

A January morning Hedges went into his father's room with a cup of tea and found him, still in his pyjamas, lying on the floor. He couldn't have been there long, because he felt warm and the room itself was icy. His eyes were wide and unwinkingly open, and blue, blue, blue. Hedges was surprised by those eyes. They were blue like paint.

"Move me, move me, move me," the old man kept muttering out of one side of his mouth. Hedges tried to lift him, but he was too heavy.

"Can't you help yourself?" he asked.

He put a pillow under his head and covered him with blankets. Fergusson was still having breakfast, and when Hedges described the symptoms to him on the telephone he said he would come round before surgery. Within the hour Mr. Hedges was in a hospital bed. He looked clean, calm, blue-eyed like a child, but silvered on the chin and cheeks. His beard was whiter than his hair. Fergusson said he'd had a stroke.

Hedges went again in the afternoon, and the old man who could do nothing for himself, except talk indistinctly out of one side of the mouth, said, "Thou shalt not uncover thy father's nakedness," as Hedges did precisely this to insert a urine bottle. A nurse stood by with a feeding cup, but Hedges took it from her. He put the spout between his father's teeth. A certain amount of Benger's Food was sucked in before the old man said, firmly, brandy made it palatable. Couldn't he have some brandy? Or whisky? It'd take the fur out of his mouth.

Hedges went morning and evening. His father had the end bed, the one nearest the door, in a ward where three of the beds had screens round them. In the others men were reading papers, listening to the Light Programme on ear-phones, staring or trying to sleep. Mr. Hedges said he was the oldest chap in the ward by a good three years. This pleased him because he would not have liked to be put with a lot of old people. King Edward's funeral, he said one evening. Another day it was Andy White.

The old man couldn't tell the story himself, so Hedges went through it for him. Three of them, Tony Walsh, Ted Sharp, and he, caught the train that got them to Paddington by about ten-thirty in the evening. They went down to Piccadilly and slept on the pavement outside Green Park, but it was so hot that it was no hardship. In the funeral procession they saw the Kaiser on a grey horse and the Russian Grand Duke who looked like George V's brother. There were emperors and kings in the sun and dust. The King of Spain, the King of Portugal, the King of Greece, the King of Belgium. People were going down smack on their faces. Fainting in the heat. He could hear the harness jingling now and the wheels grinding. A black gelding pissed. The new king on a dark chestnut. London stank like a stable.

"Sailor, gun-carriage," said Mr. Hedges.

"You took your tie off and carried your jacket over your arm. Your shirt stuck to you."

"Very hot," said Mr. Hedges. "Stretchers in the shade."

Next day it was Andy White. He lost his nerve and ran out of the line. Hedges told his father how Captain Welsh said, "Where's White, where's White? If you see White, put a bullet in him, eh? A coward in the face of the enemy." Well, Welsh himself was killed half an hour later. They saw White looking up at them out of a ditch, and the lads just went by. "In nineteen twenty-one you went up to the Christmas Fat Stock Show at Smithfield, and who should you see but Andy White on point-duty at Oxford Circus. Then you remembered he'd been a copper before he joined up. You went up to him and said, 'Hallo, Andy,' and you shook hands."

"Wouldn't take no stripes," said Mr. Hedges slowly.

"You wanted to be one of the boys. You didn't join up until January, nineteen fifteen, because you wanted Christmas at home."

"River."

"That was the summer of 'seventeen, and the adjutant offered a sovereign to the first who'd swim a river, just for the fun of it. You and the sergeant-major swam over and stood on the other bank, naked, shaking hands. You were always a good swimmer. And Colonel Quinn asked you to ride his horse down from Windsor barracks to some camp on Salisbury Plain. You got lost. In March, nineteen eighteen, they put you down for a Military Medal, but it went to a man called Swallow who married a German woman when you got to Cologne."

The old man listened intently to all this. He made a few cracks. Put his pants at the end of the bed, and he'd be in them and out of this ward. This was what Hedges under-

stood him to say. But his main interest was the war stories.
Hedges had known them all his life. Why was it men of the
'14–'18 war had this obsession? It was rare to come across a
'39–'45 veteran who dwelt on his experiences in quite the
same way. Perhaps the difference lay in the wars. In the
Kaiser's war the great division was not between the Central
Powers and the Allies. It was between soldiers and civilians.
The soldiers were never going to let you forget it.

The middle of the afternoon, he was phoned at the
office and told his father had taken a turn for the worse.
Hedges went round and found that he had developed
pneumonia and was in an oxygen tent. He breathed noisily
and rapidly. The blue eyes were shut. The sister-in-charge
lifted one of the lids and said, "You see, he doesn't know
anything. He doesn't feel anything."

But Hedges didn't believe her and reminded the old
man of that officer's servant, Rogers, who took a stray dog
into the line with him; it kept barking, and Jerry lobbed
over so much stuff that Prescott—he was a corporal at that
time—said he'd shoot the bloody animal, a sort of fox-
terrier except that he had long ears. Prescott took aim, but
just then Rogers put out his foot. His foot was smashed. He
went to the hospital and took the dog with him. Prescott
was killed in March of that year. "Where did Rogers find a
stray dog in the front line?" Hedges asked; but the old man
just went on fighting in the tent. Seventy-five last Sep-
tember.

Hedges couldn't bear the sound of this fighting. He
didn't want the old man to see him crying, so he went out
of the ward and lay on a bench in what he thought was an
empty waiting-room until he noticed the thin woman in
black sitting close to the window. She might be thin and
pale, but there was something very tough about her. Hedges

noticed the strong hands. She wore no ring. It occurred to him she was Death and at any moment she would go out of this waiting-room to collect his father.

If he'd been through his father's war he might have been tougher-minded in the William James sense (according to Brush). That is, he might have been readier to take life as it came. He could never have been like Brush, though. He could never have been so contemptuously amused by a bit of high-mindedness. Brush had been right. The high-mindedness concealed a murderous intent. Even the Kaiser's war wouldn't have given Hedges that shrewdness, but it might have spared him the embarrassment of loving women who didn't love him and asking stupid questions of parsons in trains or urging himself on this never-ending hunt for something Peacock described as trying to run up your own backside. His own very ordinary adventures as an ack-ack captain in the Hitler war were nothing to the mysterious terror the men of his father's generation came back from. They seemed to be talking about it all the time. They weren't, really. They made too many jokes. But they spoke out of an experience the civilians couldn't quite understand. Survivors of the concentration camps, they spoke out of an experience the rest of us couldn't quite understand either. Perhaps this was all a human being was left to aspire to: to be Lazarus.

The thin woman was still sitting close to the window, so Hedges went back to the ward, where the sister said his father might go on for days like this, and it would be only sensible if he went home and got some rest himself. If there was any change they would phone. Hedges put his hand under the plastic drape and felt his father's hand, wet and firm. The old man was fighting hard, and it came into

Hedges's mind to say out loud that this time the enemy wasn't the Kaiser and he wasn't worth fighting, not if it cost what it seemed to be costing. He pulled this hand out and kissed it.

There was a light in the kitchen when he reached home. He walked in to find Prudence, in a red and white check apron, peeling potatoes. Through the open door there was sight of a suitcase in the hall.

"How is he?" she asked.

Hedges shrugged. "How did you get in?"

"I climbed through the window."

She had peeled three potatoes and was tackling a fourth when Hedges stopped her. "One potato's enough for me, and I don't suppose you can manage more than two. What are we doing for meat?"

Prudence said she'd found some chops in the larder. Hedges nodded and went out to inspect her suitcase. He didn't ask what all this meant. He hadn't told her about his father's illness, but Amos had put a piece in the paper. So perhaps Pru had learned that way.

He went back into the kitchen and stood just behind her. "I can't eat anything. He's dying."

"I can't eat anything, either." Five months pregnant and looking it. "I thought you'd like a meal." After a pause, she turned. "I've come to live here now, if you like. We can get married."

What did Lazarus say to this? Hedges kissed her, but he could think of nothing at all to say. He still did not understand why she had come. He loved her, but he didn't want her that particular night. He would have liked her to go. He wanted, for that one night, to be alone.

"I've treated you badly," she said.

He took her suitcase up to the top bedroom, but the bed was stripped and the window had been left wide open. Even if he could find aired sheets and blankets, the mattress might be damp. Of course, she could always sleep in his room and he could have his father's bed, but the arrangement was not one that appealed to him. After they had eaten the chops, Hedges explained that she was going into his room and that he would sleep on the settee to be sure of hearing the phone if it rang.

"There's room for both of us in this bed," she said, after she had inspected his room. "We can leave the door open. We'll hear the phone all right if it rings. I'm a light sleeper."

This really dazed Hedges. He watched her unpack the suitcase and put clothes into an empty drawer. Without any self-consciousness she began to undress. She sat on the edge of the bed and removed her shoes and stockings. As though she was alone, she stood and began to drag her dress over her head. Leaning on the chest of drawers, Hedges just stood and watched, feeling very tired, a hundred years old and not exactly defeated but mortally wounded, perhaps, on the field of victory. She was almost as thick across the belly as she was wide. She put on a red dressing-gown, picked up a towel and bare-footed made for the bathroom, leaving Hedges with the realization that what he had thought was the rustle of undergarments in reality was the rain. The wind sprayed it against the window. He thought how it must be driving against the windows of the ward, too.

"What's your father's Christian name?" she asked when she came back. Her face was a scrubbed pink; against it her eyebrows were almost invisible. Her features seemed to have gone. Her pale hair was in a tight net, and her face

258

bobbed beneath it like a toy balloon. She removed her dressing-gown, kicked off her slippers, and slid into bed. Hedges
went and wedged the door open and stood looking down at
her.

"I'll just take my shoes off."

"What's your father's first name?"

"Edgar."

He took off his jacket as well as his shoes and stretched
himself at her side, on top of the bed-clothes but beneath
the counterpane. The bed was so narrow there was only
just room for both of them. He pulled at the light cord and
they lay in the dark, listening to the weather. Her right
shoulder and hip pressed against him, and when he moved
his right hand a couple of inches it fell out of bed. As soon
as she fell asleep he privately decided he would make for the
settee; otherwise one of them was going to finish up on the
floor. Not a flicker of movement from her. She lay on her
back, breathing regularly. He lay on his back, breathing
regularly. After quite a long time of this, Hedges was cold
and uncomfortable. He thought he had a cramp coming
on.

"Pru," he whispered.

"Yes?"

"I just wanted to know if you were awake."

"One synonym I'll never use again is 'sleeping with,' "
she said.

They must have slept because Prudence had to shake
him before he heard the phone ringing, and his first reaction
was to try and shut the noise out so that he could go back to
sleep again. But by the time he had one foot on the floor a
jab of fear had roused him. For a moment he could not
move his tongue and his legs would not support him. He

became aware that he was groaning and tried to stop it. Having pulled the light cord, Prudence now sat up and said, "I'll come down with you."

"Stay here."

Going down the stairs he missed a footing and jarred his right heel. The shock exploded somewhere at the front of his brain and was still confusing him when he had the receiver at his ear.

"Mr. Hedges?"

"Yes?"

"I've got some bad news for you." A woman's voice. The sister on night duty.

"I'll come straight away."

"That's up to you, of course, but now that it's all over I think you'd be much wiser to wait until the morning."

"What time is it?"

"Twenty to three."

He thought for a while. "O.K. I'll come in the morning," he said. "Thank you for ringing." And he hung up.

He did not need to tell Prudence because she was crying already, and the sight of her, hunched up in bed, her head looking big and bald because of the hair-net, enraged him to the point of saying, "Oh, for God's sake! It isn't your father."

Seeing the shock in her face, he apologized and said he didn't know what he was saying. What he had thrown at her, he saw now, was the opposite of the truth. It *was* in fact her father she was crying over. If it had been Hedges's mother and not his father who lay dying, would Prudence have come to the house, cooked his supper, and told him that at long last she had decided to marry him?

"I ought to have stayed at the hospital. But they said it might go on for days."

At the very last, surely, you were entitled to expect—if not some glimpse of the chariot descending—at least a moment to gather the threads of life and offer them up: the horse-dealing, the killing of many beasts and some men, the nudgings into marriage and procreation, the five quid each way on Bahram and surviving the Kaiser's war and Hitler's war. He didn't even know he was dying. So it all meant nothing, really.

Prudence made him put on his heavy woollen dressing-gown and lie at her side under the eiderdown. They kept the light on but did not talk. Hedges stared at the ceiling. His bones ached. Perhaps his own death, when it came, would be so quick he would be unaware of it and he would never get nearer to a real facing of himself than here and now. The identification with his father was so strong he felt he had gone with him. At the same time he knew he was accompanied by a woman and an unborn child.

"Lazarus, come forth," said a voice with such stunning loudness that Hedges himself cried out and sat up suddenly, displacing the eiderdown so that it fell to the floor.

"What's the matter?" said Prudence.

"Didn't you hear that voice?"

"What voice?"

"A hell of a loud voice. You didn't hear it?"

"I didn't hear anything."

He got out of bed and walked excitedly up and down the room, until at last he came and knelt at Prudence's side of the bed and slipped his left arm over her belly and murmured, "It was just as though somebody was here shouting."

"We'll call the baby Edgar."

"It might be a girl."

"Then we'll call her Charlotte."

And it really did seem to Hedges that, after a long interval, his heart began beating again. He could think of his father and the baby, and of Prudence and himself, all four of them calmly. They would all be calm for ever and ever. Whatever happened, they would love each other and so be happy for ever and ever. He believed it. He had complete faith in it.

Somehow they were going to carry his father forward into this happiness.

There was no past. It was all gathered into an upreared wave that broke at the crest in the moment before flooding onward.

Soon after the marriage and not long before Brush's case came up at the Assizes, Hedges received a handwritten note on Athenæum notepaper, saying,

Dear Hedges,

A reckless word in your ear, but then I can't resist it. Often have I thought of that splendid sword fight and your gallantry. I really think it was at that stirring moment the idea of Perstowe University hardened in my mind. I'm not an absolute fool, but I attach importance to the feel of a place, don't you? Did you notice the white scar just to the right (as you are looking at me) of my mouth? I too have fought. I was two years at Heidelberg in the 'twenties. You must remind me to tell you. Anyway, you will as Secretary of the Perstowe University Promotion Committee be receiving an official letter in the next day or so to say you're going to have *the bloody thing, and the real purpose of this communication (which I beg you to burn) is that the Powers want action in the life of this parliament, before the General Election campaign gets into gear, and if that means*

262

*students in disused railway coaches that's all right by them
and Dr. Beeching too, if we only had time to ask him. I
address this to you on the assumption the fellow lived and
you've not been hanged or incarcerated. If you'd like sug-
gestions for a Vice-Chancellor I'd be glad to oblige.*

Yours,
Jacob   Bream.

He showed the letter to Prudence, who was still in her
dressing-gown and standing before a pile of washing up. She
said her father had been expecting it and bore no malice.
The Brewchester committee would study the Perstowe
plans and make theirs complementary. If Perstowe went for
the physical sciences they would go for the biological, and
vice versa. He was sure Bream was wrong about the Grants
Committee choosing between Perstowe and Brewchester.
There was going to be a real university explosion. There
might be some advantages in having two new universities
sited fairly near one another; they might even share certain
facilities. And he assumed, anyway, that Perstowe would
make such a mess of their university there might be considerable public demand for another university in the neigh-
bourhood that could profit from its mistakes. Hedges said
that what, in all this, interested him was the information
that the old man bore no malice.

"Anyway, he likes to think he's a founding father of
Perstowe, too."

Hedges kissed her fondly and went off to work. Now
that Prudence had given up teaching, she was able to get on
with her novel. It gave Hedges a glow to think of her
dividing her thoughts between her writing, the housework,
and the state of her pregnancy. What—he thought, as he
drove off into the rain—greater comfort could a husband

have than the knowledge that his wife was dealing with the chores, was physically fulfilled, and had her fantasies disciplined by the requirements of art?

He thought he'd drive to the office via Toplis's place, on the chance that he had not yet left for the works. His route took him up Mythe Hill with fierce wind and rain at his back. But there was still snow on the northern side of Toplis's hedges. The conservatory looked milky against the spinning black clouds but not much more permanent than the snow. Even a February sun, if it could get through this murk, would turn it into vapour.

The door was opened by a red-faced woman with a scarf over her head and a duster in her left hand; but immediately behind her Hedges saw Nell, also in a headscarf and wearing a fluffy yellow jumper and shiny black corduroy trousers. He was so surprised to see her there that he just gaped.

"Gideon's in bed with a chill, if that's who you want," she said. "I don't feel too well myself. This bloody weather. When Gideon's better we're going to Morocco for a month. Like me pants?" By this time he was in the hall, and the Russian peasant woman had closed the door behind him. Nell pirouetted so that he could see how her rear filled out these shiny pants. "Didn't expect to see me up at this time of the morning, eh, boyo?"

"If Toplis is ill I'll clear off. I'd got some news for him, that's all."

The truth was that he had quite forgotten Nell was living with Toplis. No, that wasn't quite right. If he'd been asked where she was these days he would have known the right answer. But the moment that front door swung open and he had seen her standing there, he was surprised and had to go through a process of remembering. It would not have surprised him now if she had told him to clear off. But she was, remembering the hell he'd given her at their last meeting, surprisingly friendly. Perhaps she was just irredeemably stupid.

She led the way up the wide oak stairs and down a passage where the footsteps were silent in the blood-coloured pile and where the radiators gurgled. Toplis was in an expensive modern imitation of a cheap Victorian brass bedstead, with an unlit cigar in his mouth, reading the *Daily Telegraph*. The other bed in the room had an enormous satin shell at its head, and Hedges assumed that this was where Nell spent her nights. He wondered whether Toplis was waiting until they were married before he got a couple of beds that actually matched. It would be just like Toplis to wait. Hedges didn't want to be hard on him. After all, Toplis would need to do something to mark the occasion.

"Hallo, I feel awful," said Toplis, without removing his cigar. When he did, he looked at Hedges over his half-moon reading-glasses and remarked, "I was deeply sorry to hear about your father."

"Thank you," said Hedges.

"He loved butchering, and it's a rare thing nowadays for a man to love his trade. My father once sent some of his sausages to a friend in New York. They were bad when they got there."

"That was before air freight."

"Sure, sure. He made the finest pork sausages I ever tasted. Give me that lighter, will you, dear?" Toplis lit his cigar, and Hedges watched the lines of bitter distaste appear around his mouth. "I haven't shaved, either, and that makes me feel like a monkey. A funny thought's just struck me. This is the first time I've ever seen you two together. Nice couple. Nice people. Makes me wonder what went wrong."

"I apologize," Hedges said to Nell, "for what I said to you about my father."

"What was that?" asked Toplis.

"Let's forget it, shall we?"

Nell sat on her bed and crossed her legs. Hedges noticed for the first time that she was wearing white satin slippers with scarlet heels; but what chiefly struck him about the present moment was that Toplis should have chosen to talk about sausages, and Nell had once told him she objected to the way Brush ate them.

"That's all history," said Nell to Toplis. "He didn't even recognize me just now."

Hedges did not comment.

Nell waggled one of her satin slippers. "You know how you'd have liked it? You'd have liked to come into that hall and look at me rather hard and say, 'I can't remember the name but I never forget a face.'"

Hedges turned to Toplis. "I've had a letter from Bream. But I imagine he's been on the phone to you."

"What about?"

"There's a go-ahead for the university."

"Well I'm damned!" said Toplis.

"He wrote to me because he thought I was still Secretary. It was an unofficial tip-off. The real letter is coming later. Then you'll know what's envisaged exactly."

Toplis put his cigar down saying it was no good, he couldn't smoke the filthy thing. "What do you mean, *you'll* know what's envisaged? I never took your resignation very seriously. As you know, we never appointed your successor."

"It just means nothing to me personally, that's all. I'm delighted the university is going ahead. But it's nothing to do with me personally."

"It isn't because—?" Toplis nodded in Nell's direction. "Good God, no."

Nell began to laugh. "His wife's going to have a baby. Well, she may not be the only one."

"Shut up, girl." Toplis eased himself into a sitting position and revealed gold facings on his blue pyjamas; he looked like a lion-tamer in decline. "You were always such a one for the New Jerusalem."

"I had other problems too."

"I never did like that Moody and Sankey approach. Billy Graham notwithstanding, it just isn't possible any more. Supple swallowed it, but Supple is practically extinct. What with the Bishop of Woolwich and the abolition of resale price maintenance, a God-fearing grocer like Supple will be rubbed into the mud by religionless Christianity and the supermarkets. You were impressive, Hedges, I must admit, when the prophetic mood was on you. What about those students in council-houses?"

"The Kingdom of God is within us; I suppose that's what it comes to."

Toplis stared at Hedges and then rasped away at his unshaven chin with the palm of his hand. "You got Bream's letter with you?"

Hedges handed it over. After he had read it, Toplis lay back and cackled until his upper set broke loose. He made Nell read the letter. "What I always liked about Bream was his sporting instinct. If we'd had a bull in the High Street and Arthur Supple dressed up as a matador, Bream would have seen to it we not only had our university but that in the plans for Armageddon Perstowe was marked down as a Regional Seat of Government. Well, it's a headline: 'Local Government official wins new university with the sword.' "

"Somehow I can't imagine the University Grants Committee attaching that much importance to a bit of sword-play."

"Then you seriously underestimate Jacob Bream, my boy, and what's more you don't know how the world wags. Have you turned religious?"

Toplis was trying to sit up again but Nell pushed him back, took his *Daily Telegraph* away, and said he'd done enough talking for one morning. She could see by the look of him his temperature had gone up a couple of degrees, and if it was religion they now proposed talking about he'd be in for a relapse.

"Quiet, girl, I've made my will and you're provided for," said Toplis. "Have no fear! Did you hear what I asked you, Hedges? Have you turned religious?"

"No."

"Then why do you look so bloody smug?"

"I'm late for the office already." Hedges stood up. "When the official letter from Bream comes, I'll send it on and you'll deal. O.K.? Naturally I'm terribly glad Perstowe is getting its university."

"Terribly nice of you, old boy." This came out as an ironic whinny.

"I'd forgotten that New Jerusalem line. I'd forgotten about the students-in-council-houses idea too. It was all phoney. I mean this talk about a university being an organic part of the community. I was projecting my own problems. I saw myself a bit broken up. I wasn't talking about the town and students and society and all that. I was talking about myself."

"You always did," said Nell.

"Truth seemed important because I'd been deceived, I suppose. But I'm all right, now."

"Jack," added Nell.

"Look," said Hedges, trying not to get angry, even with Nell. He was a man who had learned to enjoy the world aright, the sea in his veins, clothed with the heavens, and crowned with stars. There wasn't much chance of communicating that sort of experience to this pair, but at least he ought not to scream at them. From now on his attitude was going to be relaxed and genial. "Look, it wasn't an unworthy ambition. I've got nothing to be ashamed of. A bit of inflated idealism turns out to be rooted in somebody's disease. Mine. So! I was not disinterested."

"All I ask," said Toplis, "is for you to face up to the fact that you're human like the rest of us."

"I'm not trying to set up as a Guru."

"Whatever that might be." Toplis closed his eyes, and this had the odd effect of making his skull seem a lot smaller. Momentarily Hedges saw him as a shrunken head on a pole. "If your decision is really final, I'd like to thank you on behalf of the citizens of Perstowe. You played no small part in the founding of our university."

"Thank you."

Nell said, "What fascinates me in all this is the way you don't differentiate between the state of your soul and the state of the universe."

Hedges could see she was building up one of her attacks. He remembered the signs. Her eyes were astonishingly wide open, and the wings of her nose quivered. It was like watching an old film and trying to recapture old feelings. But he scarcely took in what she was saying.

"You had one or two nice qualities," Nell said. "Always the orchid in the little cellophane box on our wedding anniversary. But basically you were only interested in yourself. The orchid was given to yourself, really; and the money and the clothes and the show of love, it was all a sort

269

of self-regarding masturbatory exercise that only somebody who was just crazy about himself could go in for. You've got the pride of Lucifer. I suppose it's that I had to get my nails into. You're so proud you patronized me even after we were divorced. I doubt whether anything or anybody is very real to you except what goes on in that swollen ego of yours."

"You don't have to do this, Nell. We're not married any more."

"I just want to justify myself."

"There's no need. I've already let you off the hook. You're in a state of grace. Remember?"

"He talks about the New Jerusalem, and all the time he's really talking about revenging himself on whatever has affronted the splendour of his own psyche. You make me want to throw up. I can forgive you for being such a bore, but what I can't forgive you for is your hypocrisy. I'll bet the first time you had that school-teacher of yours you thought it was mainly to do her glands good."

"If you really want to know, I regarded it as the first real thing I ever did in my life." He stood up to go. "It was a unique occasion. For physiological reasons it has not so far been repeated. When it is, I'll be glad to report on my emotions and thoughts. And before I depart I'd like to tell you, in the presence of Toplis, just how much money I subscribed to you after our divorce went through. It is four hundred and forty-five pounds exactly."

"I'll be pleased to give you a cheque for this amount," said Toplis, still with his eyes closed.

"Excellent. I'll take it with me, if you don't mind. I'll give it to the university appeal. Then I really will have got the last three years off my back."

* * *

Prudence took the line that he was silly to withdraw from the Promotion Committee at this stage. It would occupy his mind, for one thing. Hedges told her he didn't want his mind occupied more than it was. He had his job, he had his father's estate to settle, and he had (though he didn't tell Prudence this) some spiritual exercises to devise and practice. He had tried to read Loyola but his mind kept skidding off the surface of the words—sin, judgement, hell, election—and he felt he had to discover some ritual closer to his own needs. The word "exercise" implied, to him, bodily exercise.

After his morning bath he tried lying face down and naked in the bath-room, while trying to conceive a state of nothingness. This was followed by five quick press-ups. Nothing very remarkable, either physically or intellectually, happened, but he calmly realized one morning that his sudden disappearance from this planet would inconvenience remarkably few people—in fact, only one: Prudence, and she'd get along pretty well without him. He doubled the number of press-ups. The blood roared in his ears, and when he stopped the self-torture he couldn't immediately remember why he was doing it.

Prudence, who didn't know about the exercises, said this was no time to withdraw into himself. The death of his father was a great shock, but he mustn't mope. It was no good telling her that he was not moping, that he felt very happy about his father, who had enjoyed a hell of a good life on the whole and lived to a good age. Prudence would not understand talk like this. He had to burn a lot of bills, account books, ledgers, business letters, tea chests full of bank statements and cancelled cheques, bundles of photographs of unknown men in tight trousers and women in enormous hats, clothes the moth had been at, pieces of

271

harness that had gone green with age, and even the broken skeleton of a cherry-wood trap his father used to drive when Edward was King and which he had preserved behind the garden shed. He had melancholy bonfires at the bottom of the garden and was kippered by their smoke. There was so much of the stuff he could only burn a small proportion at a time. The old man loved a fire in the garden. Hedges remembered the way he used to lean on his fork and gaze at the flames.

The great surprise had been finding over twenty thousand pounds in his deposit account. The bank manager said he'd often tried to persuade him to put a bit of it into some good stock. The old man had War Loan, Defence Bonds, Savings Certificates, and quite a lot of government stock of one sort or another, but no industrials. He had half a dozen houses in various parts of the town. Altogether it came to just over fifty thousand pounds, which was quite enough, Hedges told Prudence, even after death duties were paid, to permit him to throw up his job and go off, the pair of them, to some other part of the country where they would buy a little business and——

"Are you serious? What sort of business?"

"Get a first-class butcher's business for ten thousand quid."

"I'm not going to live over a butcher's shop."

One February evening there was a ring at the front door, but when Hedges opened it and switched on the porch light there was nobody there, only a cardboard box about eighteen inches square tied with what looked like a piece of sash-cord. Hedges went down into the road. There was no one about. It wasn't actually raining, but he could feel the damp settling on his face and hands; because of this wet mist there was no seeing beyond the next lamp post. He took the box into the kitchen where Prudence and he were having supper and found that it contained half a dozen reels of tape and a recording machine with a strap for slinging over the shoulder. To begin with, they thought the box had been left by mistake. The next day somebody would turn up and claim it. That evening, in any case, Hedges was working against time on a report for the County. It wasn't until the following evening that he thought to have a closer look at the machine. He put on a tape, turned the knob to playback, and heard a Mr. Punch voice coming through the tiny loud speaker. It took a bit of getting used to. Eventually, quite clearly the voice said, "There's some talk of a threepenny rate, but in my opinion it's the government that ought to pay, not the public," and it suddenly came to Hedges that this must be Brush's machine and tapes. He looked at his watch. It was eight-thirty.

"If I'm not back by ten-thirty," he said to Prudence, "go to bed, there's a good girl."

He drove down town and, finding the double doors to the baker's yard standing wide open, drove straight in. There was no light in the flat. Hedges tried the door but it was locked. There was no light in the bakehouse on the other side of the yard either. Hedges went down the steps and sat on the bonnet of the car, thinking what to do. There was a tobacconist's round the corner, and he was on his way to ask if Brush had been in for his daily ration when he remembered the place would be shut. There was nothing for it but to drive round to the police-station.

Five minutes later he was back with a couple of police-men, who proceeded to force the lock on the front door of the flat. Brush was not there. The place stank, the bed linen lay in a heap on the floor, there was dirty crockery in the sink and empty corned beef and salmon tins in such a monstrous pile that Brush must have given a lot of thought to building it.

"He's skipped his bail," said one of the policemen.

"That'll cost you five hundred quid," said the other.

"If he's alive," said Hedges.

They were jumping to conclusions not because Brush was missing—he could have been in some pub or gone up to London for a couple of days—but because he had left his recorder and the tapes with Hedges. It was a gesture that said, "I'm off. If it's any consolation to you, hang on to these."

Hedges went home, leaving the policemen in charge. There was nothing for him to do, except hand the gear to the B.B.C. The police would make the routine inquiries. Nell would come first. They would ask her, probably with Toplis looking on and chewing his cigar, when she had last seen her husband. They would check with his publisher. There were railway booking-clerks, ticket inspectors, railway police, and anyone else they could think of to question. Ports and airports would be warned. With a little encouragement they'd drag a river or two. The fact that he seemed to have taken his clothes with him persuaded the police that he had simply made a bolt for it; but Hedges wasn't so sure. He could imagine Brush supposing the police would think that way.

At the end of a fortnight, there was still no hint of his whereabouts. If he had left the town, the police had been quite unable to establish how. A brother in Clapham said he hadn't seen Christopher for three years. And, as the days went by, Brush, instead of fading altogether from Hedges's mind—where in any case he'd scarcely any human and living attributes—began to glow with an eerie radiance as though a life that Hedges could recognize was returning. He had to make a formal appearance at the Assize court. The dock was empty, and Hedges was directed to pay over five hundred pounds because of it; but Brush was there all right. Curiously, Hedges could feel that he was really there. This was all the stranger because it was the exact opposite of what had happened at the preliminary hearing, when Hedges had listened to the hoarse croak of the real Brush and been unable to convince himself that the man still existed. He dreamed about Brush. They were fishing from a punt and Brush was using a float as big as a football. It bobbed below the surface and Brush, his line bending, yelled that he had caught a monster (and it was a normal yell, obviously pre-throat-wound), but Hedges declared the float was just too heavy. There was no monster, there was nothing, just Brush and a football-sized float that was probably stuffed full of lead shot.

On March second a picture postcard arrived, showing an antique statue of Hercules, shoulders back, paunch forward, as he fondly watered the ground. "No doubt," the message ran on the back, "the god is bringing fertility, but I hope that he also implies a little contempt. I'd have written a fiercer word, but I can't spell it. Neither can I give you the exact quotation from Petronius that floats at the back of my mind. Please send me my *Concise Oxford Dictionary* c/o American Express, Rome. I'm tired of wondering how many *n*'s there are in bunion. Caesar was deaf and I can't spell. And I must work. C.B."

Hedges supposed that he had better give them a ring at the police-station, where they showed only mild interest; Brush's offence was not one he could be extradited for, and until he turned up in England again there was nothing the police could do about it. Hedges said the sergeant had

misunderstood the purpose of the call. He wanted to know
what had happened to Brush's belongings. The sergeant
went off to make inquiries. Another voice came on the line
and asked who the caller was and what the query might be.
So Hedges had to go through the explanation again, only to
be asked what Brush could want with an English dictionary
in Italy. The police voice said it was funny to him, a man
who was supposed to be a writer not being able to spell.
Anyway, all Brush's gear had been cleared out of the flat
and handed over to his wife for safe keeping.

"What, Nell?" said Hedges, surprised.

"Up at old Toplis's."

Hedges did not think it worth encountering Nell again
and bought Brush a new dictionary, which he got his
secretary to pack up and post that very afternoon.

The only person who got really angry because of this
development was Prudence. She was in her seventh month
and spent a lot of time these days lying in bed and writing
her novel on pieces of ruled paper pinned to a square of
hardboard. Didn't Brush realize his departure had cost
somebody else five hundred pounds? It wasn't the money; it
was the principle. To write a postcard from Italy asking for
a dictionary and making no reference to the five hundred
pounds struck her as quite extraordinary. It was only
slightly less extraordinary than Hedges doing as he was
asked. Was there no end to his masochism? Could he
pretend that he would have done so much for a man who
didn't happen to be his first wife's lover? She didn't believe
Brush couldn't spell. She thought the statue of Hercules
offensive and was surprised the post office accepted such a
picture. This wasn't the last they'd hear of Brush. He'd be
sending for money next.

Hedges sat on the end of the bed, looking miserable.

"No, this is the end of it. I sent the dictionary as a last thank-offering."

"For what?"

"For Brush being alive."

"You thought he'd done away with himself? Not that type. He'd hang on to the withered branch by his long and abnormally hairy arm. He's a lot tougher than you are."

He kissed her and said he'd go out into the back yard and burn a few more papers. Still angry, Prudence began writing again, and Hedges stood and watched the pencil moving along the lines. He knew that Prudence's heroine had just become secretary to a hard-drinking M.P., and he wondered if Prudence's remark about Hercules indicated a shift of moral tone in the narrative; if so, it was none too early. Prudence was able to write and talk at the same time. She told him to have fun with his bonfire. The pleasure he took in burning things, anybody could see that was what he wanted to do with everything and everybody, pile her and his whole life and the unborn baby and the house, money, books, civilization on a great pyre and set a flaming torch to it. Didn't he realize he was tending his father's funeral pyre?

"Make me a corned-beef sandwich, darling," she said, after a bit. "I'm ravenous."

He brought up the sandwich and a glass of Guinness, patted her writing arm, and said if he was going to get rid of another instalment of the stuff he'd better take it out to the yard now before it grew too dark to see a struck match.

It was six o'clock but already so dark he had to draw the curtains back from the kitchen window so that the light could shine out on last year's runner-bean poles and the two rows of raped and tattered Brussels sprouts. He lodged an electric torch on a couple of bricks and carried a washing-basket full of old account books, bills, and tax returns to the ashy patch where so much of the like had already been offered up. It had been freezing since early afternoon, when the wind changed. The old Brussels-sprout stalks trapped pellets of ice along their lengths, and they stood up, catching what light there was, like jewelled and beribboned batons. No smell but frost in the hard, clean, and starless night.

The bundles of bills burned easily but the ledgers were slower fuel, and Hedges could see their browned pages turned by invisible hands on the other side of a smoky flame. Wilsher, Amos, Griffin, Studds, Bowler, Taylor— these were the Perstowe names set down in his mother's handwriting, and the shillings and the pennies, a quarter of a century before. He threw in a handful of prize-winner rosettes from the Perstowe Fat Stock Show: Christmas, 1921; Christmas, 1922; Christmas, 1923. The fire gave off enough heat to set the icicles on the garden shed dripping.

Prudence must have dumped Brush's tapes with the rest of the rubbish, for here they were mixed up with a lot of wiring to do with the tropical-fish tank his father once had in the shop; angel-fish, neons, guppies. Hedges remembered how the air bubbled up through the water weeds and children were stood on the counter to peer in. Once he'd been asked why he went in for geography, and he had blamed it on these exotic fish. He supposed there was little truth in it, really. He liked drawing maps, and that was about all there was to say.

What about these tapes? They'd burn like mad. They'd frizzle like fat bacon. They'd flare like acetylene.

There were half a dozen reels. He carried them, three under each arm, back to the house and up to what had been his father's bedroom but where he had now moved his desk and quite a lot of his books. It was his study. The tape recorder stood on a bamboo-legged table in a corner. He began playing the tapes and was still there three hours later. Either Prudence was still writing or she had fallen asleep. Maybe she looked in and saw he was busy. He had been listening to everybody from Jacob Bream to Jimmy Pigge and back again; he had listened to himself talking in what sounded like a busy railway-station about the New Jerusalem. Toplis did his stuff about education and industry.

Then, suddenly, a hoarse voice, recorded very close to the microphone in a room without resonance: "Hedges, this is Christopher Brush speaking. Nuts to you, I say. Nuts. Farewell, dear heart, for I must needs be gone. Do me a favour—hand this machine and tapes over to the B.B.C. I'll pay you the five hundred quid out of my Nobel Prize. I will now sing an old song. 'You'll get no promotion this side of the ocean, so cheer up my lads—' "

Hedges looked up and saw Prudence at the door.

"I've been listening to all this stuff about the university. I suppose," he went on, after a pause, "you're right. It would seem odd if I really did drop out of the show at this stage."

"Who was that singing that song?"

"That was Brush."

"Don't you think you ought to come to bed?"

"What's the time then? It's only ten."

"Don't you think you ought to come to bed?" she repeated. "You're beginning to look transparent."

Finally, Hedges did get his lunch at the Athenæum with Jacob Bream. They had cold smoked trout, roast ribs of beef, cheese, and a bottle of Château Margaux, 1952. During lunch they talked business, which was all about starting a university and a kind of form you had to fill in which Bream said was intolerably complicated and not at all the sort of thing to be tackled without the preliminary tuition which he, Bream, was about to give. Hedges could then pass it on to the committee. Bream confessed that as he was now sixty years of age and on the point of retiring he would like to be a little injudicious in the advice he was about to give. So far as Colchester, Norwich, Canterbury, York, Lancaster, Coventry, and Sussex had been concerned, his attitude had been impeccable. They embodied no single one of his ideas. But would Hedges think it presumptuous of him if he, so to speak, meditated aloud and permitted any little bird in earshot to make of his views what it wished? The day was cold, and Bream was wearing a solemn-looking suit cut out of some black blankety material with a lot of shiny buttons. He sported an old-fashioned silk stock secured with a pearl pin. He had a handkerchief up his left sleeve and a white gardenia in his left lapel. His bald head seemed larger than ever and even more unadorned, ostentatious, challenging. At the touch of a button, the lid would fly up and another bald head appear which in turn would open to reveal—

"I'd be sorry to think Perstowe was going in for any kind of gimmickry. What I say to you, dear Hedges, is strictly unofficial. I am just an old party burbling. And if you quote me I shall deny everything you say. I am simple. My simplicity is provincial. I've always regarded my role as being the provincial in Whitehall. Hence my accent. I would like to think that at least one of the new universities in this grand old country of ours was being conceived with certain fundamental ideas in mind. What would you say were the fundamental ideas?"

"Well, I——"

"There are a number of facts about existence. We are

bodies inhabiting a society with a feeling of doubt and anxiety. What do you deduce from all this?"

"I wouldn't like to argue," said Hedges, who had had two whiskies before lunch and three glasses of wine with it, "until you've developed your position a little more clearly."

"Ah! I can see your game." Bream actually wagged a finger. "You know how to draw me out. Well, medicine for the body, economics for society, and theology for the soul. See what I mean? I knew Maynard Keynes well. Knew his father, know his brother. They were a family obsessed with the essentials and getting to grips with them. So what happened? Maynard became an economist, Geoffrey went in for medicine, and if there'd been a third brother he'd have been Archbishop of Canterbury and eating apple sauce with his roast pork on the other side of this room just as the present Archisbishop is doing at this moment. Let's go up to the library and have some coffee."

Over coffee, Hedges asked him what he was driving at. He didn't think there would be many men in the running for the Vice-Chancellorship if you insisted on a mixture of Maynard Keynes and Albert Schweitzer.

"What I like about you," said Bream, "and it's probably the reason we got on so well together, is that basically we are the same sort of creature. Did you know I was sexually impotent?"

Hedges was startled. "No."

"I have never talked of this openly before. But then I've never come across anyone in the same case. Shall I tell you what my experience is? It's marvellous, really. We have never lusted. We have never known the sadness of what, according to Shakespeare and Spinoza, is lust appeased. We see more of the play than the players. We are not understood. Our weapon is irony. Our defect is vanity."

Bream spoke in his normal, penetrating, North Midlands twang, and Hedges could only suppose that his physical disability was the most widely known secret in London. The smooth-faced, smiling man reading *Mind* opposite them must have heard every word. He appeared to be not greatly interested.

Bream went on to say that he had been impressed, on his visits to Perstowe, to note how much talk about Hedges there had been. He was a much-loved figure. Did he realize that? People warmed to what they regarded as nobility of character. They were proud of him.

"Is this what Toplis said?"

"Toplis had gland treatment. That was why he wants to marry that woman you were married to. He denied that he'd had the treatment, of course. Always claimed to have been a bit of a goat on the quiet. He was too much under my influence for that. Ever since Cambridge he modelled himself on me. Now he wants an heir. Does he speak to you about these things?"

Bream wanted to know how Hedges had worked up enough courage to marry in the first place. Or didn't he know he was inadequate?

Hedges probed the chasm that had opened before him. "You say all Perstowe knows this?"

"You're a folk hero. People naturally wondered why a young wife should leave a local government official for that unshaven man who interviewed me on his tape recorder."

"And my second marriage?"

"It is well known that the child won't be yours. There was one woman I met after that Lack Hall fight who said you were as near a saint as she'd ever met. I told her I had been spoken of in much the same terms, but she didn't take the hint."

"You don't remember her name?"

"Mrs. Kidwelly," said Bream. "I never forget a name."

"I had no idea she was so well-disposed."

"I must admit," Bream added, after some reflection, "that she conveyed a sense of not necessarily thinking well of saints. But the general opinion is in favour of them. This is how Perstowe thinks of you. It is understandable. Ask around if you should doubt me. I asked around. I have a theory that the old prejudice against impotence is lifting. In a few years' time we should be as well thought of and as fussed over as homosexuals, if only it could be established that we were socially harmful, which of course we're not." Bream looked serious. "Quite the contrary. So the pansies will always have the edge on us there."

He accompanied Hedges as far as the front steps and showed him where he could catch a bus to Paddington. Last seen, he was turning like a dolphin, back no doubt to a leather chair where he could drink cognac and talk scandal with some professor up from the provinces before putting in a couple of hours at the office. He was nearly at the end of his trot. In a few months there would be no office to go back to, and Hedges imagined him repairing instead to the library, where he would work away at the writing of some unexpected book: a study of royal taste and patronage from Elizabeth I to Elizabeth II, or it might be something fiercer, like a secular version of Newman's *Idea of a University*.

Bream's assessment of the regard Hedges was held in and the reason for it could be checked with Amos, but as Hedges sat in the corner of his first-class non-smoking compartment his mind went back to the journey he had taken with the Reverend Mr. Warp. After Slough the countryside opened up. The Thames winked a pallid eye as they crossed Maidenhead Bridge. On the other side of

Reading, the winter-scoured hills flexed themselves like muscles. Apparently naked copses were full of buds that shone purple in the March sun.

But for himself, the compartment was empty. Had he wished he could have spoken aloud to the Reverend Warp. Instead he hummed tunelessly. Why had he made no attempt to get in touch with Warp? Why had he not introduced him to Bream so that he could listen to their conversation? Why had his first thought on entering the Athenæum not been to look round for Warp who, a guest at Lambeth, might surely be expected there? Why, for that matter, had he let Cuthbert Simms, who had risen from the depths of the past like a pious sea slug to deny he had set fire to that barn, sink out of sight again without insisting that he stand and deliver himself of the true doctrine?

None of these things had been necessary, that's why. And it hadn't been necessary to stop Bream in his tracks and assure him that he, Hedges, was not impotent; and it wasn't necessary now to go to Amos and ask questions about the opinion the citizens of Perstowe had of him. What if, as was likely, Amos said Bream was right? What was Hedges to do? Put a notice in the paper?

He wasn't going to contradict. He wasn't even going to find out whether the public view of him was worth contradicting. He wished everyone well. Also he had good wishes for all those unimaginable masses of people who lived on the back of technology in great cities and kept more secrets from one another than in any civilization since the beginning of the world.

All a man could do was not deny or declaim too much but send out his insignificant shaft of love and only sink his teeth into anybody's throat when it was that or too much hell for too many.

And trusting all these people to love you back. The child would be born. In the course of time there would be another child. After that a third child. So much for reputation. The body stiffened and the children danced. The Earth swung between Venus and Mars. Mainly, though, the job was a watching and giving and being gay in the day-in, day-out fostering of a kind of bated expectancy.

No, he wasn't going to deny publicly he was a saint.

Prudence had her son on May third, and they all lived more or less happily for quite a long time after.